GENESIS VEIL

Genesis Veil:

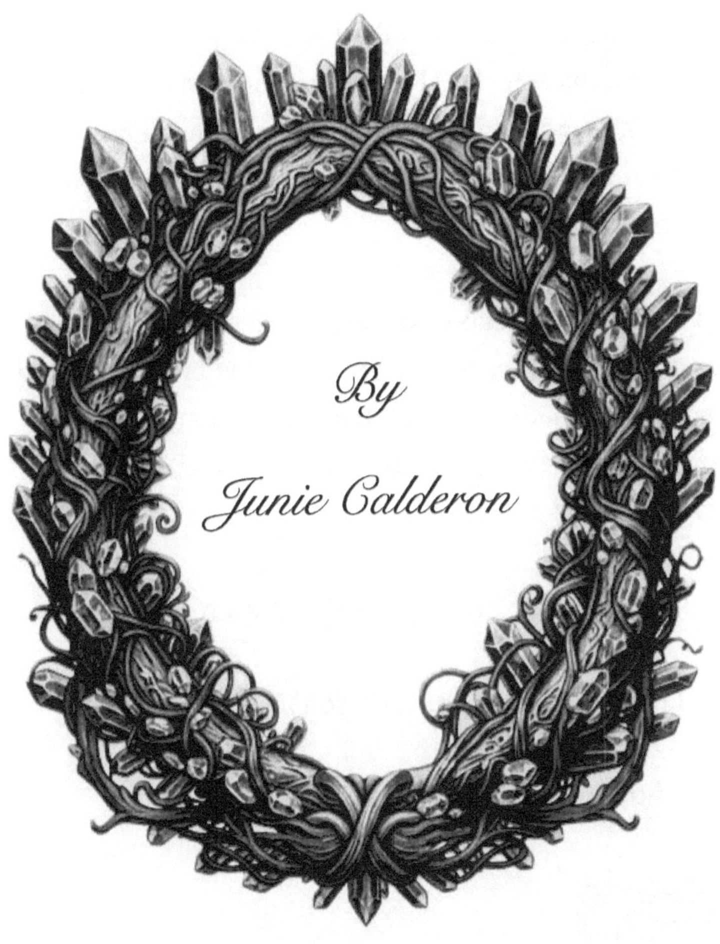

Astra and the Sapphire Mora

Genesis Veil: Astra and the Sapphire Mora

Publisher: Covert Collection Books, New York, NY

Print Edition ISBN: 979-8-218-86536-8

First Edition: January, 2026

"For I know the plans I have for you," declares the Lord,
"plans to prosper you and not to harm you, plans to give you
hope and a future."

PROLOGUE

ong before Genesis Veil was fractured by fear, there was a time when magic and mortals lived as one in harmony. Where skies bled vibrant aurora fields that glistened with untamed magic. A world parallel to our own—a realm of color, consequence, and magic—that has been broken for centuries. Its true architecture has been corrupted, and its rightful sovereign has been erased from memory. The only sign of this forgotten history is an imprint, a persistent, spiritual drag often felt in the quiet moments. An undeniable calling, a whisper in a dream, a shadow passing in the corner of your eye. The final stand for Genesis Veil is about to begin.

GENESIS VEIL: ASTRA AND THE SAPPHIRE MORA

CHAPTER 1

Unveiling the Layers

Bright red and green lights flash in the distance, guiding me as I'm running through an alleyway ignited in fire. I reached the end of the hall and tried to climb up a wall. There was a big, black creature on four legs watching me, its sharp teeth dripping with saliva and blood. Three dark, levitating, black-hooded figures floated above the wall. I was trying to get over it, but the sheer height intimidated me.

I climbed back down and turned the opposite direction. One of the black-hooded figures moved with me and led the way. It took me to a door, touched my shoulder, rested it for a second, then opened the door in front of me. The doorway led to a place outside, but there was daylight, in contrast to the night we had just been in. Piles of rusted armor, covered in green slime spread out on the ground.

A beautiful field of fresh meadows, filled with magnolias and lavender, sprouted across the grassy grounds below. The wind rustled through the leaves as we passed through and headed toward the fields. I looked at the black-hooded figure I was following and somehow felt safe, even though I didn't have a clue who it was or where it's leading me. Unknowingly, I started doing these strange gestures with my hands in my pockets.

Instantly, I noticed there were invisible figures walking throughout the land. Invisible buildings, trees, and other things that once were, now reviving and revealing themselves again. You could notice their silhouette as they moved around, but at a certain angle, they would become invisible to the eye again. We arrived at a river streaming with thickened blood bursting with air bubbles as if reacting to being watched.

Looking closer, as if staring at my own reflection, I saw colorful, bright orbs of light hovering around my head. I quickly turned, noticing they were all around me. The black-hooded figure was nowhere to be seen from where I was standing. The orbs circled around my body a couple of times and illuminated, then slowly started to fade, glowing a spectrum of colors as each one flew by. I laid to rest for a moment down by the river flowing with the blood.

As I gazed into the thick crimson color, I noticed a deep bubbling coming from underneath. I leaned back for a moment until I realized it was a blue fish trying to escape death. A squid twice the size of it wrapped long coiled tentacles around the fish as it frantically struggled for survival. The fish's effort to break free enticed me to reach in and lend a helping hand. I unraveled the squid's gripping tentacles, allowing the fish to make an escape as some of its scales fell off like falling leaves during the change of seasons.

I felt a slight tingling in my hand, but I didn't think much of it. While walking along the river, I saw a massive dragon lying on the ground, its body the color of deep, cold ice. Upon getting closer, I realized this dragon was dead. It had been badly wounded, and its blood had been seeping into the river, causing the water to be overcome with the crimson shade. I rubbed my hand across the dragon's face, feeling sorrow that such a beautiful creature lay lifeless in front of my very eyes. A shock of energy pulsed into my arm.

The tingling began to sting with a coldness, sending a shiver up my arm. I looked down and noticed an icy but muted shade of blue running up my arm, changing its color. I rubbed my hand vigorously over it, trying to scrub the color from my skin, but it remained the same. Walking down the stream of dragon's blood into oblivion, not knowing where I would end up, but somehow knowing I was still heading in the right direction. Soon, I saw rocks forming in a spiral formation, going downward into a hole in the ground.

Thinking to myself, 'Is it really a good idea to wander down there?' I started walking up to the levitating structure while taking one last look at the dragon pumping the end of its life into the river. I stepped onto the first rock, then the next, and continued until reaching the bottom. Every inch of space was filled with mirrors and led to an old wooden door with a heavy doorknob that was cold to the touch, right at the end of the tunnel.

I opened it and was immediately bombarded with a strong smell, telling me something was dying. The stench was enough for me to turn away. Nothing but pitch darkness looked back into my eyes, staring into my soul. I turned around and headed back out the door, closing it behind me within seconds, and started going back the way I came.

Trying not to panic and freak myself out, I started to speed walk and noticed, while passing by the mirrors, that there was a dark shadow following my reflection. I started to pick up the pace and ran toward the spiraled stones. Heading up, jumping and climbing over stones in a hurry, I fell down, back to the mirrors. The sound of my voice yelling for help echoed in my head, then stopped once I realized I was alone, with no one around me—not even mirrors or shadows for that matter.

A forest filled with trees stretching high into the sky surrounded me. The smell of fresh cut grass took over my mind's thought process, and I almost forgot that I was yelling for help a moment ago. Waves of water started to pass by my feet. I felt its intensity continuing and rising higher up my legs as I stood there, trying to make sense of where it was all coming from. I climbed onto a wall, using the stones and random objects stuck to it for leverage, and pulled myself up and away from the waters. Pots, chairs, teapots, bottles, books, and just the most bizarre objects were fused into the wall.

At first I questioned its existence, but after noticing these items were saving my life, I began to just go with the flow. A small house sat on top of a tree stump larger than the house itself. The rings on the tree were disappearing as soon as I stepped on them, moving toward the house.

Realizing the energy around me felt rejuvenating, I didn't hesitate to walk further into the door without even knocking, as if I owned the property. Candles were lit all around the inside of the main hallway, which led up to the dining room. The tall candles created a light that was almost uncertain and nervous. A viscous, golden wax spread in an irregular puddle, hardening into a smooth disc.

I called out, "Hello, anyone there?" Nothing but the echo of my voice bouncing off the walls. As I scanned the room for anything that would stand out to me, I noticed what seemed to be a strange, empty picture frame beginning to fly toward my direction. While standing in front of the picture frame, I noticed big green vines growing from behind it, sprouting and attaching themselves to the walls. A Pink fairy came out of the center, from what looked like a tiny portal opening in between the wall and the frame.

The Pink fairy pulled out two leaves that were wrapped around the frame and placed them on the nearby table, which was covered in salt and baby's breath. Looking at me with its soft, mirror-like eyes, I could almost hear a voice telling me to hold the leaves. I gently picked them off the table while keeping eye contact.

The fairy has a bald head with a design in the shape of an eye on the back of it. I gently put the leaves in my hand, and it began to hover around the leaves I was holding, fluttering around in circles, going faster and faster and creating a small gust of wind around me. Its wings were transparent, but you could see the intensity in the colored veins starting to cause a halo-like circle around my hand.

A feeling, as if I were being tickled and scratched at the same time, started in my hands. Then, in an instant, it stopped, and out flew two new fairies, one from each hand. Hovering in front of me now were these three colorful fairies. The two who were born from the leaves had wings that resembled them. One was red and the other green, both as radiant and intense as the Pink fairy.

The fairies resembling the leaves flew closer to me as the pink one gazed into my eyes, then returned into the empty picture frame. They stood right by my side, not making a sound, just hovering right beside my right shoulder. I kept walking through the house, noticing that on just about every wall there was an empty picture frame. Some were colored with beautiful shades of the ocean, while others were simply made of wooden and metal materials. I heard my name being yelled from a distance, "ASTRA!"

I glanced out the front door and saw a girl with short, light brown hair. She was running at such a high speed toward me. "Ouch!" I yelled out.

She forgot to stop and bumped right into me before I could even think to move out of the way.

"Astra, it's you, I'm so glad to see you here," she said.

I looked at her with a puzzled expression, unsure of who she was, she began to talk again.

"Hello, it's me, Xara, your trusted friend," she said with a smile stretching across her face from ear to ear.

Although I couldn't fully remember her, the name resonated within me and felt familiar. Xara and I have known each other since forever, it felt. For some reason, my memory seemed foggy, and I couldn't remember much of my life before this.

I picked her up off the ground while just looking at her with a blank stare and thought to myself, 'Why is this girl following me?' I didn't know what to think of anything, really, as so much felt like it was happening all at once.

"Astra, why is one of your hands blue?" Xara asked, her tone seeming both peculiar and frightened at the same time.

"Oh right, my hand," I replied, remembering my hand had changed colors. "I'm not sure what actually happened."

I told her, thinking to myself that it had to be the dragon-blooded river that caused it to turn this blue color. Talking to her, I could feel the fairies hovering throughout my long, curly hair. I lifted my shirt slightly to circulate some air inside and help relieve some of the heat I was feeling from being nervous.

Xara looked puzzled and responded, "Still, I absolutely admire it."

The fairies stood hidden in my hair, finding a way to camouflage into it as if they weren't even there. I didn't know what to do to get them to reveal themselves, so I just brushed it off without mentioning it. Xara headed to an empty, white picture frame hanging on a wall nearby. She gave it a light dusting with her sweater sleeve, revealing a switch right above the top right corner of it. The frame turned into a mirror, showing a tree sitting on a hill in the middle of a scorching hot day, but snowing underneath it at the same time.

In the distance, I could see floating rocks in a spiral formation. I immediately remembered running through the mirrored hallway, trying to get back up the floating rocks. It all felt like a distant memory. Wherever we were, it didn't feel like home, that's for sure.

I tried to shake the thought away and told Xara to walk with me to another picture frame and maybe one of them would have some type of clue to figuring out why we were even here to begin with. As we headed over to the kitchen, I saw the table dripping with blood. A letter written out to me laid flat against the center of the table while blood continued to leak off onto the hardwood floor, as if it had just recently occurred. We looked at each other, both shocked, as we made out what was written. It read:

ASTRA,

THE CYCLE IS ENDING.

FATE HAS DELIVERED YOU TO THIS MOMENT.

THE SILENCE THAT PROTECTED YOUR NAME IS ONCE AGAIN BROKEN.

THE THREAD OF YOUR DESTINY IS IN MY HANDS.

RECKONING HAS BEGUN. YOU SOON SHALL PERISH!

I noticed the blood from the letter starting to drip down into a perfect stream toward the basement staircase. We followed the trail of blood until we got to a circular vent in the floor. I lifted it open, and a hidden passageway revealed itself. Inside was a small ladder, broken halfway down. Footprints stepped in blood led my curiosity to go further down and investigate what was going on in this house.

"I think I can jump down safely from the end of that ladder," I said.

Xara didn't seem so sure that heading down there would be the best idea for us both and insisted on staying behind to find something to pull me back up with when the time came. She ties up her short brown hair behind her neck with a strange looking black ribbon while I prepare myself. Possibilities as to what could be down there began to race in my head as I stared down into the vent. Xara places her arm around my shoulder and tells me not to worry.

Her thick-rimmed glasses kept falling off her nose as she looked down into the vent with me. Constantly having to push them up she removed them for a moment while holding in her hands, scratching at the bridge of her nose. They gave her gaze a certain gravity, emphasizing her steady eyes and the sharp, playful curve of her smile. The frames were bold, anchoring her gentle features with a touch of confidence.

CHAPTER 2

Descent into the Unknown

glanced over at Xara before heading down and nodded my head at her. I inhaled a long breath of air as I grabbed the ladder and climbed down. I climbed as far as the ladder allowed until I felt it stop. I looked down before I jumped, aiming for a successful landing, only to fall into a puddle of blood.

"Are you okay down there?" Xara called out.

I responded in a loud voice, "Yes! I think I'm okay, but it's terribly bloody down here. And now that I'm thinking about it, maybe you should start looking for a rope or something to get me out."

I really hadn't thought this through and was slowly starting to regret my brave decision. Looking around as I tried to figure out which direction to head toward, I remembered the two fairies hiding in my curls. I yelled out to Xara one last time before I started walking, "Don't forget about me down here!"

As I started hearing Xara walk away, I shook my hair vigorously, hoping the fairies would come out and assist me in some way. They were a big part of the reason I had the guts to come down here in the first place. I found it strange how the two fairies matched my red and green hair. With one side being red and the other green, the fairies hid in the corresponding side of hair to blend seamlessly. As they revealed themselves, they both brightly lit up the darkness with red and green lights, emerging from my colorful locks.

The presence of the two fairies was almost comforting enough to make me forget the surrounding blood and the unforgiving eeriness that began to creep up my spine. The blood kept streaming down the tunnel, which we followed straight ahead until we came to a junction with four different paths to choose from.

I looked at the fairies with a puzzled and confused expression. They both took the path on the far right, and I followed close behind them, trying not to lose sight. While going down the path, I noticed scattered human skeletons across the floor. Embryos of small animals, perfectly organized in jars filled with water, sat on shelves. Everything around me was quite disturbing. I decided to walk up to the animal embryos and examine one more closely.

I grabbed a jar, feeling the outside and removing the dust, revealing a label that read, "Llama fetus, bury for good luck."

"That's strange—a llama fetus for good luck?" I wondered who would even put such a thing down here. I placed the jar gently back onto the shelf and continued looking around. I grazed my hand across a few jars, slightly wiping the dust off to get a better view of what was inside.

Nothing would have seemed out of the ordinary to me if this were upstairs in the house. I wasn't as surprised to see this as I thought I would be. Everything being so organized felt safe, like it was there for protection, besides the llama for luck. I started to wonder if Xara had found anything to pull me back up the vent with by now. It seemed like I'd been down here for quite some time.

As I continued down that path, I began to feel a cool breeze pass my shoulder and go down my back. I turned around quickly, thinking someone was behind me, and suddenly I saw blood rushing toward me. A vast pool of blood collected on the floor while I gazed deeply into it, almost mesmerized. Suddenly breaking my concentration, I heard a glass being shattered. While I glanced around to see where the sound came from, I saw a fallen embryo surrounded by shattered pieces of glass on the ground.

It was a tiny pink elephant, which I hadn't noticed on the shelf before. It looked so beautiful and peaceful lying there within the blood. I didn't know how to properly dispose of it, but I just didn't want to leave it lying on the ground like that. I untied a cloth hanging over a shelf and used it to pick up the embryo without touching it or getting blood all over me.

I held the pink elephant and looked for an empty jar to put it in. Holding it in my hand and looking around, I felt a burning sensation so hot I couldn't contain myself and dropped it. I looked at the ground, and there it was, being sucked into the pool of blood on the floor. All of a sudden, the elephant slowly started reaching its trunk out of the blood. Unsure of what to do, I simply reached down and put out my arm to help it latch onto me.

It wrapped around my arm as I grabbed it and pulled it out of the blood. The elephant was alive and breathing. I held it against my chest for a while to help it feel safe. It was so adorable and helpless I couldn't resist feeling sorry for it.

Covered in blood, I held it in my hands, keeping it calm, and looked around. I noticed that the elephant was no longer pink as I started to wipe the blood dripping from its face. A cerulean shade of blue consumed his whole body while I watched the color changing before my very eyes, as if everything had been in slow motion. It looked exactly like the color of my right hand for a split second and got me thinking again about how exactly my hand changed this color. It had to do with something involving that dragon or its blood.

Memories were flashing back into my head. Walking toward a wooden chair placed in a corner of a wall, I turned it around to take a seat. While I was sitting, I noticed the floor underneath me start to slowly open up, slightly creaking, as if it were another passage beneath. I got up quickly and watched as it continued opening. I saw a bright red light as I stood there looking at the floor, which was lowering and glowing, flaming bright red, like there were flames down there.

I could start to feel an intense heat, making breathing feel like a struggle. The chair remained exactly how I left it, and very slowly the ground lifted itself back up as if nothing happened. It's as if the chair was there to be used as some sort of Venus fly trap, a human-styled execution. I wasn't amused, and at this point, I just wanted to leave; relaxing for even just a moment wasn't an option. I've officially had enough of being down in this vent.

The colors from the fairies' lights began glistening in the room around me, getting brighter and pulsating faster with each passing moment. I couldn't seem to see the fairies in plain sight but knew they were around. I shook my right hand in my hair, holding the baby elephant in the other, and kept shaking, hoping the fairies would drop out, but nothing happened. The heat down here was starting to become extremely uncomfortable. I turned around and went back the way I came, past the shelf of embryos and out of the tunnel, back to where the vent I came down from was.

"XARA!!!! XARA!!!! Where are you?" I yelled from down below the vent.

I noticed that the vent wasn't opened anymore and had the cover over it, only allowing a few slivers of light to shine through. I can't believe what I'm seeing. Did Xara really just abandon me down here? Did something happen to her? What in the world is going on right now?

I'm in complete shock, but I need to relax and find another way out of here, and find those fairies too. I turned to the tunnel where the four paths are, with the elephant in hand. I stood in front of the tunnel on the far right, the one from which we came. I turned into the tunnel right beside it, thinking I should just check every tunnel one at a time. As I walked into this tunnel, my anxiety began rising. The flashing colored lights were starting to distract and confuse me into just wanting to lay on the floor and fall asleep.

I kept walking and felt microscopic spiderwebs rub into my mouth, sticking onto my tongue. I tried picking it off, scraping my nails against my tongue while dripping saliva. The strands of web felt like a sticky, sugary floss clinging to my taste buds.

"Disgusting!" I yelled out.

There was a dark section of the tunnel that the fairies' light did not illuminate. A black and yellow leather coffin was standing up against a wall, with hundreds of rusted nails sticking out around the wall. I noticed a handprint dented into the front of the coffin while I placed my hand over it. Before I could remove my hand from the coffin, a force in the room started spinning everything around.

After the spinning came to a halt, I realized the tunnel from which I came was blocked by a wall. The room spinning somehow turned itself around. As soon as I removed my hand from the coffin, it sprung open, hitting me in the face. The baby elephant in my hand woke up and started moving around, so I put it on the ground. It looks as if there's only one place to go. I stuck my head into the coffin and looked down to see a wooden staircase barely holding itself together.

Looking at the elephant as it looked up at me, I said to it, "Do you have a name?"

As if a voice whispered in my ear, I heard a strange name while repeating it. "Rylo? Is that it?" I asked.

The elephant just looked at me with gleaming, big, watery eyes.

"Alright then, Rylo it is."

"Come on, see if we can find a way out of this place," I said in a deliberate, even tempo.

I bent down to pick it up in my arms again and went into the coffin, stepping onto each step of the staircase with extreme caution. The third step was missing, and so was every other step after that, making going downstairs a nerve-wrecking moment. As I was getting closer to the bottom of the staircase, I could smell the scent of someone baking bread. A very sweet, clean, yeasty aroma that somehow smelled warm, like you were inhaling a cozy blanket on a cold winter's night.

We reached the bottom of the stairs, and it led to an outside tunnel. The walls of the tunnel were covered in vines, and grass was growing through the concrete on the floor. I noticed a voice in my mind that was telling me to look for marbles. "Marbles are in the area," I kept hearing.

As it repeated over in my mind, I began walking around in search of any marbles I could find anywhere. I told Rylo, "Keep your eyes peeled, okay?"

Straight through the tunnel, I could see a marble sitting underneath a stone sundial. The marble resembled an abstract combination of blues, greens, and yellows that swirled as they blended together. I held the marble close to my eye, keeping the other closed, as if it were a kaleidoscope. The colors from the marble, seen through the sunlight, showed me a vision of a beautiful grand castle.

The castle had several large gargoyle statues hovering on the corners, which had water pouring out their mouths into the large pond underneath it. The pond had lavender-colored water shimmering with sparkles of iridescent light shining on the surface. I could see creatures swimming underneath very peacefully without disrupting the water's surface. A pool to the left side in front of the castle splashed with water as small fish were swimming playfully around.

Every window was glowing a bright, fiery light from within. A large tree stood in a forest nearby the castle with vines hanging low into the magnificent lavender-tinted water. The castle had an array of windows with elaborate tracery on the exterior; I could only imagine how luxurious the inside looked.

Suddenly I dropped the marble, and before it hit the ground, Rylo sucked it into his trunk and blew it up into the air. It grew in size, big enough to engulf us both, and in an instant, both of us were inside the marble, flying through the tunnel, breaking through, up, and out of the ceiling. I made eye contact with Rylo and applauded him for doing a spectacular job getting us back on the move. My ears started to give this crackling and popping sound as we began soaring higher through the sky.

I saw nothing but muted colors of the marble from the inside of it, not knowing where we were going. As I began to let my guard down and relax, something reached in and grabbed a hold of us, both falling into mid-air.

CHAPTER 3

The Feather and the Key

While mid-air, I saw a winged creature flying towards us. It immediately swooped underneath, catching us on its back. The hairs felt extremely sticky, like glue, and we were immediately stuck to it. Not being able to move, I started to panic. The creature was flying at full throttle. I began to look, trying to catch a glimpse of the creature. Its head was that of a cat.

The body was striped as if it were a hairy zebra. Its tail was full of elongated feathers, all resembling its body's zebra print except for a few that were silver. The winged creature made a loud screeching noise, separated the clouds, and dove straight underneath the water. For a moment, I held my breath as we rapidly moved through the waters until I realized I couldn't feel the water or even the wetness of it. A force was pushing the waters aside, creating a passageway for the creature to fly through.

It looked back at us, making sure we were still there. Looking around inside the ocean, I noticed the floor filled with wonderfully colored marine life, simply existing as we passed by. I reached my hand out to see if I could break through and feel the water, but it was blocked by the barrier and speed force, making my hand repel. I could see fast-swimming creatures with beautiful, long hair flowing in the nearby waters. I was almost certain they were a group of mermaids, but at the speed we were going, I couldn't be too sure.

The zebra-printed, cat-winged creature came to a stop and made another loud screeching sound, revealing a door in front of us. This door was almost invisible but present. We all entered it as the creature began pressing its silver tail feathers onto a wall. Faster and faster, the feathers hit the stone, engraving a message in a foreign language we knew nothing of. It stood there until the wall was filled with symbols, while the dust that remained on the floor turned into a small golden key with two notches at the end. The top of the key was in the shape of a skeleton.

Fussing about, I managed to get myself and Rylo unstuck from the sticky hairs of the creature. I grabbed the key as I fell to the floor and held it in front of the creature as if I were holding some kind of weapon.

"Stay back, I'm warning you now!"

"Where the hell have you taken us?"

"Say something!..."

The creature opened its mouth and began to speak. "Hello, I am the one who will bring you to the answers your spirit seeks. You are the one who has awakened me from my slumber by finding the marble I've been trapped inside."

"My name is Iscana, and I've been imprisoned inside the marble you found by a powerful sorcerer named Nedos. He killed both my parents out of fear they would put an end to his evil ways. He then cursed me, turning me into this creature and trapping me inside that marble, all because I wouldn't take his hand in marriage."

"Are you serious? You can actually talk? Did this all really happen? I have to be dreaming," I replied, my eyes widening.

"Listen to me, this is very important. Nedos and his army will be looking for you once they realize I'm no longer trapped and you have the artifact. It is the key to my family's tomb. I need you to take it, awaken them, and tell them about me. Tell them I'm safe and alive, and I need their help. Then we'll be able to defeat Nedos for good."

"Iscana, this all honestly sounds very confusing. How will I even find your family tomb? I don't even know how I ended up here."

"Don't be frightened. That small elephant of yours has been in my family for generations. He was also killed and trapped by Nedos due to his extreme loyalty to my family and immense amount of magical abilities. His name is Rylo—you must have heard him speaking telepathically to you. That's how he communicates."

"Oh, so that was him whispering his name to me when I asked what I should name him? Speaking of names, I don't think I ever told you mine. I'm Astra."

"Astra, you must listen, there's no time left for getting acquainted. Take the key and keep it tied around your neck with this."

Iscana turned her neck toward her large tail full of feathers. She bit onto a long, thin, sparkly silver feather and ripped it straight out of her body. Taking it in her paw, she handed me the feather, keeping my hand warm and closing her eyes while doing so. In an instant, once she removed her hands from mine, I could see the feather shaking and moving as if it had a heartbeat of its own. She took the feather and, with her mouth, slipped the key through one end. I tied it around my neck.

"This feather will help you along the way," those were the last words I heard from her.

A deafening sound coming from the door we were behind started getting louder. I could see tons of mermaid creatures surrounding our area from outside.

These mermaids had large, transparent tails exposing every single bone in their lower half. Each mermaid had bright-colored coral attached to their arms, using it as some type of armor or decoration.

Their skin was a light, minty green, and their hair was mixed and entangled in seaweed. The eyes of these mermaids were glowing like a bright lighthouse in the middle of the night. All at once, the mermaids started banging against our invisible shield behind the door we were in. The coral on their arms created a thunder-like glow onto the barrier of our shield, allowing the barrier to become visible. The more they attacked, the more I noticed the area around us turning brighter and brighter.

I started feeling a drip of water fall onto the top of my head. The mermaids looked extremely violent, without blinking. They focused their concentration while holding hands, forming a circle around us. The top of our barrier continued to leak, causing more and more water to enter.

Iscana made another loud screeching noise, and a smaller door revealed itself in the room. It didn't look as if she could fit inside of it, but before I could ask any questions, the door opened up and sucked Rylo inside. I was pulled in right behind him, falling down a long metal slide into a dark area.

Looking up from where I came, I didn't see anything, not even Iscana. "Where did she send us?" I asked myself.

The air grew thick and heavy against my skin, while a faint, flickering pale light shimmered in the distance like a dying star. The area had a large, spacious nest in the center of it. It looked as if someone or something was living here. The nest was primarily made of large tree branches, grass, mud, and long feathers that resembled the zebra-stripe print on Iscana's tail.

Rylo picked one up with his trunk and waved it in front of me, bringing it closer. This made me realize this was where Iscana used to live. But why would such a beautiful creature want to live down here in this dark tunnel willingly? If she ever lived here, it wasn't by her own choice and had to be by force. I couldn't understand why. Unless, maybe, she was hiding from someone.

So many questions were left unanswered, but it was just the beginning. Making a way closer towards the light, there were two gated doors with large medieval padlocks. Behind each gate, I could see torches lit up against the walls, illuminating through and allowing me to see further into the distance. I bent over and tried the key given to me by Iscana on the door to the right, but it didn't work. I tried the door on the left, but nothing.

I turned around and just stared into the darkness ahead of me. A sensation of light-headedness brought me to a loss of balance, causing me to fall to the ground. Holding my hands on my head, I began to feel trapped once again, with all hope fading away. I started pinching myself to see if I would somehow wake up from a dream.

Tears started falling from my face onto the floor, absorbing into each drop. I continuously tapped my foot on the ground, trying to come up with an idea. Lifting my head up to wipe the tears streaming down my face, I looked to get a view of Rylo. I could see him playing with a shiny object on the ground. I crawled over to him and grabbed what appeared to be a broken piece of glass.

Sitting on the floor still, I held onto the shard of glass in my hand and laughed. At least I can entertain myself for a while with this, I thought to myself. I started to carve a small flower into the ground and noticed the image burning with fire, then causing a hole in the ground in the shape of a flower. Immediately, an idea crossed my mind. I went over to the gate blocking the passage, took the padlock in my hand, and drew a line across the handle of the lock that attached it to the gate.

The padlock fell off onto the ground, and the gate started slowly rising up shortly after. I could hear the loud metal clanking from the chains that lifted it open. Inch by grudging inch, the gate rose, dragging a curtain of dust and dried leaves along with it. I placed the broken glass carefully in the front pocket of my dress and looked over for Rylo as we both walked side by side through the fire-torched passage.

Walking with my eyes fixed on the ground ahead, as if anticipating a trip wire or trap, I could feel my heart pounding against my ribs. The gravel beneath my feet crunched with each tiny pop, seeming as loud as a gunshot. Cautious with every breath, I came to a halt and watched three furry brown balls rolling over in our direction. Out popped three hairy creatures with short, pointed ears and glowing brown eyes, giving them a whimsical, harmless nature. They walked on two legs while laughing endlessly, sounding like tiny chorus bells.

Their footprints left behind a glowing trail as they ran around me in circles, which began to slowly vanish. One by one, the footprints evaporated into the air, leaving behind no trace. One of them reached into my pocket, grabbing the broken piece of glass and running with it. "Hey! Give that back to me," I yelled as I ran after it.

The three hairy creatures rolled back into a ball shape and moved further away, making it even more exhausting for me to catch them. I couldn't even tell which one stole the glass from me; they all looked the same. The little brown balls of fur began taunting me, rolling all over the walls and floors, completely out of my reach. I stopped when I noticed a dark area ahead of us.

The torches were no longer lit, and the laughs of these furry balls kept getting further away. I lost sight of them completely. I really wish I knew where those fairies were right now; I could really use their assistance right about now. An overwhelming feeling formed in my stomach, as if a knot were being twisted and tied tightly. I walked back towards the torched path we came from, towards the gate, and tried looking to the other side to see if I could see anything.

I wondered what could be on the other side of the locked gate for a while. Looking at the broken lock on the ground as I sat there with Rylo for what seemed like forever, I finally got up and grabbed hold of it tightly, the broken, hard edges digging into my palm. I'm sick of being here, and I have to find the courage to walk through the darkness. It was the only way to move forward. I threw the broken lock hard against the wall; the impact of it echoed in the silence.

Grabbing onto a torch and continuing down into the unknown darkness extremely carefully, I could feel Rylo brushing up against my leg while walking. I saw a long, narrow piece of wood planked across the floor as a bridge to get to the other side. Beneath the wood were broken, crumbled pieces of the ground itself, fallen and scattered around, making a chaotic field of wreckage. It was deep enough that if I fell in, I knew I wouldn't be able to get out—that's if the fall didn't kill me first.

I second-guessed my own weight and whether I would be light enough to get across to the other side safely. I bent down and picked Rylo up while holding onto the torch. One foot in front of the other, one step at a time, as I held my breath. I entered a calm, almost meditative state, focusing only on the next step. We got across safely, discovering bloody handprints dragging across a wall.

CHAPTER 4

A Ghostly Gift

Looking closer at the wall, I noticed the rusted splatter of blood with a darkened, dull smear, as if it had happened some time ago. I touched it and was immediately brought into a vision of a woman with hair colors similar to mine, holding her shoulder while running down this exact passage. She was crying and had an open wound oozing blood. She removed her hand covering her shoulder and held onto the wall as if about to faint. She then took her time feeling along the wall, pressing into it, looking for a certain brick. She pushed firmly onto one brick, opening up a secret staircase from within the wall going upstairs.

I snapped back into reality, remembering exactly where the woman in the vision had been. I went to that spot and began to examine the wall closer, pushing against every brick near the dried blood. I finally pushed the right one, and the staircase came out from behind the brick wall. Since the area was illuminated by the light from the torch flames, I left the one I was holding behind.

Quietly, I began tiptoeing up the stairs, wondering what I would run into next. I could feel my hands shaking uncontrollably. I could tell this wasn't a good place to be. Why would Iscana send me here? It didn't make any sense to me. I bit my lower lip as I got closer to the top of the staircase. I took a big gulp of saliva and exhaled deeply but faintly.

I turned my head both left and right, looking to see exactly where I had ended up and how to get myself out of this forsaken mess. It looked as if I had ended up in a castle of some sort. This whole area was a dungeon maze full of both men and women, with heavy padlocks covering their gates. Every person had an enigmatic essence, and their gates were covered in green slime. As I walked by, watching the suffering look on their faces, I couldn't help but feel helpless, as I couldn't be the one to save them. This was so unacceptable. It was as if the slime worked as an invisibility barrier because no one made eye contact with me, nor did they utter a word.

I made a few turns and ended up losing my sense of direction. Straight ahead, I noticed another staircase. My fear was slowly turning into anger with each step I took. As I reached the top, I looked around and saw a detailed framed painting on the wall. I stared at it for a while and began to touch my own face, feeling as if there was an uncanny resemblance. I couldn't escape the feeling that the woman in the painting was keeping a secret. The purple garment she was wearing gave an illusion of depth and richness. It looked exactly like me. That can't be me.

An icy kiss of air caught Rylo's attention. He ran toward its direction and led me to a hall filled with more paintings, lined up in a straight row on the wall. One was an empty white canvas that had a beautiful silver frame around it. I looked at it with anticipation, as if something would happen. Right when I turned to walk away, I glanced back at the empty picture, and what was once white was now mirrored.

I could see my reflection clearly in the mirror, and I could also see the two fairies, both red and green.

"What happened to you guys?" I asked, looking straight into the mirror.

They explained Nedos was the cause of their entrapment and that they now had a specific time limit for being outside of the mirrors before they got pulled back in. It didn't seem right, but I was surely thankful that I had found them, even if they were trapped. I felt useless in their situation but knew I had to help them somehow.

The fairies emerged from the mirror and hovered around me, flying with great speed and excitement. I followed them to the next passageway as they led us through the halls up to another staircase. One thing stopped me from continuing: the sound of a man's voice. I could hear someone speaking in the distance. I whispered softly to the fairies, "Shhhhhhh."

Both fairies turned around and went back into my hair, one on each side, to avoid us being seen. The voice sounded very deep and ominous. I walked slowly towards a half-opened door and peeked through the crack on the side.

Two men were drinking wine and sitting with their feet up on a round wooden table, both wearing armor made of gold. From the look of their faces, I could tell they were related in some way—perhaps brothers or cousins. While I watched them, I covered my mouth tightly, as I didn't want to accidentally give myself away.

They started talking about how they were going to take all the prisoners to the top of the castle during the new moon and sacrifice them all, offering their blood to Nedos in order to strengthen his fleeting powers. These despicable, cursed men really had another thing coming to them if they thought they'd get away with something so heinous as this.

I started to feel the feather Iscana gave me loosening from around my neck. I tried to hold onto it, but I wasn't quick enough. The feather with the key attached to it began levitating in mid-air. It started to go towards the wall to the side of the door, close to its hinges. I noticed both their swords were standing against a corner near the door. I could hear the men starting to get up and walking towards the door. I dreaded being caught. I slammed the door shut and shoved both swords underneath the sliver of open space between the door and the floor.

The two men were now both pushing with all their strength on the other side of the door. "What is going on over there?" I heard one of them say as he tried to both pull and push at the door while the other kicked at the sword's sharp blade. As I kept watch on the swords, making sure they weren't pushed away, I noticed the feather go up to the wall and start engraving a message:

FIND THE ORANGE FUR CANDLE ...

What? A fur candle? That just didn't make any sense. I couldn't think straight right now. I needed to get away from this area before I was caught and something bad happened to me. Filled with anxiety and the sound of those men struggling to escape behind the door, I grabbed the feather and key and placed it back around my neck. Continuing on my path toward the opposite direction, I stopped in front of a window of great magnitude. It was as tall as an ancient oak tree and felt as if it were a gaping eye looking out towards the forest.

The grey afternoon light filtered through the thick, grimy glass panes, making the room feel cold and unwelcoming. It was wrapped in moss that was covered with drawings of evil, dark-looking shadows, almost as if they were drawn by a child. I picked one of the pictures, tearing it off the window to get a better view.

The picture was drawn all in black and had a couple of fingerprints on it. I started ripping off every single drawing and dropping them all onto the floor. I glanced down and could see Rylo dodging around the falling paper and even jumping onto a couple, making a game of it. Once I finished, I sat on the floor to carefully examine them all. I knew I didn't have much time, but this could be something important. I continued glancing through the drawings as everything around me started to waver like a reflection in a heat haze. Getting dizzy, I gazed into a trance.

Quietly, I saw the images from the drawing coming out of the paper and forming into physical bodies. They stood in a line like an army ready for battle right in front of me. I dug my nail into my wrist to try and wake myself up from the pain, but nothing happened. I continued pushing the edge of my nail into my wrist as

I was making eye contact with the leader standing in the upfront position.

"Thank you for releasing our souls from that haunted window. For centuries, we have been taken and kept prisoner here. Our bodies have been sacrificed by Nedos, then our souls were cast into these drawings, serving as his dead army."

"He took all of our magic powers, but we are no longer held captive, and to properly thank you, we have a gift to bestow upon you."

"Please, it's no problem at all, seriously," I replied.

"Do not be worried; hold out your hand." I trembled with fear, but without thinking, I could feel my hand reaching out.

The leader touched my hand, and I could feel a sharp vibration run up my arm and throughout my body. A lightheadedness overcame me, and I could feel myself levitating off the ground, leaving my physical body behind. It still had its hand holding onto mine, and I could see it now getting smaller as I continued to rise up toward the tall castle ceiling. Then the hand removed its grip from mine, causing it to snap right back up into itself as if it were made out of elastic. I noticed I was in control now and got used to the feeling of flying around. I managed to get myself back down to the ground and went toward my body.

"This gift is yours. Do you accept it?" I could hear the wind whistle into my right ear, almost with a high-pitched quickness.

"Yes," I responded.

"Once returned back into your body, you will have this ability to fly around just the same. The only downside is you cannot take your physical body with you. So whenever you decide to go on a flight, remember to keep your body safe and secure."

I woke up on the floor from the feeling of Rylo's cold feet pressing against my stomach as he smelled under my nose, making sure I was still breathing. I smiled and told him what happened. Even though I was scared, I had to figure all of this out and figure out how I could save these innocent prisoners and get out of this foul place.

Suddenly a thought crossed my mind: What if I fly through the door where the two men were locked behind? I wonder if the candle is there? How did I even activate this? The shadows didn't leave any instructions. What should I do? I just thought of it and closed my eyes, but nothing. I looked at one of the drawings again and held it for a moment, and still nothing.

I scratched my head in front of the window and saw a black dot on my hand in the reflection. When I looked at my hand close up, I could see it was shaped like a heart. What is this black heart doing here? My hand was already blue, now this. I touched the heart and immediately felt my body drop to the ground and my spirit rising into the air.

I thought, this must be the exact spot I was digging my nail into when the monsters first revealed themselves. Levitating in the air and looking around, I decided to peek into the room where the two men were to see if they'd notice me. Much to my surprise, they didn't notice a thing.

Moving past them, I tried to see if I could spot any candles lying around the room. I didn't see anything that stood out to me, but I continued to look around. The vast mahogany table was full of silverware and pewter goblets in the center of the room. A plate on the table where the two men were eating had nothing but the remains of half-eaten chicken on it. I began to notice a series of small, scattered white flecks of salt glistening in a serpentine path. While following it, one of the men walked across it over to a window, making a faint crunch underfoot.

I could hear him talking about how strange it was that both their swords had become lodged into the door, causing it to jam shut. He looked out the window to see if anything seemed out of the ordinary. As a guard walked by from down below, he whistled sharply, creating a sound resembling a boiling teapot about to burst. He gave a hand signal and went back to eating at the table while watching around the room in suspicion.

There was a corner of the room releasing a putrid stench. As I came closer to it, I could hardly catch my breath. The floor was scattered with dried, brittle red flower petals across the floor like forgotten promises. As I turned back around, I could see one of the two men directly in front of me.

He didn't have a clue I was sharing the same air as him. I pushed through his body, going unnoticed with my ghostly existence, which I was beginning to feel an excitement from. I caught onto a long, draped crimson-colored curtain and pulled at the base of it, causing the whole structure to come down. A loud, shattering thud echoed as the velvet collapsed into a heap. The man at the table flinched as the curtain fell down, his gasp lost in the clatter.

It felt good for a moment, causing a bit of havoc while in this form of my body. A black box about six feet high revealed itself from behind the curtain. The top of the box was covered in orange melted wax mixed with what seemed to be blood. The box had three switches on the bottom of it. I flipped the switch on the left, and the box lit up with fire from the inside. I flipped it back. The second switch I flipped in the middle made the box illuminate with bright blue lights; the intense coldness just by standing near. Before I could hit the third switch, both men came to fix the curtain that had revealed the strange structure.

While they were placing the curtain over it, I could start to hear the clink and rattling of metal armor far in the distance, getting louder with the march. A rhythmic thumping began vibrating through the stone floor as I watched the specks of salt losing their shape.

About a dozen guards wearing identical plated armor rounded the corner, entering the room, their steps all perfectly synchronized. The guards' arrival abruptly ended the calmness within me, and the fear inside began stirring. I had to get back to my body quickly before someone noticed my body laying on the ground. I gave one last glance around the room and exited from where I entered by passing the guards as they stood there speaking with the two men. They gave orders to sweep the castle halls on this level, looking for intruders or anything out of the ordinary.

CHAPTER 5

The Orange Fur Candle

As I returned to the area where my body lay, I saw an indigo-colored, transparent shield around the two of us. It was shaped like intertwined stars, spinning so fast it seemed to be moving in slow motion. I called out to Rylo, whose head was resting on my stomach, "I'm back!"

The shield around us began to fade when I yelled. I placed my hand over the black heart on my body and transferred back into my physical self. Next time, I must remember to hide and sit down before trying to use this magic again. Although it came from the shadows in those drawings, it felt as if a part of me had returned home—an unexplainable feeling that was always meant to be there.

I began to hear the rumbling commotion of footsteps getting closer. I gave Rylo a tug and signaled him to stay nearby with a slight hand gesture. Walking down another hallway away from the approaching noise, I noticed a strange luminescent orb of light fly across the window. Faint lines of ancient writing were etched into its surface, glowing from within.

It drew my attention toward a tall statue in the distance that seemed to command the center of the garden, looming over the flowerbeds. Hearing the metal clatter of the guards armor, I froze in fear, realizing they were closer than I expected. I quickly picked up my little companion and headed in the opposite direction. There was another window at the end of the hall, with nowhere else to go. I saw the same orb fluttering by the window beside me. I got a feeling it was trying to get my attention, leading me somewhere.

The orb began circling around the corner of the window outside. I pushed the side of the window, and it sprung open. Looking down at the space between my feet and the grassy ground below, it seemed too far of a jump—jumping down would surely lead to my death.

Rylo went out the window and walked along a narrow balcony, following the orb and making a clearly visible path for me to follow. Using my foot to quietly close the window, without leaving behind any suspicion or evidence of having been there, I moved along. Holding tightly onto the walls and the vines attached to them, I pressed my whole body against the side of the castle. My feet carefully slid side to side as I was plastered to the wall, my hands gripping each vine with desperation.

A red and black ladybug landed on my hand for a moment. I looked at it in admiration, having never seen one this close. A quick vision crossed my mind: a dark female figure with long ears and a green light glowing in her chest, running through trees, hopping and swinging around their branches as if they were an obstacle course. I snapped back into reality, watching the ladybug take off, leaving behind a small trail of glitter on my hand as it flew into the distance.

I didn't dare to look down, focusing only on the soft scraping sounds my shoes made from the crumbling ledge. The orb of light continued to lead the way while I followed Rylo, who was playfully dashing along. A long vine connecting from the castle to the ground lifted up and opened out a wide-reaching leaf. The orb flew over it, and we both jumped onto the leaf as it began slowly lowering us safely to the ground.

The air was thick and sweet, smelling of the nearby blueberry bushes. A sea of lavender stretched around us. Marigolds of yellow and orange hues blazed beside fragile, tissue-thin poppies and baby's breath that all danced with the slightest breeze. I had never been in a garden so captivating and beautiful. The plants were green with red and purple horizontal stripes. Some of the flowers looked as if they were made completely out of water, while others resembled fire. A small, secluded corner held chrysanthemums, which glowed as the sun's light beamed into the petals, illuminating their vibrant pink colors.

Everything felt magical, yet also strangely confusing to me. I walked over to the area where I had spotted the massive statue that the orb had brought to my attention. I came across a small bridge where the dirt below was completely dried out. A scatter of broken glass spread throughout the ground underneath the bridge. The shards were like tiny icebergs emerging from a sea of brown mud.

As we got across, I noticed a snail crawling under the bridge. It grabbed onto a piece of broken glass as it dropped its shell, wrapping its body around the shard. Immediately, right in front of my eyes, I watched the snail grow and transform into a human. Shocked and not believing my eyes, I stepped closer to the young man, who was covered in clear slime and hiding behind a bush.

As I got closer, I began to examine him and realize what had just happened. "What in the world? How did you? Who are you?" I asked in confusion.

"I'm sorry to meet you this way. I was certain you would have walked past the bridge without noticing me," he responded. "I'm Ceju. The snail you witnessed me transform from isn't my true identity. I'm from another realm. I've been waiting here at Wormwood Castle for you, us both meeting isn't a coincidence."

"This glass was placed here under Nedos' commands to serve as a trap if anyone were to cross over that bridge. I've been strengthening the bridge at its base for some time now, awaiting your arrival."

"I don't understand. So you came here from another realm and transformed into a snail?" I asked.

"Yes, I couldn't risk being noticed by Nedos or his guards. But now that you've arrived, I can finally release myself from snail form."

"Nedos has become obsessed with power ever since becoming immortal, and his mission has been to get rid of all magic beings, sacrificing them and absorbing their magic. Although immortal, his powers are fading, and he has to keep absorbing from others in order to maintain their strength."

Listening to him speak was becoming difficult to focus on as I noticed him trying to reach behind a set of leaves. He grabbed a nearby leaf and wrapped it onto a piece of glass pointing out from the ground, without removing it. It transformed into a jumpsuit in the same color as the leaf: green with red and purple stripes.

I didn't know if I could just trust anyone around here. This wasn't the best place for me to be in at all.

"I want you to know that you can trust me. Take this." He handed over a small, junky-looking bottle, beaten and with a ton of marks all over it. I twisted off the lid and poured the contents out into the palm of my hand.

"What's this supposed to be?" I said.

There were two burned pieces of wood inside. The wood had a mystical feeling of power as something began shining from within.

"This is O-Wood, the key to the statue that I'm sure you're heading towards. The statue won't open up without it; it hasn't for centuries. But I can see you are the proper soul."

"Proper soul?" I repeated, confused.

"Quiet! The guards are coming closer. We must hurry along the path. Head straight towards the statue and don't look back. I'll be right behind you; I just want to make sure our friends following us aren't able to find us." He said while giving a wink.

Ceju started gathering pieces of glass in his hand. He tossed them across the other side of the bridge. I watched as enormous purple flowers with human tongues sticking out began growing right where he threw the glass. As I headed towards the statue, I turned around and could see Ceju not too far behind me.

While both of us headed towards the statue, I could see the mutated flowers continuing to grow, their tongues dripping huge amounts of what seemed to be saliva down to the ground below. Those flowers should be able to buy us some time as they look really intimidating and completely block the way.

In front of the statue, I stopped to catch my breath. I began noticing that what I thought was moss covering the statue was actually some sort of fur material, which resembled that of an animal. As I pressed my hand up against it, feeling the base, it felt like a body, as if alive.

Perhaps this was my mind playing tricks on me. I hadn't believed my own eyes for a long time today. Everything had been quite strange. Out of nowhere, I started to give the statue a gentle rub, as if I were petting a loved animal.

Ceju caught up with us and stopped next to me, wheezing while catching his breath. I immediately asked what exactly those tongue-having flower monsters were that he had released by the bridge. He laughed and told me they weren't considered monsters where he was from.

"They do nothing but allow people that are in front of them to see exactly what they would see if they had nothing to look for."

"In better words, they're just an illusion, a disguise. You and I can see them from behind, but from the front, they're completely invisible, making the bridge and this whole area where we're at unfindable to the naked eye."

"Let's say one of the guards happens to walk into one of the flowers. Their tongue would lick that person, leaving them absolutely clueless while wiping their memory. Seems pretty harmless to me," Ceju mentioned.

"Now, the bottle with the two pieces of O-Wood, place one facing the north side of the statue and the other on the south, both pointing upright."

I did exactly as Ceju directed me, but nothing happened.

Ceju came over to where I was and started moving around the grass that had been overgrowing on the ground. Underneath it was a cemented brick with a cut-out shape inside of it, the size of a small rectangle, perfectly enough to fit the O-Wood. I went around the statue and ripped through the grass to find the other cemented brick and placed the O-Wood inside. The moment I placed it, I watched it immediately disappear.

"Did we do something wrong?" I asked.

"No. Look up," Ceju said.

The wind howled through the garden, causing the branches and leaves to roar. A sudden gust sent a flurry of leaves to spiral into a whirlwind of color. My sight became gritty, turning to a red-brown blur as the wind shrieked and shoved a fistful of dirt straight into my face.

I closed my eyes for a moment until I could feel everything coming to a halt. When I opened my eyes, I wiped the dirt from my eyebrows and shook out my hair. My eyes teared up as they worked furiously to flush out the grains of dirt. Everything around us lingered with small leaves in the air, floating down ever so gently. There was a small pillar with an orange candle on top of it that presented itself.

"The orange fur candle. This is what you need to help Iscana."

"How do you know her?" I replied.

"Iscana and I have known each other for many moons. She reached out to me, sending sound waves through the ocean. I was able to make sense of her despair while I was in snail form getting a drink of water."

"It's a lot to take in, but just know this strange candle is a very important object. You must guard it with your very life," Ceju explained. "This is no ordinary candle. It can bring back the dead momentarily. It's been protected by this statue for as long as I've known."

"When Nedos took over Wormwood Castle, I removed the two pieces of O-Wood from it. That caused the statue to go into lockdown protection mode. No one would ever be able to know its secrets without the O-Wood. Not even Nedos could reveal its secrets. I've been waiting for this exact moment in time. We have to get to Iscana's family tomb. Awaken them with the candle and have their powers lend their strength to Iscana. Until then, we don't have a chance against Nedos."

"Unfortunately, with the candle in your possession, it will start to attract all types of obstacles heading our way to stop us from fulfilling our purpose. We must hurry and leave this place," he explained.

"But what about the prisoners in the castle? I can't forget about them. We can't let them suffer and be sacrificed."

"Don't worry about them for now. Soon, once Nedos realizes that the orange fur candle has been restored and is in our possession, he will start to unleash his anger, forgetting about everything else. He'll stop at nothing to put an end to us and our plans."

"But don't you worry, my friend. I have everything we need, and so do you. We just have to do a bit of training first before things get serious. Let's stay here in the garden for a while," Ceju said as he walked into another area of the garden with a large open space.

There was a small plant on the ground, and Ceju walked up to it, examining it for a moment. He pulled at a stubborn weed until the fine, brittle roots were finally exposed, yanking it free with a shower of dirt. Ceju tossed it in the air with a piece of glass from under the bridge. He had saved a large handful in a leather pouch that hung from the side of his jumpsuit.

He turned the plant into a dark moon and covered up the sun, turning day into night. The stars immediately started revealing themselves one by one. As if I were controlling their appearance, everywhere I turned, I would notice another star forming.

"Okay, now that we're completely covered by the darkness, let's do some practice moves," Ceju hinted towards me.

CHAPTER 6

A Diamond in the Palm

As we stood in the open area of the garden not too far from the statue, I thought about what kind of training was about to happen.

"That arm of yours, it's blue for a reason. Do you know why that is?"

"If I had to guess, I'd say it has something to do with a dragon."

"Dragon's blood, yes, but so much more. Your arm is blue because it stores the blood of an Ancient Frost Dragon. Its blood fused into yours, causing your arm to not only turn blue but to harness the powers of Frost."

I looked at Ceju with excitement, amazed at each word that was coming out of his mouth. Looking back at my hand and noticing the shade of blue again, I started admiring it with awe.

"Trace the shape of a diamond into your blue palm with your other hand. This will grant you the ability to harness the Ancient Frost Dragon's power," Ceju said.

I looked up to the night sky as I turned my palm toward the pinpricks of silver pulsing melodically. For a moment, I felt inexplicably connected to the universe and everything around me all at once. Seeing the stars' reflection in my hand, I took my pointer finger and started tracing the shape of a diamond into my palm.

Once I drew the shape, a cold, freezing temperature came from my fingertip, spreading outward toward my elbow, but not extending beyond the colored area. I started wiggling my fingers slowly to catch the feeling inside them and noticed the colder it felt, the more I wiggled.

"Focus your energy on the coldness and let your imagination connect with it!" Ceju yelled out.

I didn't know what that meant, but as he said it, I looked into my hand and thought of a bear. I put my hand out and continued pushing from the inside out, feeling the coldness spread from my palm into the air. I watched as the bear in my thoughts came to life in the form of ice. I had no clue what I was about to get myself into. The bear was made completely of ice but was still able to move and sound like a real bear.

It scratched its back on a nearby tree, causing shards of ice to expel from its body in every direction. I gave a crazed glance at Ceju, my eyes widening in fear.

"What are we supposed to do now?" I asked.

"Control the bear and make him bend to your every command," he responded with a grin.

"WHAT?" I exaggerated my question as I stared head-on toward the bear.

The bear glistened like glass, both jagged and fractured with razor-sharp edges. When it walked, you could hear the shattering of ice underneath its feet as frost bloomed onto the surface below.

I gave another pulse out of my hand, this time thinking of a wolf. An ice version of the wolf I imagined appeared next to the bear. It was transparent, its internal structure swirling with a ghostly vapor, while a coat of fine frost covered its body. Its paws left no tracks in the ground as it walked over to me, smelling my hand covered in the cold ice. It had sensed that I was its creator, and once it had realized it, so did the bear. Both just harmonized right in front of me while I watched the magnificent magic I'd performed.

"The real training begins now. You seem ready with the two animals you conjured." Ceju reached into his leather pouch and carefully picked out a shard of glass, placed it on top of a rock on the ground, and then placed another rock on top of it. It transformed into a wooden dummy figure, mimicking the armor from the guards at Wormwood Castle. I squinted my eyes to adjust my focus on the dummy and try to make some magic.

I clamped my eyes shut, trying to block out the distraction and turn my focus inward. With my eyes closed, the noise of the ice crackled while I took everything around me into one deep breath. Feeling the palm of my hand, I noticed it burning with coldness. Looking down, I could see a large icicle forming from the center. Ice was poking out of my hand, like an iceberg in the middle of the ocean.

Holding it in front of the dummy, I began to press the pressure from within my hand, and shards of ice started shooting out toward the dummy. Out of the array of shards that I expelled toward the target, one missed by a razor's width. My head lowered in disbelief, then I immediately went for another attempt. Once the shards of ice dug into the dummy, both of the ice animals began attacking the target as well.

The wolf jumped from side to side, attacking at the base of the wooden structure, holding onto it and shaking with a mighty grip. I could see the wood starting to form ice around it, the wet crunch of its icy teeth against the wood ringing in the air. The bear charged with aggression toward the back of the target dummy, clawing at the neck and shoulders. With every attack, the sound changed, and the damage accumulated. The target became more scared and less resistant.

I started to charge my hand again, pressing this pressure from within and giving that cold feeling a sensation of freedom. I expelled it from the icicle forming out of my palm. By that time, both the ice animals stepped back to allow me a chance to strike at it. Multiple shards cast out of my hand with intense force, and I was able to get a direct hit on the target's facial area. I looked over at Ceju and gave a mischievous smirk. I pulled out my hand and pushed pressure from within, making one large shard of ice come out of my hand at once. It pierced into the chest of the wooden dummy.

I did the same thing once again, but this time the shard of ice was immense. It impaled the neck area, decapitating the dummy's head and sending it rolling onto the ground. The ice wolf walked up to the head and licked it, suddenly turning it into hard rock ice.

"Is that good enough training?" I asked.

"I thought it was. That was truly remarkable for your first time," Ceju said.

"So now what happens with the wolf and the bear?" I asked.

"They can either stay here and melt away or come back with you, your choice."

"How cool would it be to have my own ice minions? I certainly would like to preserve these two creations." Raising my blue-toned, cold ice hand out toward the wolf, thinking of a way I could bring it back, I started pushing the pressure within my hand and watched as the wolf slowly faded into a cloud of snow dust and retracted back into the diamond shape in my palm. I did the same to the bear, and it went back with ease in a whimsical gesture.

Looking around, I could see the huge mess left behind, as if there had been a snowstorm recently. I noticed my hand starting to feel normal again and could feel the warmth of my blood returning throughout the arm that was once of ice.

"Ceju, let's go back to Wormwood Castle," I nearly begged him.

"Even with your training, you still aren't ready for the troubles that come with that place. Honestly, you're lucky to have made it out there alive."

Ceju started moving around the wooden dummy laid out on the floor and made a small fire in the cavity of its chest that was impaled by the ice. I watched as the evidence of us having been there slowly melted away all around us. Normally, I'm always the first person to feel the chill in the air and get cold easily.

Ever since I had my hand altered, I haven't experienced coldness the same way.

Eating something right about now felt like a must, as I was starting to feel weak. I asked Ceju if he could make something to eat with those shards of glass he kept. He picked out a shard and asked what I would like.

"Surprise me. No, how about you make a pie—that's it, a nice blueberry pie," I requested.

Ceju ripped off a piece of wood from the bottom of the wooden dummy and pierced the small shard of glass into it. He held it in his two hands, both spread out, pressing together with both palms upward facing the night sky. The wooden glass melted into his palm, and out came a pie big enough to fit perfectly in both of his hands. I thanked him as he handed me the pie. Breaking it in half, I insisted on sharing with him, but he refused, making a disquieted face.

"You need all the energy you can get. Eat it all. I added some strengthening properties to it as well." I broke off a small portion and placed it on the ground for Rylo to have with me.

As I was finishing up, stuffed with pie and rushing to swallow a mouthful, I heard a raging commotion.

"What's happening?" I asked.

I could feel the ground trembling underneath us and could sense something bad was about to happen. I ran toward where we came in from, just to see if anything was coming from that direction. Before I could get too far, magenta smoke started rising up into the air. The flowers protecting the bridge were destroyed.

Panicked, I turned around and headed toward Ceju, grabbing onto his clothing and running without saying a word. Brushing up against every branch and leaf along the way, Ceju led us into an overgrown area. We continued running until we reached a body of water, surrounded by moss-covered rocks. Running through it, I could feel the water becoming deeper. The leaves around us started falling from the trees, like autumn happening all at once. The trees around us stood bare as the leaves on the ground were swept away by the forceful breeze.

We weren't easily hidden anymore. I turned to check on Ceju, and he had his whole body submerged under the water. I grabbed onto his leg and tugged at him. He came up quietly and pulled me under with him as Rylo followed. Holding our breath underwater, we swam slow and steady without making much movement to the water's surface.

As soon as we came up to catch our breath, I could see the guards from Wormwood Castle standing around near the body of water we came from. The water seemed to have connected from one pond to the next. It felt impossible that we were on the other side without swimming that far. I tried to go back underneath to not be seen, but it was too late. My colorful hair must've stuck out like a sore thumb since all the leaves and plants had fallen.

"To the other side!" yelled one of the guards.

Both Ceju and Rylo jumped out of the water behind me, and we continued running down a dried dirt road path. Its clay-colored surface was cracked, like having been sun-scorched for long periods of time. It seemed thirsty, as if it were begging for any type of moisture. Our wet footprints quickly absorbed into the ground.

Ceju pulled out a shard of glass and threw it onto the floor in front of us. A sunflower grew from the cracks in the dry ground. As it sprouted open, a swarm of monarch butterflies came out, fluttering all around us. Completely surrounding our bodies, a cloud of orange and black began taking over our sight.

"This will cause a distraction," he said. "Could you hurry and grab onto that ribbon hanging over by the light post there?"

I could hear the commotion of the guards as they tried to get to the other side. Some guards began throwing weapons and yelling toward our direction. I ran quickly over to the light post, grabbing the black ribbon and handing it over to Ceju. It had a weird texture to it, almost like moist sandpaper, like a cat's tongue. I saw images etched in black and white on the ribbon, but I couldn't make out what was on it from all the butterflies still fluttering around.

Ceju took the ribbon and said an incantation, "Jessu Dessu Kessu Lak." A dark shadow came out from the ribbon and transformed into a black creature on four legs. Its body was extremely furry all over, completely black, and had some spots that sparkled in iridescent shades of purple and blue.

Frightened by the sight of its looks, I grabbed Rylo and held him close to me, making sure he wouldn't fall prey to this creature. I watched as the creature began to scramble through the monarchs and across to the other side. Mangling and tearing apart the guards to pieces, my jaw unhinged in disbelief. The sound of their screaming pain hit through me like a sharp dagger. Although they were the bad guys, it hurt me having to hear and see them killed before my eyes.

"I wish they didn't have to die, especially the way they did," I said.

"Better off them than us."

I gasped for a breath of air and held onto Rylo tightly. I could feel him shaking his ears against my stomach. Ceju came over to us and wrapped his arms around us. For a moment, I felt my head resting on his shoulder, giving me a feeling of security and solace.

"You guys are safe with me," he whispered into my ear as he held onto us, feeling his heart beat through my body, pressing himself against my shoulder.

The creature on four legs came over to us with blood dripping from its mouth and claws. It didn't see us as a threat, but still looked like it was going to kill again at any given second.

"Climb on its back. We're headed to the X-Graves. He will be our transportation there," Ceju explained. "This is the guardian of the dead. His name is unknown and has been around longer than time itself. Give him a drop of your blood, and he will transport us. From there, you can find Iscana's family tomb and be another step closer to putting Nedos and his evil plans to an end."

"Only people from this realm can enter the X-Graves, and I am far from where I belong. I can go as far as the entrance gate with you. From there, you'll be on your own. I'll wait for your safe return."

"You have my word," Ceju said as he got on the back of the guardian.

Rylo and I both held on tightly as we adjusted to its silky soft, hairy body. We began moving at a speed so fast I could almost feel as if we were moving in slow motion. Shades of green, glistening lights floated around us. Blackness enveloped behind it, being consumed entirely.

I could start to see the colors of my hair begin to glow as we continued pushing through the darkness. On top of a darkened mountain, I saw an ancient-looking rusted gate with garden snakes wrapped around each point. The iron looked as if it had been corroded into the color of dried blood. Its sharpened edges seemed impossible for the snakes to be wrapped around without being killed.

The area gave off a feeling of menace and abandonment. The guardian lowered its body, and we came off one by one. Thanking it with a simple bow of my head, I walked toward the gate's entrance. Noticing another black ribbon tied to the gate, it resembled the one used to summon the guardian to get us here.

"Don't forget about the training. You'll be fine alone. Just remember that you have more strength than you may think," Ceju said.

"Now that you'll be on your own, just know only you can stop this, so be fearless and conquer."

Ceju began to get comfortable on a bench he made from a small bug on the ground that he transformed with a piece of glass from his pouch. The bench still had legs and the texture of the same bug in bench form.

"Thank you," I gave him a big, long hug as I prepared for what lies ahead.

CHAPTER 7

The X-Graves

ooking up at the tall, blood-rusted gate, I notice a metal sink in front of it with overflowing water that never reached the ground. I run my hand under the running water and watch as the gate opens. My hand never got wet; the water simply repelled against my skin. Beads of water ran in the opposite direction from where they splattered.

There is a large projection hologram of a pixelated beast, holding an old-looking book. It begins reading from the very beginning, using its claws to guide along the page. An unnatural, gnarled, vicious growl escapes it, a sound that is otherworldly.

The gate continues to open more and more. I slip inside while it is still opening. A terrible lament escaped the gate as it continued to swing open; the gate's hinges were like a pair of screaming lungs coming out of a newborn child, continuously crying as its first gasp of air was taken, being brought into the physical for the first time. My hands begin to tremble as I look ahead without moving.

An ominous screech let out from the gate as it slammed shut behind me, pushing me closer inside. It felt as if it were a warning, but I couldn't turn back now. Not after I'd come this far. Rylo is walking in front of me, acting as a source to follow. "Can you sense the family tomb of Iscana?" I called out to him, not expecting a response. I follow.

As I walked cautiously into the gate's opening, I scanned the area for anything that might stand out. Aged tombstones stood perfectly aligned, surrounded by thorny bushes that appeared as ghostly figures in the dim light. Every shadow began to move out of sight as I noticed them, keeping me on edge. Rylo stops and stares off toward a foggy mist heading our direction. A splintering crack suddenly echoed in the distance.

"Hello, anyone there?" I called out.

The dense fog creates an almost blinding sight before our eyes. Everything around us begins to be consumed in shades of grey and white. The cracking sound gets louder in my head as my muscles stiffened. Flickering figures glowing from afar began taking shape as they got closer.

Right in front of us stand figures made of wax, looking straight at us. There is a path not too far ahead from where we're standing, with small lights aligned on the sides of it. The figures start moving closer together, melting with each move they make. They didn't have any eyes or any features on their faces.

I sprinted past them, escaping from being trapped in the middle, watching as they continued to walk closer toward the center. They all morphed together into an epic entity. The size of this figure was about the size of a grand willow tree.

My eyes filled up quickly, watering as if I couldn't even control my emotions. A chill in the air sank into my bones; I could feel my arms trembling and shaking, almost ready to give up from the pressure and fear. I see Rylo in the corner, scared, hiding behind a decayed fallen branch, half submerged in a pile of dead leaves. In that moment, I forget everything, and my fear melts away.

Yelling loudly at the figure, I try to intimidate it, but it doesn't seem to help. Drawing the diamond shape into my palm, I activate the frost dragon powers within me. Multiple sharp icicle daggers begin to shoot out from my hand, piercing the wax figure. It continues moving toward me, throwing heaps of hot melted wax in my direction. I call out to the whispers I can hear in the wind, "I'm not afraid of you," I yell as I try not to get covered with the hot melted wax.

The figure starts to form a large ball of wax in its hand, looking ready to toss it at any moment. I try to

muster all of my strength, pushing out from my hand—
I don't know what I was thinking, just to protect
myself. A wall of ice formed in front of me as the wax
was thrown. I took no damage, watching as it melted
slowly against the iced barrier. I realized that the wall
was able to resist the melted wax successfully.

I tried to do the same thing on another side, with
the plan in my head to trap the wax figure behind four
walls of ice. The only thing is I didn't know how to
make the walls connect. Running out of time, we
started heading toward the lighted path. I turned
around and gave one last try; if this didn't work, then
I'd have no choice but to continue running away.

I forced an iceberg-sized glacier of ice to form from
my hand, starting off as small and gradually getting
larger. It continued growing in size while aiming it at
the torso of the wax figure. In an instant, I shot it
through its chest as if I were shooting an arrow. The
mighty wax has fallen under my magic ice, turning into
a flat piece of hard wax spread underneath it.

Rylo started heading down the illuminated path
without me. What I thought were mini lights from afar
were actually small mushrooms that gave off a UV sort
of color, enhancing the gravely texture of the road.
The hum of insects filled my ears as we pushed
through, making an obvious noise with each step.
There was no sneaking around here, that's for sure.

I can still hear the sounds of the pixelated beast growling that opened the gate for us. I see up above the sky is like a pixel vibrant green-colored static, feeling as if this whole place is computer-generated. I follow the lit path, passing by rows of weathered stones, each a monument to a story I would never know. The path comes to a fork in the road, while the scent of wet stone and decaying death lingers in the air.

"They all look the same. Which way should I go?" I call out to Iscana, "If you can hear me, help us find the path to your family." Nothing came from the feather tied around my neck, just when I needed it the most. I guess it wasn't a two-way communication device, but it was worth the shot trying. I feel the energy as I step along each path, trying to get a glimpse of what could be if chosen. I get the strong urge to stay on the right-hand side; we continue down the path.

A wide-reaching hedge maze sits in front of us, walls covered with scorpions of all colors and sizes. They're crawling from side to side as if guarding the area. I walk closer through the entry, thinking what would be the smartest way to get through here safely. As I looked around for a moment while biting on my lip, thinking, I thought of sending out some ice owls to aid me.

Drawing the diamond shape again into my blue-tinted hand, I begin concentrating on bloodthirsty, savage owls. Four ice owls begin to fly outward from the palm of my hand as I concentrate on them, each one being outsized by the previous one. I look up as the owls fly in circles around the entryway. Their slow controlled movement suggests a sense of dominance.

Before I start walking through, I expel a small amount of ice toward one of the countless scorpions. The owls began to focus on their target soon after, allowing me to feel safe while walking through. The owls are picking at each scorpion that looks to come my way, decapitating them one by one. The bigger owls even take a couple bites, eating some whole.

I start to feel this inner compass inside me; no longer lost and confused, I head along the path across the maze. There is a sea of green spread out in front of me, nothing but a straight-ahead path for now. I start to pick up the speed and begin running. The light continues to change as it erupts through the thickened hedges, changing from vivid to dark, being filtered through the branches while creating a ghostly effect.

I make a right turn, then another right, and continue straight ahead. The sharp talons of the ice owls grab onto the scorpions and spread them right in front of me, bit by bit—just dead scorpion bodies hitting the ground. As we headed through, I can hear the furious beak clacking of the owls as they target their next prey.

Forgotten statues covered certain corners of the maze with their eyes covered by moss dark as blood, and thick woody vines coiled around their limbs like serpents, never to escape. The statue reminded me of the one in the garden at Wormwood Castle. I reached into my pocket to feel and make sure the candle was still there. I didn't feel a thing. I can't believe it.

"I lost the candle! No, I couldn't have!" I cry out.

Beginning to panic, I started digging everywhere I could while looking around in circles. I stop and take a look at Rylo and notice him holding onto the orange fur candle with his small trunk wrapped around it tightly. I sigh in relief and allow him to continue holding it. So much time here would've been wasted looking for that candle if it weren't for him. He's more aware of things than I expected.

There's an eerie feeling brewing around here, as I get further into the maze. Sounds that seem to come from everywhere and nowhere at the same time. Thorny branches snag at my clothing as the walls begin to form closer together. The scorpions are no longer present, but I can still see the owls digging through the hedges and scanning the air. I turn left and head straight, then make a couple more turns, losing my sense of direction and inner compass.

The crushing weight of repetition consumes me, and I try not to allow myself to lose it mentally. After walking hopelessly, the last few turns started feeling identical to the others. Walking in a daze of confusion, I stare up toward the static pixels in the sky. The static above starts to form a faint arrow pointing toward the east. I stare at it until the arrow burns into my memory, and I start to go in that direction, almost feeling hypnotic.

There's a dark, heavy wooden door straight ahead, hanging from a single piece of wood. I run toward it, hoping it will be the end to this wretched maze. Placing my hand along the splintered wooden door while catching my breath.

"Ouch! A splinter!" I yelped.

My hand jerks away from the door while I clench my teeth, looking down at my hand. As I try to pick out the splinter from my hand, a relentless, nagging sensation formed around the splinter like a voice whispering from within. The pain in my hand starts becoming hot and angry to the touch. I couldn't focus, but had to continue moving forward.

The wooden door was extremely weathered and splintered, looking almost as if it would deteriorate with a single push. If only I'd paid attention to that before holding my hand against it. I turn the knob to open the door, but it's jammed shut. I bite at the splinter in my hand, trying to remove it as I look around thinking. As I pull my hand away from my mouth to examine the splinter, I turn my hand and notice the black heart on the side of my wrist.

This time I was ready, I sat on the floor and crossed my legs. Rylo watches and comes closer to sit with me. He holds onto the candle with a tight grip even as he comfortably lays between the gap in my legs. I focus on the heart and press my finger hard against it, as if I'm pressing a button of some sort.

My heartbeat slows down, and I can see my spirit rising up above my body. As I'm in the air, I can immediately sense the smell and taste of blueberries flowing harmoniously. I go over the side of the jammed wooden door and realize there were two large boulders blocking the way. From the looks of it, it seems to have been intentionally placed there to block intruders.

Pushing with all my strength on the boulder, I began to notice my strength isn't as strong as it would be with my physical body. My body's spirit floats around, looking for anything that could be helpful with moving those boulders. There's a tree in the distance with bottles of vivid colors hanging from it. I glide over to get a closer look at it as the colors mesmerize me. In an instant, I can feel myself being sucked into a bottle. I try to pull away, but the force is too strong.

Green-tinted glass envelops my surroundings; my every movement is consumed by it. Everything seems to be sealed off as if I'm trapped in a glass bubble. The colors of the surrounding hanging glass shine in the night with the glistening of the night stars from up above. The sky here was different from the rest of the grave. I look at the heart on my wrist and shake my head in disbelief. Look where you've gotten me, I speak to myself.

I start to nod off, getting sleepy. I try to fight the urge to fall into a deep sleep. My eyes are starting to feel weighed, as if resisting gravity. Struggling to keep my eyes open, becoming more drowsy. I can feel a haze coming along my vision, causing a blurring around the edges of my sight. I shut my eyes tight and start rubbing them, which seems to just make me more exhausted.

Yawning starts to overcome me, causing my eyes to tear up and burn. As sleep approaches, thoughts become dreamlike, and my internal battery begins to deplete. Inside of this fortress, I can see a woman outside by the tree, examining the boulders blocking the wooden door. She approaches the tree where I'm encapsulated. My vision goes in and out; with each time I open my eyes, I can see her getting closer. She's holding up a blue-tinted bottle as it hangs from the tree. While looking inside the bottle, she begins to laugh. Darkness suddenly consumes my sight.

CHAPTER 8

The Glass Snare

⌒

Awake inside the green glass bottle, lying on my side, I began to stand up with every bit of energy left inside of me. A sharp rap from the glass shattered my concentration, causing me to look at the source. The persistent bang against the glass continued, a rhythmic annoyance that grew into an alarm. She came over to me and plucked the bottle, which was hanging from a tree. Holding me in her hand, she walked over to her small wooden cottage.

Darkened with age and silvered by the moon, her cottage glowed in the night. Dead, blackened flowers filled the small window boxes lining the front of the house. A dramatic gothic crimson red door pulsed brighter and brighter with each step closer. In the center of the door, a brass knocker engraved with the symbol of a cross caught my attention.

The twisted doorframe looked like a welcoming smile but, at the same time, felt like a dreadful trap. I stayed still and watched as the woman placed me on a tabletop counter next to a bowl of dried beans. I overheard the woman talking to a raven sitting at her window.

"Go and give this to Nedos," she spoke.

She handed a small scroll to the raven's claw, and he took off, gripping the parchment. As the woman walked towards me, I could smell the scent of blueberries once again enveloping my senses. She took a teapot and poured hot water onto a dead flower sitting on the window. From inside the flower, a golden powder poured out along with a small golden egg that rolled onto her hand. She placed the egg in a skillet, cracked it open, and cooked it until it was ready. Then, she took the pan and placed it by an open window to cool off.

Grabbing a sharp knife, she headed over to the window and cut into the egg, eating it piece by piece. I could see her aura around her beginning to glow a bright purple color. The radiant glow started to blind me for a second before the intensity of her aura lessened, making her seem more rejuvenated.

I gave a knock on the glass from the inside, and she turned her head towards my direction. The woman grabbed a metal pole sitting on top of the counter and struck the bottle, breaking it on impact. I was freed and grew back to my normal body size. Before I could thank her for releasing me, she whispered, "He's listening."

I didn't question her and carefully followed behind her into a room covered with a variety of wind chimes. A tranquil serenity overflowed through this area, creating a constant, shifting melody. It was almost as if there were musical ghosts in every corner of the room. The sounds felt more like a presence than a noise, as if they seeped into your bones, filling the empty spaces of your mind.

She began to elaborate, "Nedos is coming after you. He knows you have the candle and that you're looking for Iscana's family tomb. I have been secretly against Nedos for centuries, awaiting his downfall."

"Finally, there's hope. You must, under no circumstances, speak of this to anyone. If word gets out that I helped you in any way, our hope is over, and most of all, my life will be."

She began moving her two long, gray strands of braided hair over the side of her shoulders, braided ever so neatly; not a single strand of color remained in her hair—it was as pure white as snow. Precious amethyst shades colored her eyes with a mystic radiance. Her face, though mature, still remained youthful with little signs of aging. I could see the crow's feet gather at the corners of her eyes, scrunching up with each movement of her face. The black lace dress she wore had holes in it, as if eaten by moths, from the bottom of the dress to her long sleeves.

Holding onto my hand, she told me to watch out the window with her as the sunlight started to break through the night sky. The sun's rays shone down only onto the tree covered with glass bottles, leaving the rest of the area cloaked by the night sky. She pointed towards the tree with the hanging bottles. One by one, small explosions inside each bottle began rising with blackened smoke, filling the air with enough smoke to simulate a fire being extinguished.

With a brutal swiftness, the wind disintegrated the smoke as it scattered throughout the sky.

"What was that?" I asked calmly.

"Those are the trapped evil spirits being broken and destroyed. They come out at night. The sun is the only thing that destroys them completely."

"The vivid colors of the shining glass bottles attract their curiosity while trapping them inside. Once trapped inside the bottles, it's only a matter of time before the sun demolishes them for good," she clarified.

"Is that why I was trapped as well, because I'm also a spirit?" I asked.

"Correct, my dear. This can only work on spirits. Luckily, you caught my attention before it was too late for you."

I sighed in disbelief, thankful that I'd escaped such a fate. A dry click echoed in my ears as I swallowed air.

"I'm Astra. Thanks for saving me."

"Yes, it was my pleasure. I'm Ferna. You should get going before someone notices you're here."

Ferna began to rummage through an old treasure chest: "Here, take this with you."

She handed me a pair of sai weapons, both looking like miniature tridents. Holding onto them, I started feeling their heavy weight and sharpness. The end handles were wrapped in a tough black leather with a red rope hanging from their ends. Intricate carvings displayed across both blades showed words of a different language, glowing red with each breath I took while holding them.

"This is the sai weapon I used when I was once a fighter. I've kept it hidden since living here under the watch of Nedos. I beg you not to use any magic until you exit the X-Graves. Using magic will only bring him closer to catching you. Use these weapons until you return back to Genesis Veil."

"They can destroy the toughest of enemies. This weapon alone isn't strong enough to defeat Nedos, but it is powerful enough to help along the path to freeing Iscana."

"Take the sai weapon and go. When you head out the door and back to your physical body, make sure you head north and don't get distracted. Also, whatever you do, don't look up at the sky. The arrows formed in the sky will only confuse you, leading you in the opposite direction."

"I don't know if you'll get lucky again as you did when I saved you, so be warned, evil is spreading around you. Nedos knows enough and has already sent his followers. The raven you saw earlier is headed to Wormwood Castle now to tell him that I still haven't caught you but still lighting blueberry candles to lure in hungry spirits. Hurry, my dear!"

"One more thing, and most importantly: the pixelated beast that granted your entry into the X-Graves is the time keeper. Once he is done reading from the book of the dead, the gates will close and won't open from the inside."

"I once tried to do exactly what you're doing now. My only mistake was following the signs in the sky; don't let them imprison you. When you hear the beast let out a loud, thundering high-frequency sound, that's your first warning to start heading back to the gates to exit the same way you entered. It will give out two more that will rumble the grounds beneath you. At the sound of the third eruption, the gates will be sealed."

I grabbed the sai weapons and began to head out of the room filled with the wind chimes. The silence outside the room was so sharp you could cut it with a knife. A deafening sound enveloped my hearing with a faint ringing in my ears. I gave Ferna a hug, feeling not much in return due to my body form at the moment. I smiled at her and nodded my head before heading out. She placed her hand over my head and said a silent prayer, moving her lips; I could barely make out the words.

Turning around, looking back at the crimson door, I watched her close the door behind me with a sense of relief, thinking soon one day everything would be alright. The energy and mood within her shifted; at first glance I perceived her as wicked, but after our brief time together, I realized she was actually a loving, gentle soul.

I floated past the bottled tree that once captured me with great caution, not flying too close as to get trapped again. I went through the wooden door and entered my body again. My heartbeat became noticeable again as I started to feel it racing and beating as if for the first time.

I sat there and gathered my thoughts for a moment as Rylo stretched his body from his nap. I looked to my side and felt the sai weapons on the ground, one on each side of me.

"These weapons are our way out. This is the only thing we can use now," I explained to Rylo by habit of talking to him, certain he could understand me.

A small cloud of brown dust burst into the air as I slapped off the dirt, grime, and grass clinging to my clothing. Ready and eager to start all over again, I adjusted myself. The growling sounds of the pixelated beast continued as it resumed reading from the book of the dead. I glanced up above me for a slight moment; feeling dazed, I started noticing an arrow forming, pointing towards the west.

This time I wouldn't be deceived so easily. I shook it off as I turned my head and body, telling myself not to fall for the confusion and traps set before me. It was almost as if some kind of magnetic pull was trying to avert my eyes upward. The ice owls guiding my way were left unattended for too long. They began to melt away, turning into a puddle of glistening water, shapes blurring into nothing. A slight, delicate cold vapor misted from the puddle as it evaporated into the thin air. I could hear the screeching of the owls one last time.

CHAPTER 9

Shifting the Balance

Gathering ourselves, we headed north, clinging only to the hope that this direction wouldn't betray us. The maze's hedges began to lower as we continued straight. We hit a blockage, forcing us to turn left. I had a strong feeling that this path was dangerous. Suddenly, the maze opened up, its design disrupted, freeing us from its confines. As we stepped out, the hedges rapidly closed in behind us, minimizing until they vanished completely.

A gate made of tangled barbed wire appeared ahead, bearing foreign script across its top. I drew my sai weapons and noticed the similar markings on the blades. Both weapons began to glow a brilliant red. I gently pressed one of the glowing sai against the gate, and it slowly creaked open. We continued straight until we walked directly into a dense, ghostly grey fog.

The lack of wind sent a prickling sensation across my skin, raising the hairs on my arms as coldness pebbled my flesh. A primal alarm bell vibrated in my chest as I crept along the path. I found myself unable to blink as I peered ahead, noticing a pair of luminous green eyes fixated on me in the distance. The muscles around my eyes began to twitch as I struggled to keep focus.

The eyes began to spin continuously, accelerating until they formed a bright green ring of light around us. Clenching my weapons, I charged straight into the ring. Just as I was about to break through, the spinning stopped. Standing before me was an elegant, illuminated green fox, sitting upright. From the ridge of its back down to its tail, it bore captivating, lime-green, peacock-shaped feathers. It was almost transparent, with long, pointed ears reaching toward the sky. I slowly began to lower my weapons.

The moment my hand dropped, the green fox lunged, its wide mouth open in the air. I threw myself out of the way, dropping my weapons to the ground. They were now out of reach and sight; I saw nothing but the fox's glow through the thickening fog—it was the only thing my eyes could focus on. Instantly, I felt the weapons slide back against my back. I grabbed them and struck toward the fox.

"Stay back or you'll be sorry!" I yelled.

The fox's anger intensified; the feathers on its spine rose up, shaking with a rattling noise. For a moment, I gave up, but in a split second, a fearless power surged within me. I dodged the fox's attack again, this time slicing a cut across its back leg. Green smoke bled from the wound, mixing with the fog. Avoiding the fox's path, I ran, attempting another strike. The fox outran me, stopping right in front of me, face-to-face. My hands stiffened at my sides, my legs rooted to the floor. I pushed with all my might, the power of the sai pulsing through my veins, and stabbed the fox swiftly in the throat. The green fox slowly melted away, fading into smoke that lingered in the air.

The sai began to glow, the writing on it becoming visible after the contact with the fox. A loud, thundering, bellowing roar—the one Ferna had warned me about—consumed my senses. Time was running out, and I still hadn't reached the tomb. Through the multi-colored fog, I could make out a pixelated black wall. Eyes, surrounding the pitch blackness, began revealing themselves one at a time.

The wall was staring back, its eyes following my every movement. I pushed my hand through an area to see if it was a hidden door. My hand went seamlessly through, feeling soft to the touch, almost as if the material were melting. There was nowhere else to go, and time was of the essence.

Headfirst, I stepped into the dark, eye-covered wall with Rylo. Walking straight, I could barely see anything. The ground felt textured but slick. A bright blue outline sliced through the darkness ahead. I could make out a light coming in and out of sight—the awning of a door. The outline resembled a flash of lightning momentarily illuminating the area, pulsing like a rhythmic heartbeat.

We stood in front of the door, flanked by two fire lanterns burning with a soft, gentle glow. The ground was embedded with marbles: mostly silver, blue, and white, with sporadic red ones. I felt uneasy, but detected no immediate danger. The key, wrapped with the feather around my neck, levitated into the air. A keyhole appeared in the center of the door. With a swift movement, the key unlocked the door, and its light remained steadily lit without a pulse.

I entered, feeling a sense of ease that Iscana's family tomb was finally found. The room was completely surrounded by walls of falling water, creating a distorted, waterfall-like view. Above, long drooping plants with white poppy flowers hung perfectly still in metal chambers, completely covering the ceiling.

A lever with a ridged bar handle sat in the corner of the room. I made my way toward it, pressing forcefully downward on the end of the handle as it groaned and screeched. Bracing myself against the ground, I placed all my weight on it. With a sudden lurch, the wall of water in front of me slowly lifted upward, revealing the inner chamber of Iscana's family tomb.

My eyes were amazed by a magnificent, polished granite tomb, stained with mold and moss. Carved inscriptions covered the front arch of the doorway. The two glass windows in front were covered in a thick layer of dust. I wiped one to glance inside before I entered, but the dancing dust motes prevented a clear view. Upon entering, I was greeted by a stray spiderweb that entangled across my face. Brushing it off, I began to dust everything inside the tomb out of respect.

"Hello, I was sent by Iscana to awaken you," I called out into the cavernous space.

The muted, muffled noises from the falling water outside continued. I kept looking around, touching almost every surface, until I triggered a switch that opened a hidden compartment in the floor toward the back of the room. Iscana's feather around my neck sent vibrations down my spine.

Reaching in, I felt something moving inside. The sudden movement made me flinch, and I stiffly pulled my hand away. I placed the orange fur candle on a long, empty candlestick wrapped in orange cloth. Taking a flame from one of the lanterns at the front entrance, I lit the wick. It crackled, and the room began to glitch, flickering as if it were about to disappear.

The air was cold, carrying the scent of damp stone and old dust. Iscana's silver feather floated off my neck and dove into the ground where I had felt the movement. Two beams of light shot up, each containing the shadow of a woman and a man. The hole in the ground closed up, and the shadows slowly began to reveal features as the light beams around them faded until they were completely gone.

A woman and a man stood before me, wearing tall, jeweled crowns that created a striking silhouette. The jewels flashed as they held their heads with perfect stillness. They both had pink-tinted skin and gleaming, dark-pitched black hair. The hair was equally long, reaching to their legs and spreading across the floor. Rylo ran over to them, jumping for joy at the sight of his lost family.

"Iscana is in trouble!" I yelled immediately. "She's been turned into some kind of animal, trapped by Nedos, and she needs your strength to escape."

"I'm Astra, by the way... Nice... to..." I paused, interrupted by the familiar rumbling roar echoing in the distance.

"That's the sound of the pixelated beast guarding the gate; it's about to lock us in permanently if we don't get to the entrance quickly. We don't have much time. Can you help us, please?" I trembled, thinking this would be the end of us all.

Iscana's parents each took a long, thick section of their hair, throwing it toward Rylo and myself. It instantly wrapped around our legs. A shock of darkness overcame me, and my head tilted back. Moments later, we were transported to the gate's entry. I saw Ceju on the other side of the gate, waving his arms at us to hurry as the opening rapidly shrunk.

At the last possible moment, we escaped the X-Graves. I was overwhelmed that we had made it out, feeling the reality that we could have easily been trapped. Iscana's parents stood side-by-side, emotionless, watching as I dramatically rejoiced, trembling uncontrollably.

"That was too close for comfort," I sighed, catching my breath.

"Did everything go alright there?" Ceju asked.

"For the most part, yes, but look—I found Iscana's parents. I don't think we were properly introduced," I said, turning to face them.

"I'm Astra, and this is Ceju; we're friends of Iscana."

"Pleased to meet you both," they replied in unison. "We are Onisa and Eiko, both celestial beings."

"Do you know where Iscana is right now?"

"No! I actually don't. I know there's a castle where she could be. Nedos trapped her and refused to change her back to her normal form because she wouldn't marry him."

"I've seen the chambers given to her in that castle, but she wasn't there. The last time I saw her, she sent me to Wormwood Castle to see things for myself. The thing is, I really can't tell you where she could be," I said, holding my hand to my head, trying to recall anything of importance.

"The mermaids, I remember now. Last I saw her, we were underwater in a capsulated room. She pulled out this feather and wrapped it around my neck with this key I used to find you two. Next thing I knew, I was heading down a small door with just Rylo."

"We will send vibrations through the waters to search for Iscana then," they replied. "Be cautious on your journey and hold tight the memory of Iscana; you're stronger than you know."

They both lifted their heads toward the pixelated sky, their long hair wrapping around themselves completely. They vanished within an instant, without even a strand of hair left behind.

"Ceju, I found them! It was insane in there; I can't believe I'm standing here in front of you. I really didn't think I'd make it out of there alive."

"I knew you would, Astra," Ceju nudged my shoulder as he responded.

"You know, I met an interesting person there. Her name is Ferna, and she gave me these sai weapons." I pulled them out from my sides, swinging both carelessly into the air.

"Wow, these are not ordinary weapons. These are from ancient times; look at the inscriptions," Ceju said, grabbing one and running his finger across the lettering.

"Ferna, you said her name was?" he asked.

"Yes, do you know of her?"

"No clue, but I do know this writing. She has to be a Holy Ancient."

"There was a time long ago when the Holy Ancients would heal and help people. Some would travel galaxies away just to breathe the same air. Some believed that a Holy Ancient could see glimpses into the future, aiding you in your troubles."

"Ceju, there's another thing. I saw her talking to a raven; she gave him a scroll to send to Nedos. She's working for him in disguise. We have to help her. If it weren't for her, I wouldn't have made it out of there."

"If we don't make it out of here now, we won't be able to even save ourselves. We'll be back for her," Ceju bellowed.

He started to unwrap the black ribbon from the side of the lamppost by the gate. Watching while he removed the ribbon with ease, I began preparing for the guardian of death to arrive. He took the ribbon and began to recite the incantation: "Jessu Dessu Kessu Lak."

CHAPTER 10

Cost of Salvation

he guardian of the dead that brought us to the gate was summoned before us once again, glaring with its malevolent gaze. We jumped onto its back, and this time, I pricked my finger with the sai weapon onto its black fur as our form of payment. We held on tight as we were taken to a place with nothing but sand and a compact tent.

"Why did the guardian of the dead bring us here? I thought we were going back to Wormwood Castle?" I asked.

"We'll be there shortly. I just need to gather some equipment." Ceju rang a small bell on the top of the tent with his finger, slightly.

Out sprung a tiny, wobbly old raccoon, wearing red goggle-glasses and holding a distorted, burned leather book in its hand. It scratched vigorously at the front of the book, turning it into a different shape. What once resembled a book now became a cup filled with hot, steaming liquid. The raccoon took a cautious sip before making eye contact with us, adjusting the goggles on its face.

"Hello. We've come a long way to ask for your help; there's someone we have to save from the X-Graves."

"There isn't much I can do in that situation, I'm sorry." The raccoon took another sip of its beverage and scratched at the side of the cup with its sharpened nails. The cup transformed into a bundle of white-tinted plants, neatly wrapped with twine. It pulled out a match and lit the stick, letting smoke form around us as it waved the bundle around our bodies.

"Please, isn't there anything you can do for us? She isn't dead—she's the only one there that's actually alive!" I shouted, making the raccoon give me its full attention.

"An eye for an eye," it said as it slowly stopped waving the burning plants.

"What are you talking about?" I responded.

"I need an eye. Only then will I be able to help you. You want to save a soul, don't you?" The raccoon explained.

"I'll do it," Ceju interrupted.

"Are you crazy? Don't. Let's go, we're not doing this." I pulled at Ceju as he pulled away, choking on the dry desert air.

"This is the only way to help that I know of here. Trust me, everything will turn out okay."

"No, you've done too much already. Why do you have to put yourself through this? It isn't necessary; we can find another way."

"I've made my decision, Astra. Please..."

He crawled into the tent with the raccoon, leaving me alone outside with nothing but my thoughts. I sat in the sand for what felt like an eternity; the sun was out, but there wasn't any heat. I could feel my nerves coming and going as I bit at the skin around my fingernails. Rylo played, making a small heap in the sand, completely oblivious as to what was going on inside the tent. I didn't hear anything but the sound of mechanical metal clinking from inside.

Ceju finally came out of the tent with his left eye covered by a bloody bandage wrapped over the top of his head. The raccoon behind him handed him a vial.

"Pour three drops into your new eye once you leave here. It will give you the power to pry into anyone's life, like a two-way mirror. It will also give you the ability to save one soul from damnation. Upon arrival, you must give your new eye and have that person consume it in order to escape the X-Graves without the pixelated beast noticing."

Ceju nodded his head at the raccoon's command. I held my hand over my mouth in pure disbelief. I don't think I would've given up my eye. Why would he do such a thing? He doesn't even know this woman. We said our goodbyes to the manic, eye-obsessed raccoon. As it turned and headed back into its tent, I could see the mess left behind: a shelf filled with jars of eyeballs stretched around the top. The tent closed, and I hugged Ceju tight, rubbing his face with ease.

"I can't believe you did this," I said to him as I pulled away, looking into the eye freed from the bandage.

The raccoon came back out of its tent and brought out a drawing done in black paint.

"This was drawn by my son when times were different, before Nedos took over Genesis Veil and we were a family," it said.

"We were all separated during the takeover. While everyone escaped, some made it to the human realm, Starfall. My wife was trampled to death by the stampede of people rushing through portals. I looked all around for my son until I saw Nedos and his guards surrounding him, taking him prisoner. He doesn't know it, but he holds magical powers."

"I'm unsure what it may be exactly, but magic is bound to our blood," it said. "My son is alive, I can feel it. Please, if you see him on your travels, can you give him this?"

The raccoon handed over the drawing. Ceju mentioned that he had heard of the takeover of Genesis Veil and had come to aid in its revival. That's why he transformed into a snail to avoid being found on Nedos' radar near Wormwood Castle the day we met. He was just waiting for the day he came across me. It was as if I was so important, but I didn't understand why. Hearing Ceju say that, the raccoon looked more relieved.

"I'm Nexus the Alchemist, as you may or may not already know. My son, Vex, was probably too young to remember anything, but I know that once he sees this drawing he made of our family, he will. Please, will you do that for me? It's not safe for me to leave Desert Driftia yet. Until I know for certain Nedos can't harm again. Besides, there are so many others who come here for my magical aid. This has been my secret relocation for some time, and although it's been quiet lately before your arrival, I believe I could still be of help. I would be useless if taken by Nedos," Nexus said.

"Of course, we will do that for you," Ceju responded as he grabbed the drawing, folded it, and placed it carefully into his pocket.

"Vex has one white ear, by the way; you'll easily be able to notice him. He will be at the age where he's able to harness his powers from within. Showing him the drawing should be enough to help," Nexus explained. "One last thing, be careful when walking through the sands; there are strange creatures living here."

"How do we get out of here, Ceju? I don't see that black ribbon anywhere around here." I looked around, seeing nothing but open space in the desert area.

Ceju pulled out his pouch filled with broken shards of glass and crushed one in his palm, throwing a fine mist of glass into the air. As it dispersed in the wind, the glass created a prominent line above us, then faded away. The spot where Ceju's new eye would be was still covered, making him unable to see properly.

"We should head that way," I said, pointing in the direction indicated by the glass.

We thanked Nexus one last time before heading off into the desert distance, unknowing what lay waiting for us. Nexus stood in front of his tent, watching as we got further into the desert until we were completely out of sight.

"The black ribbon that will transport us should be along the way if we continue straight," Ceju said.

As we walked side by side, I couldn't help but look over at Ceju's eyes. I wondered what it would look like once revealed. He didn't seem to be in any pain, walking with his head held high. The scorching sun created a shimmer of heat around us. The sand slowly became a nuisance, flying into my teeth, and I felt the gritty crunch as I tried to get it out of my mouth.

We passed along the sands to a dried, cracked land, as if it had once been a body of water. A tall rock was off the path where we were headed, and I pointed it out to Ceju.

"If we get on top of that rock, we could get a better view of the area," I said.

"No, Astra, trust me. We shouldn't stray from this path; this is not a safe place to venture around." As he said that, I could see the rock in the distance growing closer.

The rock became close enough for me to notice its shape forming in front of my eyes. A dingy, rustic-looking robot revealed itself, shifting from the rock form it hid in.

"What brings you to Desert Driftia?" it said.

"We came to find a lost friend of ours," Ceju said swiftly.

A loud explosion caught our attention in the distance. Other robots were heading our way, acting destructively, causing the ground to tremble beneath our feet. Ceju pulled out a shard of glass and created a small memory card chip. As the robots continued heading towards us, he jumped onto the leader robot's back, removed what was there, and placed the memory card in a slot behind its neck.

The robot turned around slowly to look at the others, and they all stopped in their tracks. Once Ceju jumped off, the robot began to hold out both its hands, causing two holograms to pop up. Unable to make out what the holograms were, I drew the diamond shape into my hand and poured out ice toward the floor, creating a barrier between us and the robots. Immediately, the ice started to melt into the dried, cracked land, creating a flowing river.

"Hurry, before they override the memory card I placed in the leader's neck," Ceju said as we started running along the side of the river.

"There, I can see the pole in the distance!" I yelled out.

That had to be the pole with the black ribbon attached to it. The robots came back to their senses and chased behind us. Robot hands began breaking through the ground as we ran past. As they emerged, the others became angry and formed around us, closing in. I drew the diamond shape into my hand, creating a group of ice wolves to attack them.

I pulled out the sai weapons Ferna gave me, and the robots backed off, allowing us to reach the pole. I couldn't tell if it was the weapons or the wolves, but I was relieved we didn't have to endure any fighting for now.

"Okay, let's go find Iscana," I said as we walked toward the pole tied with the black ribbon, pulling the wolves back into my palm before they melted completely.

CHAPTER 11

The Well of Oversight

We used the black ribbon once again to summon the guardian of the dead. After Ceju said the incantation, we hopped on, and I pricked my finger as we headed toward Wormwood Castle. From a distance, we could see the castle on the other side. I pulled out the eye drops for Ceju and immediately started unwrapping his face, causing his eyes to close shut.

"Whatever you do, just don't be startled, all right?" Ceju's hands were clenched tight.

"Okay, open up. I'm going to put the drops in."

As he opened his eyes, it looked like the entire eye was covered in blood. I squeezed the drops directly into his eye; a sizzling, burning sound emitted, causing him to drop to the floor in agony. I knelt on the ground, holding him in my arms until the pain from his eyes subsided. When he got up, I tried to get a better glimpse of the eye he'd had removed. The cornea resembled a golden-yellow star.

"How do your eyes feel? Can you move them?" I asked, trying not to stare too much.

"Surprisingly, I feel great after those drops. I just have a slight headache, but that's nothing," he responded, moving his eyes all around to make sure both functioned correctly.

"Yeah, I can move them all right," Ceju said, glaring toward the castle.

"Look, there's smoke..." Ceju pointed at the rising smoke, heading into the clean air.

The smoke rose, becoming thicker each moment, and now held a magenta hue, hanging in the air like a ghostly veil. I watched birds flying away from the castle's direction, heading toward us by the forest. The new moon phase approached, drawing closer to the sun. We headed toward Wormwood Castle, ready for a fight. I noticed something catching my attention in the corner of my eye.

I glanced to my right as we walked and noticed an oval-shaped mirror hanging on a nearby tree, held by a nail. I walked up to it, leaving Ceju for a moment. The Red and Green fairies who were once hidden in my hair appeared in the mirror's reflection. As soon as I saw them, they emerged from the glass, fluttering around me, buzzing with joy. Both flew back into my curled hair before Ceju could notice.

"Don't be afraid of them," I heard their whispers from within my hair.

"Are you all right over there?" Ceju called out, looking confused as he watched me touching my hair near the mirror.

I headed back toward him, continuing straight to the castle. Before we got any closer, I asked Ceju if he could use his new eye to locate Iscana. He held his hand over his face, leaving the star-shaped eye exposed as he stared blankly into the distance. He was zoned out for a moment before dropping his hand to his side, returning to himself.

"She's trapped in an underwater cave with some kind of reptile guarding her. I can see her just lying around; she looks really weak."

"Oh, we have to hurry!" I picked up the pace as we headed forward.

Running now, I lost my balance and fell, knocking my head on a sprawling heap of old branches scattered across the ground. Getting up, I realized I was alone, surrounded by fire in a narrow alleyway. I ran down the wall and climbed it, using the slight ledges from the unevenly laid bricks—just enough for me to lift myself up.

A prickly sense of familiarity washed over me: an overwhelming feeling that I'd been here before. Every movement felt like a familiar groove. I started walking as if I knew exactly where I was headed, guided by my inner senses. Slowly, I started seeing movement forming in mid-air, as if someone were trying to get my attention. Invisible figures walked toward me, revealed only by their flashing, blue, transparent outlines.

The whole area around me was consumed by invisible figures, structures, and nature. A twitch in my leg jumped repeatedly from the sudden nervousness I began to feel.

"You're Astra, aren't you?"

"Yes, I am. What is this place?" I asked.

"You're in between worlds. You knocked yourself unconscious, but we have something important to show you."

The invisible figures carried me; I floated slightly in the air high above their heads in a sitting position, feeling almost like I was sitting in a comfortable chair. A long, thick red line of marble spread across the ground, dividing it. As we crossed over to the other side of the line, everything around me began to form its color and shape.

I began to see the invisible figures who were once carrying me; all were women. Their faces and bodies were uniformly tinted blue. Each had dark-blue hair, all the exact same length, as if they were replications, except one that only had one eye. Piercing blue eyes blended with the other blue features on their faces. The mysterious blue-eyed, blue-bodied figures placed me on the ground, all staring at me blankly.

"Follow us to the well," one of them said as they all guided me along the path.

"The Well of Oversight. It will give you answers to your soul's awakening."

"My soul's awakening? I don't understand what you're talking about. What kind of awakening can my soul possibly have?" I chuckled.

"Take this stone. Hold it close to your heart for a moment, focus on it, absorb it, and become one with it. Then cast it into the well."

I took hold of the stone, questioning whether or not I should do as they said. I examined it in my hand: a blue stone with silver, sparkling shards inside, giving it a grainy texture, as if it could crumble to pieces if I squeezed it hard enough. Without overthinking, I held the stone against my heart and closed my eyes. A spinning sensation formed around me in circles as I focused on the stone, causing me to get dizzy. I pulled the stone away from my body's grip and noticed it gleaming in my hands, glowing with an inner light.

I tossed the stone into the Well of Oversight that emerged from above the ground. I listened but didn't hear the water splash until after a brief moment. Rushing water began bursting into the air, creating a mist above. Images started to form in the sky mist, almost like watching a faded memory.

"What the... who is that?"

"You don't recognize her?" one of the blue-bodied figures mentioned. "Take a long, hard look."

I stared at the misted images, trying to make sense of who this could be. An overpowering sense of hate consumed my body as I began to realize who was within the mist. It was Xara! She was standing in a kitchen, writing a letter with blood. Looking at the mist, I noticed it was the same exact letter I remembered reading some time ago. My memory still remained foggy, but I was slowly starting to piece things together.

"Why would my own friend be doing this? I don't understand." I looked over at the blue-bodied figures.

I watched Xara pouring blood onto the floor toward a basement area. She grabbed a pair of oversized shoes, put them on, and created intentional footprints in the blood heading in that direction. Shaking my head in disbelief, I felt nothing but absolute betrayal as I slowly recalled the lost memory. The dots are starting to connect in my head. Speechless, I continued gazing up into the mist in the sky.

Xara started gathering her belongings and cleaning up any signs of having been there, then hid behind a bush. The mist gradually faded into the air at that point, stopping the cinematic display. Being backstabbed by someone I trusted made me feel foolish for ever considering her a friend.

"Don't let your emotions control you; use this knowledge to your advantage," the one-eyed, blue-bodied figure whispered, as it rested its hand upon my shoulder.

"The most dangerous journey is the one back to yourself."

"Who are you all?" I held onto my head trying to grasp everything that I'm seeing.

"We are the Sapphire Mora, a race sent between realms here at The Half-Light, neither dead nor alive living in eternal twilight. The evil sorcerer Nedos was jealous of our beauty and cursed our family, causing every woman to be turned to this blue toned shadowy existence. He threw us into a sapphire colored mirror at Wormwood Castle, the place he now rules over. Our hope remains in you, Astra. Unable to travel out of this realm without our bodies turning to dust, you're the key to his undoing."

I gazed into the bewitching eyes of the Sapphire Mora, feeling a strong force pull me. My whole body felt squeezed through a tight hole. The sensation of sharpness tingled across my skin, as if passing through a cactus field. I woke up lying on the ground with Ceju looking down at me, holding my head up beneath his arm.

"You all right, Astra? You were knocked out for a while there."

I tried to gather my thoughts, remembering what had just happened and what I saw in the mist from the well. I was filled with anger as my heart raced. I tried not to think about it and let it affect me.

"I'm all right. I just need a moment, please."

I headed over to the nearest shaded area and sat on the ground, holding my hand over my temple.

"You look stressed, Astra. Are you certain everything is all right? Give me your hand."

I placed my hand in his, and he lifted me from off the ground.

"Whatever it is, just know I'm here for you. You can trust me." The feeling of doubt crossed my mind for a split second.

"Let's go, come on!" I started heading toward the smoke billowing from the castle.

The air began to smell putrid as we got closer. I had a bad feeling we were too late. We reached the side of the castle's dungeon by swiftly moving through an array of obstacles. Traps and moving razor-edged pendulums swept rapidly across multiple areas, making it nearly impossible to reach the castle. The massive gate leading toward the inside was sealed shut, its rusted teeth piercing into the stone floor.

"There has to be a way inside the castle from here," I thought out loud.

Trying to think of a way through, I suddenly remembered I could use my spirit to travel. I sat on the floor and got comfortable.

"Wait here with Rylo; I'm going to be right back."

I looked for the black, heart-shaped mark on my wrist and pressed my finger hard against it. Seeing my spirit floating above my body for the first time, Ceju watched in amazement. I was unsure how he could see me—perhaps only people equipped with magic could notice me in this form. Ferna was the only one who had noticed me besides Ceju. I pressed a finger to my pursed lips, hinting for his silence.

As I pushed through the massive gate blocking our entry, I looked around for something to release it. I floated past the other cells where prisoners had once been. Every cell seemed to be completely empty. Not a person in sight. The slime that used to cover the gates was gone as well. I feared for the worst.

CHAPTER 12

Journey Uncharted

Levitating through the castle's dungeon halls, searching for a way to open the blocked gate, I saw a shadow approaching in the distance. It's Xara, the traitor. What is she doing here? She's carrying an open box filled with brightly spotted and striped venomous snakes.

She snatched one by the head and swallowed it whole. One after another, she forced them down her throat until the box was empty. Groaning in agony, she collapsed onto the floor for a moment. I circled her, pressing against the walls, desperately searching for a secret button like the one I'd found before. One of these bricks had to be false. I saw the staircase Xara had descended, beckoning me to go up, but I couldn't risk leaving my friends—especially now that Xara was here, full of snakes. I pushed against every stone until I felt a distinct movement. I heard the prison gates rumble as they began to lift from the ground.

Returning to Ceju and Rylo, I pushed my spirit back into my physical body. As my consciousness settled, the fairies in my hair fluttered free from the entangled curls. The fairies immediately darted up into the castle toward the staircase where Xara lay struggling. I saw her there and approached to check if she was alright.

With Rylo cautiously hidden behind me, I called her name.

"Xara, is that you?" I tapped her shoulder.

She sat up, clutching her stomach and leaning against the dungeon walls. "Oh my god, Astra! I'm so glad to see you. I thought you were dead," she groaned. I was certain that's exactly what she'd hoped for. It took all my will to restrain myself.

"What are you doing here, and why are you lying on the floor like that?" I asked, feigning surprise.

"I waited for you for a while after you went down that vent, got lost, and somehow ended up here," Xara explained.

As she was weaving her web of lies, I started to form a plan. I would lure her into one of these empty cells and lock her inside until I sorted things out. She simply couldn't be trusted. I stepped into a nearby empty cell, briefly leaving the others. I drew the diamond shape onto my palm and focused on the image of a sunflower.

An iced sunflower immediately sprouted from the concrete floor. I called everyone over to show them the "Mysterious Flower." As I led the way to the cell, I turned and tried to hint to Ceju with my eyes to stay behind. He didn't fully understand my signals until I mouthed the words. He nodded and remained behind with Rylo as we went ahead without them.

Inside the cell, we walked over to the frozen sunflower and admired its beauty. "I've never seen anything like this," Xara whispered, clutching her stomach, trying to prevent vomiting.

"Where is Ceju? Why isn't he looking at this with us? Ceju, where are you?" I called out to him, pretending to be unsure of his location.

While Xara was distracted by the flower and her agony, I sprinted to the control brick and shoved it, instantly trapping her inside. The dungeon gates slammed shut with a deafening crash. I looked over to Ceju and explained why I had acted.

"She set me up. I thought she was my friend this whole time. For now, she'll stay here until I figure out what to do with her," I explained.

"This is insane. How do you know this?" Ceju responded.

"Back when I hit my head on that pile of branches, I lost consciousness and was given a vision. She's behind something sinister, and I'm going to find out," I continued.

Ceju seemed persuaded and asked no more questions. We cautiously headed up the only visible staircase. The castle felt uneasy, and as we ascended, we could hear Xara screaming and calling for us to return for her, her voice dragging, almost like a speaking snake.

The fairies' lights flashed in the distance, drawing my attention. I moved closer to their light, following them up through a slippery hall. I slid and nearly fell off the ledge. Getting up quickly, I grabbed a rail and caught my balance.

"Ceju, what do you think of us splitting up? We can cover more ground that way, and if you need to locate me, you always have your new eye to help out."

"Are you sure you'll be alright on your own, Astra?"

"I'm sure I will. I've been getting familiar with these powers lately, plus I have Rylo here to protect me," I said with a joking laugh.

Looking at each other deeply, we shared a brief, tight hug. "Be careful," I said softly as I headed in the opposite direction.

"I'll have my eye on you," Ceju replied, walking away and down the opposite hall with a torch he'd transformed from a shard of glass in his leather pouch.

The red and green lights from the fairies were flashing from underneath a small door above my head. I began stacking a few scattered boxes and climbed on top to reach it. I opened the door and saw a crawlspace passageway. Picking up Rylo, I placed him inside and climbed in behind him. As we rustled through the confined passage, I continued straight, making a few turns until I came in front of another small door.

I pushed the door open this time. Inside lay an old wooden box covered in a thick, gray blanket of dust. The hinges were rusted, and the key was still attached to the lock. It felt as if a hidden secret was waiting to be revealed. I began turning the key, opening the box while holding my breath, trying not to sneeze from the lingering dust. As I lifted the lid, it groaned under the forced movement.

Black and white photos sat neatly inside the box. They seemed to have survived a fire; the edges of each picture were tarnished with burn marks. As I examined the photos for a moment, I was transported into the memory of the picture I was holding.

I was walking while pushing a man in a wheelchair. He was extremely old and gripped a silver pocket watch tightly in his hand. I took him to a nearby park and sat on a bench, watching a tiny bird bathe in a puddle of water. Kids were playing on high rocks, climbing them and sitting on top, looking down at us.

"I remember when I used to be able to do that," the old man said, reminiscing about the past. "If only I could have that again," he started sobbing into his arms, covering his face.

"Don't you worry. We'll find a way to make you better, I promise," I said while kneeling, looking at him.

As the vision ended, it left me blankly staring at the pictures, trying to remember where I was. I focused on the picture longer and couldn't help but notice the woman in the photograph looked so much like me. The red and green flashing lights continued, leading me to another passageway big enough for me to stand and walk. I was behind the walls of the castle. I guessed this was a secret route built for traveling unnoticed.

I pushed through an opening, leading me into a bedroom with red interior decorations. The room had a table that held a beautiful, intricate mirror made of fine silver, crafted with immense detail. A mermaid was wrapped around it on both sides. As I looked into the mirror briefly, I could see the Red and Green fairy within it, fluttering around. In my head, I could hear them speaking to me.

They told me to tear up the floorboards from underneath me. The Red fairy pointed behind me toward a crowbar resting against a corner wall. I grabbed it and started ripping into the wooden floor panel, tearing it apart one by one with all my strength. Feeling a cold chill rising up, I ripped apart some more and could see a statue of some kind, covered by an oversized, dusty cloth wrapped in rope.

I unraveled the rope and pulled off the cloth, revealing a dragon statue sitting in a majestic pose. I ran my hand across it, feeling each groove of its detailed, carved scales. My hand began to tingle with a chill sensation. The blue hue from my hand spread into the statue, completely changing its color appearance to blue. I could feel its powers emerging from within me. My hand felt more powerful than it ever had.

I climbed out of the hole I'd created and walked toward the door, exiting the room. Guided by a detailed rug, I began to follow its repeated pattern as I walked along it. A row of complementary golden and red tassels bordered the rug, giving it a classic look. I exited the door, which cracked open loudly as Rylo and I slowly made our way down a checkered hallway.

Out from a window, I still saw the magenta-colored smoke spreading rapidly outside, becoming a raging torrent that almost blended seamlessly into the sky. I tugged on the curtain to reveal the full window. As it dropped, I could see someone standing on top of a roof across the view. "I really hope Ceju is seeing this right now. We have to get to that roof!" I said to Rylo aloud.

As I headed down toward the nearest staircase, a small ghost child drawing pictures on the floor caught my attention. Scattered drawings were piled up around the child. I looked and saw every drawing resembled shadows, very similar to the ones I'd seen posted on the window when first entering the castle. I called out to the child, but they didn't seem to hear me or acknowledge my presence. Completely ignored, the drawings continued.

Picking one up, I realized the same dark shadow was in the drawing—the one that had granted me the power to leave my body as a spirit. The image inside the picture started to change colors, growing more vibrant. Blood suddenly began seeping from the walls of the castle. As I looked around, I started to notice more blood dripping all around me, as if the castle were alive.

Pushing through the lobby, I could see Ceju from across the way. Cupping my hands around my mouth, I squealed his name. I kept calling out until he finally noticed me. He used a shard of glass to create a reasonably sized bridge connecting us.

"Something isn't right here. We have to get to that roof. That's where the smoke is coming from; I saw someone up there too," I said to him in a hurried tone, waving my hands wildly.

"No, we have to head back to the X-Graves!" Ceju responded swiftly. "I realized it's too late. The new moon has set, and every prisoner is now dead. The smoke of their bodies filled the air with the magenta smoke we've seen. I saw it all," Ceju continued.

"There's a box used to sacrifice them. I noticed it was drenched in blood. When I followed the path, I saw all the dead bodies lying in a pile, some frozen while others burnt."

A complete, crushing wave of guilt washed over me, a sickness in my stomach that screamed I was directly responsible. Why hadn't we returned sooner? I felt their blood on my hands, and the certainty that I had caused this tragedy made me start to lose focus.

"Astra, I know it's hard to grasp right now, but those prisoners are all dead, and that means Nedos has grown stronger. The two of us alone won't be able to take him down. We have to come back with more help."

A bowl of marbles sat on a nearby table. Rylo blew toward it, and the marbles instantly levitated above us. One clear white marble enlarged, encapsulating us all, then shot through the castle walls without leaving a mark. It zoomed into the sky, creating nothing but streaks of colored light in our wake.

He was transporting us somewhere, but I had no clue where. I remembered him doing this when I first found him, leading me to this exact castle. We ended up in front of an old, abandoned ship on an island. There was a pocket watch hanging on a tree that looked oddly similar to the one in the photos from Wormwood Castle. Feeling the ticking vibrations from the watch, I began walking closer. Without examining it, I placed it in my pocket as I looked around the island for anything else that called out to me.

"Why would Rylo send us here? There has to be a reason," I questioned silently while staying alert to our surroundings.

CHAPTER 13

The Electric Current

We all wandered around the island when Rylo started picking up a scent. He headed through a small, dried-up bush and began digging into it. Underneath, he revealed a glass barrier with Iscana inside. I knocked and banged on the glass repeatedly, trying to cause it to break, but it was surrounded by a force shield, protected by magic.

Iscana looked up and noticed us. Turning her head, she pointed toward the west. We headed straight toward the west and saw her parents lying on the sand, their long hair spread out around them in a circular shape. They were holding hands and looking up at the sky. Something felt off about their energy.

"We've fulfilled our daughter's life force with ours. When the sun comes up, we will return to the X-Graves, where we belong."

"No!" I shouted.

"You can't! Iscana said the candle would bring you guys back, and it did!"

"The candle's power can only last so long, but don't be afraid for us, child; death is only the beginning," they both replied in unison.

"Iscana is still in trouble; she needs you!"

"You will soon see the wonder we have bestowed upon her. In time."

"The starfruit hanging on the trees here will grant you the ability to breathe underwater. Eat them and follow the electric current we've created, leading toward Iscana," they both said with a gentle ease, as if slipping away with each word.

"Rylo, keep them safe," they said as they both began to remove the center jewel from their crowns.

Both jewels combined together, floating in the air, spinning repeatedly until they merged into one. While airborne, it slowly began lowering closer to the center of Rylo's forehead. As soon as it touched his skin, the jewel began fusing into him.

"You've been loyal to our family for centuries. With this jewel, you now have the ability to feel what it's like having a human-like body. Use it well, our faithful servant."

Rylo stood still while our eyes connected. He started to stretch outward, growing from his small elephant shape. A blinding light covered his body until he was fully transformed. He stood before us with an erect posture. His body was still the same shade of blue, and he had short, spiked, jet-black hair. The jewel in his forehead shined with a sparkle, highlighting the beauty in his eyes.

For the first time, I could hear words spew out of his mouth.

"I have a body! I have a human body! Thank you, thank you!"

Rylo went toward Iscana's parents, but the sun had come up and already taken them back to the X-Graves. Small clusters of bubbles floated up toward the shining sun in an organized line. He looked down at their imprint left behind in the sand and laid on top of it, thanking them and rolling around in the sand, excited about his new life ahead of him.

"Look at you! I don't even recognize you!" I said as I started examining his hands and face.

Ceju pulled out a shard of glass from his pouch and poured some sand over it, creating a beige-colored attire that he put on promptly.

"Rylo, you look so different! I can't believe it's really you in there," Ceju said as he watched in amazement.

"Alright, Rylo, get yourself stretched out and move those legs. We have to go rescue Iscana," I said as I headed over to the nearest tree, grabbing three starfruit in my hand.

"Okay, boys, this is it."

I handed each of them a starfruit, and we all bit into it, one after the other, consuming the whole fruit.

"That was actually quite refreshing," Ceju mentioned as he started licking the juice off his fingers.

"Alright, so they said for us to eat the fruit and follow the electric current path," I said as I started feeling for the electricity with my hands while crawling in the sand.

I could feel the electric pulse from underneath the sand and headed toward the ocean. We all stood with our feet touching the water as the tide rose, splashing up against our legs.

Before we headed into the ocean, I asked Ceju to use his eye's vision power to look at Iscana. He started to hold his hand over his opposite eye and gaze into the distance.

"She's sitting by a bolted door, guarded by a reptile. We still have time to get to her," Ceju said.

"No turning back now!"

We all dove into the water at once, heading into the electric current. It began to pull us effortlessly through the sea. The calming essence of the ocean depths brought a serenity like no other. Colorful schools of fish swam past in all directions. Coral sprouted from the ground, and jellyfish bounced up and down as if dancing in the water.

A mermaid following behind us, holding onto the back fin of a swordfish, caught my attention from the corner of my eye. As the electric current pulsed us through the sea, we reached the end. It led to an opening into an underground cave beneath a rocky area. We swam down toward it, then got confronted by the mermaid who was riding on the swordfish. Swimming closer to us, she spoke with great authority.

"What is your purpose here? You don't belong here, foolish humans," the mermaid spoke.

"We're here to rescue our friend Iscana. She's trapped somewhere around here," I replied immediately.

"Please, we mean no harm and will be out of your way faster than you know it," Rylo chimed in.

"It's not you I'm worried about, it's my sisters. We now guard the waters heavily since the murder of one of our sisters, protecting it from every strange, unwelcome creature that isn't from the sea. It's our nature and the only thing we've known for a very long time."

"Unlike my sisters, I'm the eldest, leader of the mermaids. I ride around on that swordfish you saw, looking for intruders. Sometime ago, I fell in love with a man on an island. He would send me gifts along the ocean shore—wonderful items from the human realm."

"I never felt anything like it. One day, he came into the water looking for me, and my sisters devoured him. There was nothing left of him. Nothing but a skeleton. From the looks of the skull laying on the shore, I could tell it was him," she said while showing sadness and distress in her face.

"They strongly believed he killed my sister and took revenge on him the same night."

"Ever since that day, I knew I wasn't like my sisters. They've become nothing but pure evil, allowing the bitterness of the unknown and humans to ruin their hearts," the mermaid continued.

"But I can feel the love you three hold, the love in each of your hearts," she said as she held her hand over her chest, which was covered in an old, torn fishing net with small red starfish clinging on, decorating her slim figure.

"I'm Merlissa, by the way. Please don't think any less of me because of my sister's doings."

"Nice to meet you. I'm Astra, this is Ceju, and that's Rylo."

We all smiled at each other and watched as a red dart zoomed right across my face. I looked around, trying to see where it came from, but couldn't see anything but the vast emptiness of the waters surrounding us—nothing but coral and tiny fish scattering around, going into hiding. A horn-blowing sound echoed through the water, getting closer, as another horn blew synchronously.

"Hurry, my sisters are near! Head into the cave. Follow the coral along the walls and head toward the bubbling rock. I'll meet you on the other side of it."

We swam rapidly through the opening and followed the coral. There was a path that led to the left and one to the right, both lined with coral against the walls.

"What do we do? Which path do we take?" I freaked out and turned to Ceju and Rylo frantically.

Rylo's jewel in his forehead started to glow while he pointed in the right direction. "This way!" he shouted.

We swam behind him. As we got closer to the end of the path, I could see the bubbling rock Merlissa spoke about. I heard the movement of the water behind us swishing around and felt the walls tumbling and shaking. The mermaids were trying to collapse this cave while we were inside. We started to bang on the bubbling rock, hoping it would move out of the way, but it was too strong for the three of us combined. I tried to use my diamond ice hand, but it was completely useless underwater.

"Merlissa! Merlissa!" We called out to her in a panic as we started to see the crumbling of the cave falling around us.

"Oh, why did we think it was okay to trust her? All mermaids are the same!" Ceju yelled as we were trying to push through.

"This is the end..." Ceju gave up.

"No! Push harder! We can't give up now! Come on!" I forced Ceju back against the boulder.

I heard a voice faintly from the other side of the tightly placed boulder we were trapped behind. "Move out of the way now!"

Merlissa crashed through the bubbling stone while riding on her swordfish. "Come on, hurry!"

We headed out of the cave in a hurry. Glancing back behind us, watching the wreckage, I noticed I had dropped the pocket watch found on the beach. Swimming back quickly, I grabbed it before the whole inside of the cave collapsed inward.

As I placed the pocket watch back in my pocket, Merlissa swam toward me.

"Are you insane? You almost got yourself killed there! Why would you risk your life for an object so small?" she said.

For a moment, I thought exactly the same thing. Why would I be so careless and jeopardize my life over this insignificant item? Questioning my own attraction to it, as if it meant completely nothing, although I still felt somewhere inside me as if it belonged to me. I didn't know how to respond; there was a sort of energetic pull the pocket watch had. I felt as if I had known it for a long time—a strange connection I was still unsure of.

"There's a bolted door past this barrier. Unfortunately, the barriers here are made with an otherworldly magic that I'm unable to penetrate," Merlissa stated.

Ceju, behind me, started to hold onto my shoulder, and we just looked at each other for a moment. While out of ideas and unable to use magic underwater, I thought of nothing but letting everyone down. I'd let Iscana down, the prisoners of Wormwood Castle, and Ferna. No one should depend on me for anything.

Rylo started to emit a glow around his body, making the waters ripple all around him. A loud, high-pitched whistling noise released from the ripples pointed toward the barrier, breaking it on impact. The jewel in his forehead glowed brightly as he focused on the magic barrier around the door, slowly fading it back.

"You're amazing! Thank you, Rylo!" I hugged him tight.

"You three, go save your friend. I'll guard the surrounding waters just in case we have any unwanted visitors," Merlissa said.

"Thank you, Merlissa. I have a strong feeling this won't be our last time together; we will meet again," I said to her as we hugged and departed toward the bolted door, which was floating weightless in the middle of the ocean.

CHAPTER 14

Threshold of Command

As we head toward the metal-bolted door just in front of us, we find three walls creating a closed space. A light up above is the only direction we can go. We swim up toward the light, and our heads break the water's surface. Looking around quietly, Ceju points out the reptile he saw in his vision guarding the door. The reptile was pacing back and forth, holding a staff with a bright crystal glowing from the top of it.

There was a big enough area for us to attack successfully. I gave the signal for us to leap out of the water, one by one, hiding behind a corner wall. I draw the diamond shape into my hand and summon the ice wolf and bear, the same ones I first practiced with on the wooden dummy by the castle. The reptile's attention was caught when I sprayed him once with a shard of ice from my hands, prompting the ice animals to attack. Immediately, the reptile lifted its staff and created a fireball fierce enough to melt both of them within an instant. I didn't expect anything like that to happen and was caught off guard.

"Intruders, come out!" the reptile said, walking closer in our direction.

We peeked out from behind the wall where we hid. Rylo stood in front of Ceju and me, spreading his arms out to protect us. A transparent, glowing shield formed around us. Blue-shaded stars, attached to each other, spiraled around the shield in slow motion as we looked at the reptile.

"We're here to rescue our friend. Let her go, please; we don't want any trouble," I tried to reason with the reptile.

"You may not pass me, unless it is over my dead body." He stood directly in front of the door.

He held out his staff and created a big, gnarly, fire-breathing horse. It approached us and tried to knock us into the wall. The horse had flames of fire instead of hair, and its legs glowed a golden red, as if melting from deep within. The shifting colors within each flame went from a deep crimson and fiery orange to an electric blue and white shining at its core. The radiance of the flames caused shadows to dance across the walls around us.

The fire horse's attack missed us completely, but then it did a rapid turn and charged at us again. I yelled to Rylo to stand in front of the water where we came from, hoping it could be used as a trap. Ceju started fussing with his leather pouch, dropping pieces of glass onto the floor while trying to find a way to help.

I called over to the horse to get its attention and have it follow me. Ceju began to transform a shard of glass into a purple flower with a large tongue, similar to the one that hid us from the castle guards. It covered us both, and for a moment the horse couldn't see where we went. It focused its aggression on Rylo and charged in his direction as he stood in front of the water. At the right moment, he jumped out of the horse's way, making it dive headfirst into the water.

The water started fizzing and rising with a shrieking sound as the horse's fire washed away, leaving no evidence of its existence. Nothing but the faint smell of smoke remained as it vanished. I stepped out from behind the flower's invisible shield and pulled out my sai weapons. The reptile and I went head-to-head, clashing our weapons against each other. The staff the reptile was holding morphed into a staff made of hard metal covered in flames of fire.

He pushed me with the weapon across to the other wall. My pocket watch dropped from my pocket once again, making both myself and the reptile stop for a moment. He placed his weapon against the wall and picked up the pocket watch, analyzing it before dropping to his knees with his head bent down.

"Please forgive me, Queen Hexia. I had no clue it was you," he said, holding out his hand, returning the pocket watch to me.

As I grabbed the pocket watch from his possession, I started to wonder what exactly he was talking about. Queen Hexia? I thought to myself. The name didn't sound familiar, but I knew I had to play along if I wanted to save Iscana.

"Yes, it is Queen Hexia. I'm in disguise, and you have done your job with utmost excellence. I will make sure to grant you a grand position at Wormwood Castle once everything settles down," I said, looking over at Rylo and Ceju with a deceptive grin on my face.

"Oh yes, Queen Hexia, thank you!"

"You can unlock the prisoner now. I came here to transport her to another location as well as testing your loyalty. You have proven yourself in the eyes of the Queen."

I smiled and held my hand over my mouth to stop myself from giggling as I looked over again at Ceju, trying not to laugh. "Yes, my Queen," the reptile stood up and waved his staff in front of the door, unlocking it with three balls of fire that zoomed across it, covering every inch of the surface, changing the door's color from rusted silver to a golden brass.

He stood at the side of the door while it opened, kneeling back down with his head facing the ground. I put out my hand, signaling to Ceju and Rylo to stay put. I went inside the door and saw Iscana sleeping in the corner of the confined space. Looking up, I could see the sun shining through the barrier where we once saw her from the island.

I walked over to her side, careful not to startle her, and gave a gentle brush of her tail. She didn't seem to notice me touching her, and I continued, slowly increasing the pressure as I tried to wake her up comfortably. Her body trembled from within, as if she was having a nightmare of some kind. I began to inch closer to her. A chain attached to her back legs led toward the wall, holding her prisoner. I used the sai weapon to pierce through the lock attaching her to the chain but was repelled by an electric shock. It was useless. I tried to wake her up again.

"Iscana," I whispered while sitting upright by her side.

"We came to save you. We're finally here." I continued rubbing her tail, then began rubbing her head.

She opened one eye and noticed me right away. Iscana got up and shook off the sleepiness, causing her tail feathers to swiftly glide across my body, tickling me. A whisper of pressure that was so light it was as if it wasn't even there, creating a sensation across my arms like a soft brush.

"Astra, you made it. You came back for me!" Iscana said with tears forming in her eyes.

"Shhh. The reptile guarding the door thinks I'm Queen Hexia. That's what helped us unlock the door to saving you."

"Come, we have to go now," I headed out toward the door, leaving Iscana behind me and calling to the reptile.

"Can you remove the enchantments and unlock these chains from her legs, please?" I asked the reptile while standing over it at the base of the door.

He walked into the room and used his staff to melt the chain and lock off her body with a swiftness. The metal melted into water that ran down the cracks of the dry floor. I followed the trail of water, watching as it ran into itself, forming a puddle. The reptile held his staff over the puddle and absorbed it completely.

Now that Iscana was free from the entrapment of Nedos, she could use her powers again. This time even stronger with the lended help of her parents. Still unable to turn back to her true form because of the curse put on her by Nedos, I was sure that with her and her parents' strength combined, we could defeat him and bring everything back to the way it once was.

Iscana let out a majestic roar, summoning in front of us a door similar to the one that led me straight to the castle the first time we both met. As it grew in size, big enough for all of us to get inside, I called out to the others. Ceju and Rylo walked into the room where Iscana was held hostage, and we all looked toward the portal door Iscana created. Turning toward the reptile, I made eye contact with him after tapping on his shoulder to ask for his name.

"My name is Heris, Queen Hexia. I never thought I'd be lucky enough to live in the days of your arrival."

"Come with us back to Wormwood Castle; I could really use your help," I said.

"It would be my pleasure to assist you, My Queen."

"Nedos is no longer to be trusted, under any circumstances. You're no longer taking any orders from him. Do you understand?" I commanded him.

"Yes, my Queen," he bowed his head in respect one last time as he joined us, grabbing onto his staff.

As Heris opened the door, we all entered, sliding downward into Iscana's section of the castle. It was dark, damp, and eerie, with cold air blowing toward us. Rylo lit the way, shining through with his bright, glowing jewel in the middle of his head. I felt familiar with this place, as it wasn't my first time here. Knowing we were with Iscana at the castle brought an ease, even with the eerie darkness around us. I pushed through with everyone as Rylo led the way; we all walked in silence.

"Wait, before we head any further, Ceju, can you check and see if everything is going alright with Ferna? Maybe we should go get her first," I mentioned quietly, almost forgetting.

He stopped for a moment, holding his hand over the opposite eye. In the darkness, I could see the star in his eye glowing with an irresistible appeal. After his vision of Ferna, he said with an urgency, "Nedos has Ferna! He has her hostage."

My mind started racing with possibilities as to what could be going on. Is he using her as bait? Did he find out she helped me? I failed the prisoners of this castle, and now it seems I've failed yet again. Ferna was such a pleasant person. She had such a loving energy. I would be so hurt if something ended up happening to her.

We passed through the bottom area of Iscana's lair in the castle and proceeded through a passage that I didn't notice the first time. The hall was lit with golden bowls filled with water and floating blue flames on the surface. Iscana passed her tail feathers around the side of one of the bowls carefully and dropped a tiny matchbox.

"Light the match and place it in this bowl of fire," she said to me.

Grabbing the rectangular-shaped matchbox, I could feel its gritty striking strip hugging against my skin. Faded floral designs covered the box with a very old feel. Almost falling apart in my hands, I pushed off the sleeve from the box, revealing a single match inside. The single match gave me a new sense of determination.

With the match in my hand, I began to raise it slowly into the air. Everyone around me, including myself, stopped breathing for a moment, hoping it would help the chances of the match staying lit. As soon as I lit the match, it fizzed out, making it useless while the blackened, brittle wood stared back at me.

"Not to worry, I can help you with that," Heris grabbed what was left of the match and lit it on fire with his staff, throwing it into the bowl of flames.

The red fire from the match started blending into the blue flames, turning into a purple shade. Every bowl of fire began changing its color to purple, one after the other. The wall where Heris threw the match into the fire opened up from both sides, pushing outward. Inside, there was a room holding shields and armor behind sturdy glass cases.

"Be prepared for a battle; we don't know what to expect with Nedos and his army," Iscana said to us all.

"Get some armor and weapons—whatever you can carry and wear. Then we can proceed to finding and defeating Nedos."

"Defeating him and breaking my curse, along with every other curse he's caused, will bring me great joy," Iscana continued.

"Remember we have to think smart; he has Ferna hostage, and we must be successful in saving her from his wicked plans," Ceju reminded us.

Everyone began placing armor over themselves as Iscana stood guard at the entry. As I was covered in armor resembling one of the castle guards, I didn't feel as I once did. My powers couldn't be accessed with my arms covered, and I couldn't move swiftly with all this heavy armor. I decided not to wear the armor but had an idea instead.

"Heris, why don't you just wear the armor and disguise yourself? This way, Nedos doesn't recognize you're here with us. It will also allow you to infiltrate his side if needed," I said to him.

"Hide your staff behind this sword," Iscana said while looking toward a sword spread across one of the walls.

Iscana's body vibrated as her tail feathers rose up into the air. A couple thin feathers fell to the ground. I tied his staff around the back of the sword tightly with the feathers from Iscana's tail, holding it intact.

"I'm wearing one of the royal guards' armor. I would've never seen this coming," Heris explained. "I always dreamed of being in this armor but always ended up doing mindless orders for Nedos."

"He never appreciated me for what I was and what I could do. Because of my image, he never allowed me to stay in the castle for too long." Heris looked heartbroken.

"Don't you think about that anymore. I accept you exactly for who you are. No matter what species you are. You're a phenomenal person with great magic abilities. I will never let you dim your light."

While we gathered ourselves, heading out of the armor room, I began to think of Xara, forgetting that we left her trapped in the dungeons. I wondered if she was holding up alright. Even though she betrayed me, I really didn't want to see anything bad happen to her. There were so many questions left unanswered. Yearning to find out more on the matter, I asked Iscana a favor.

"Iscana, I'm sorry for this detour, but can you lead us to the dungeons, please?"

"Not a problem," she said.

Approaching the dungeons, I called out, "Xara, are you there?"

I looked into the cell where we trapped Xara, but she was no longer inside. The gate didn't seem to have been lifted or manipulated in any way. I started looking into the other cells, thinking maybe we trapped her in a different one. Every cell remained empty. The sound of the pebbles scattered across the floors as we searched for Xara echoed through the empty dungeon.

"Forget about her; we have to save Ferna," Ceju said with an urgency.

"Let's head out through the back here and toward the other side of the castle. I believe that Nedos should be on the Sacrifice Tower," Iscana replied.

"Heris, you go ahead of us and try to blend in with the other guards when you see them. Do not speak a word of us to anyone," I said to him as he headed out by himself.

Waiting a moment before heading outside, I could see the shining of the stars brighter than ever. It was as if beams of light were hitting the ground, as if the stars were searching for someone. We ran across the fields and were met by a group of guards blocking the tower, all standing in a line around the perimeter of it. They started pulling out their swords, ready to attack.

Rylo was the first to make a move. He swung his head in a swift movement. His short, spiked black hair soon resembled that of Iscana's parents—long black hair. It wrapped underneath the legs of all the guards, dropping them onto the floor all at once. While they got back up, I glanced at them, making sure Heris wasn't mixed in with these guards. I drew the diamond shape into my palm, closed my eyes, and summoned up an ice rain, pouring down on them with rapid speed.

Ceju started combining shards of glass with small worms lying on the ground, turning them into a wild rose bush filled with enormous thorns surrounding the fallen, injured guards. While we made our way past them toward the tower, I noticed the small ghost child wandering around aimlessly. I walked up to it, curiously following behind, but it soon vanished before my eyes, fading into thin air.

CHAPTER 15

Tower of Sacrifices

Heading up into the tower, we looked up and saw a seemingly never-ending set of stairs. As we stepped onto the stairs and began walking up cautiously, they started to glow from within. Red lights pulsed from underneath, burning as if a fire were sealed inside. The smell of death grew stronger as we neared the top of the tower. I hadn't expected it to be so overwhelming, but I could barely handle it.

A sickening, pungent wall of strange metallics hit my senses unexpectedly, causing a prickle at the back of my nose as I desperately gasped for fresh air. Turning to lean over the handrail, holding on tightly, I gagged for a moment until I felt ready to continue. My legs trembled as I tried to manage this strange scent, and the glow within the stairs grew brighter. Ceju held a shard of glass and a small thread in his hand. He quickly transformed it into a thick cloth and handed it to me to wipe myself clean.

"Thank you," I said, catching my breath.

He smiled at me as we all continued upward. The stairs below began to retract into the wall, revealing fiery flames burning beneath. Shaking movements of the first step sliding inward caught our attention. Squinting at the steps below us, I tried to make sense of what I was seeing. It was too late to turn back now.

"Everyone, run fast now! The stairs are collapsing!" Iscana shouted from behind us as we all scurried toward the top.

The vibrations from each step being slammed into the walls continued to shake the tower, making the climb hellish. Afraid of falling down, I held onto the rails and stopped running periodically just to be safe. Everyone was ahead of me, and I wasn't moving fast enough. My dress got snagged onto a sharp edge of the rail as I ran, pulling me back. I slipped and knocked myself down a couple of stairs.

The fiery opening was only a couple of steps behind me, slowly catching up. I got up, holding onto the bottom of my dress instead of the rails, and ran with all my energy toward the top. Overexerting myself, I began to lose my breath. I could see everyone at the top of the tower now. Ceju reached out his hand, and I grabbed it as he pulled me up the last few steps.

Looking down as the remaining steps forcefully shoved themselves into the walls, the entire interior of the tower was engulfed in flames, which were slowly dying down and lowering in intensity. Catching my breath, I tore at the rip in my dress, pulling it across and fashioning it into a short, ripped skirt. Having that much fabric on me had nearly cost me my life; I wouldn't let it happen again. Ceju helped tear off the other side of the dress with me. He insisted on making me another outfit, but we didn't have enough time.

The magenta smoke we saw spreading across the sky looked like it was coming from nearby. I noticed the large, black box fixture that was hidden in the castle, with three switches on the bottom. It was dripping with blood, leaking out uncontrollably. It seemed like this was some sort of execution chamber. People were being put in there to be killed.

"Astra, it's Nedos!" Iscana said from behind me, her tail rising up, shaking, looking as if she were about to pounce and attack.

"Don't make any sudden movements, be still for now. We have to save Ferna," I said quietly.

"Well hello, my lovely visitors. Please make yourselves comfortable," Nedos spoke in our direction.

Iscana yelled at him from a distance, "Free me of this curse and return me to my body now, you wicked monster!"

"Now, is that any way to speak to your superior?"

"You still want that ridiculous body of yours back? You should be thrilled to have become such a creature as yourself!"

"Look at you, you're my best creation!" Nedos said with a grin as he pulled a black cloth from over a metal cage by his side.

Ferna sat pressing her head against the metal bars, tied up tightly with a wire that was digging into her skin, causing blood to ooze.

"FERNA!" I screamed her name while running toward her vulnerable, confined body.

"Don't you move, or I'll take her life force quicker than the blink of an eye!"

"Did you think I wouldn't notice that you tried to trick me? Her helping you at the X-Graves, leading you to your success. Do you take me for a mortal fool?" Nedos went on.

Nedos began to chuckle as he started unlocking Ferna from the cage, holding her closely with a dagger pressed against her throat. Ferna opened her eyes and made eye contact with me for a brief moment before falling back unconscious. Her limp body in his arms moved effortlessly as he held her hostage in front of us, taunting us to make a move or give in to his will. I tried to think of a way to get him to release her without causing further harm.

"Please let her go, I beg you. Don't hurt her," I cried out.

The raven that had once delivered a scroll for Ferna now flew over her in circles, as if waiting to eat its next meal. I could never forgive myself if I let another innocent life perish in the hands of this evil man. Crying out of frustration, I heard Ferna struggling to speak. Nedos wasn't allowing her to be heard, constantly laughing louder over her words while pressing the dagger deeper into her skin. A single droplet of blood dripped down onto the dagger's blade.

"Never fear, when death is near," I finally heard words escape from Ferna's lips.

She tried to move away, but his tight grip couldn't be escaped. Iscana let out an echoing, shrieking sound toward Nedos, hoping it would damage his senses and allow Ferna to be loosened from his grip. It only made Ferna suffer more pain, causing her to fall lower toward the ground. Ferna made eye contact with us, then closed her eyes and accepted her fate.

Right before our eyes, Ferna's blood rushed toward us as Nedos pierced her neck with the dagger, leaving her lifeless body lying in a pool of her own blood on the ground. My heart stopped for a moment; I felt everything around me begin to freeze, almost in slow motion. Rylo ran to Ferna's aid but was pushed back by Nedos' forceful magic.

Iscana went to attack Nedos, but there was a force field protecting him. He had the whole area protected by his magic. Unable to penetrate the barrier, I got closer and banged on it with my hands, watching as he laughed in my face. Each time I touched the barrier, I could feel a sharp shock throughout my body, causing me to feel weaker with each attempt.

"Face it, you all are no match for me," Nedos said as he began to get a better glimpse of me close up.

"Hexia, Queen Hexia? It's you, you're finally back," he spoke in shock.

I didn't know what he was talking about, but I wasn't new to this whole Queen Hexia mix-up. Going along with this persona has been the most effective strategy lately. Maybe I could make things different if I could truly make him believe I was this Queen. With no other options, I had nothing to lose. The only way to save us now would be to play along.

"Yes, it is me, Queen Hexia," I responded.

"Forgive me, my queen," he said. "I don't know what's become of me. Ever since you vanished, I've been ravished by rage and became such a horrible person. I love you. Please stay by my side once again, and we can rule together."

"I cursed Iscana because she wouldn't marry me, yes that is true, but now I see that was a blessing in disguise."

"Otherwise, I would've never found you. I didn't think I would ever have seen you again," he went on.

"Astra, don't listen to him, he can't be trusted," Iscana whimpered.

"Trust me, everything will be alright, just stay here," I said, looking back at everyone.

Glancing over toward Ceju, he started crying, trying to hide his face. Walking toward Nedos, I stood close by with the barrier still between us. My heavy heart and tears falling from my eyes began to lower his defenses. As the barrier around him retracted, I began to touch Nedos' arm softly. I didn't want to, but I had to do this to save everyone and break his curse. I knew the only way out safely was to go along with this act.

In order for this to work, I really had to commit. I'd marry him and pretend I was this Queen Hexia, play the part for a while, get him comfortable, and leave. I played over the plan in my head over and over, trying to convince myself and stop the urge preventing me from wanting to do this.

"Queen Hexia, I've waited so long."

I could feel the presence of the sai weapons pressing against my skin. The urge to pierce them through his body overcame me, but I stopped my thoughts from allowing my body to attack. I had to play this smart. After he broke the curse, I reminded myself. I could see him stare at me, gazing into my soul as if he'd known me for years.

While holding me close, he felt the pocket watch vibrating and ticking through my pocket. "You have a watch, let me see it please." I gave him the watch, and he opened it. Feeling the watch, he carefully examined it. He didn't say anything else and handed it back to me. I looked at him with a suspicious face. Something didn't seem right.

"Behold, I have my Queen. With this ring, you vow to be eternally mine," he said, holding a spiked-rimmed ring made of gold into the air. Lightning struck down onto it, causing it to change to a polished, mirrored silver.

He placed the ring onto my finger. The darkness and clouds lifted from the night sky. I could sense a change in him, as if the wickedness was lifted from his heart. Shocked by my decision, Ceju caused a gust of rose petals to fly all around us after throwing some glass into the air. Rylo stood behind him while Iscana tended to Ferna's body, trying everything to revive her.

"You're free from your curse," he said, holding out both his hands toward the sky. A beam of light shone around Iscana.

Iscana changed back to her original form. She had long black hair, just as her parents did, but her skin was a checkered pattern of black and yellow. Bright yellow earrings hung delicately down to her shoulders that resembled small chandeliers. A long, flowing dress of velvet maroon with fluffy feathers along the rim covered most of her body. Her shoulders and arms were exposed by the dress's thin straps.

A glowing light above Ceju started to pulsate. His skin became a dark shade of gray with bright neon green highlights around him, and he sprouted two pointed ears. The star eye he acquired from Nexus at Desert Driftia remained the same, and his hair was bright red, tied up on top of his head. Pointed black spikes stuck out from his spine and down his arms as he stood shirtless, wearing long black pants tied with a rope. Since Nedos was no longer a threat he decided to change into his true form and stop hiding.

Rylo watched in amazement as the two people we once knew completely morphed right before our very eyes. Although, it shouldn't have been much of a shock. The energy all around us shifted; everyone seemed to be happy and at peace. Although I was happy that the curses were broken, there was an inner sadness growing within me.

As I looked over at Ferna's body lying lifeless on the floor, I began to notice her blood being absorbed back into her body like a sponge. She filled up with life once again and sat up on the ground. I hugged her tightly and brushed the dirt off her face and hair.

"Ferna, I'm so glad you're alive! Thank you so much for everything you've done for me. I can never thank you enough," I said, holding onto her for a moment.

"Everyone, now that the curse is lifted, I vow to never speak another curse into existence," Nedos said loudly.

I began to daze off into a distant memory as the noise around me started to silence. I was standing in a room with Nedos, both of us watching as servants painted the walls, adding decorative designs that spread across the borders of the walls and ceiling. Nedos was smiling at me when I took his hand, holding it as we watched toward the horizon together. A woman walked over with a tray of hot beverages and set it aside.

I snapped back into reality, not knowing whether that was a glimpse into the future or the past. Starting to feel worried, I had a look on my face I couldn't hide. Iscana noticed something was wrong and came over to me and Ferna. Kneeling down toward the ground, she helped me pick Ferna up back on her feet.

"Look how beautiful everything looks from up here," Iscana said while spreading her hand toward the castle's direction.

Ferna looked at the sun and raised her hand above her eyes, blocking its shining light from blinding her.

She looked down at her blood-soaked clothing, disgusted by what remained. The mark on her neck from the dagger Nedos used to kill her was completely gone. Not even a trace of dry blood on her neck, as if nothing had happened. The only reminder was her clothing. Ceju made an exact copy of her black laced dress and handed it to Ferna.

"Why, what a thoughtful gesture. Thank you, my dear. I will cherish this garment; it means so much to have my dress repaired."

"I haven't seen the sun for so long, or felt its warmth against my skin," Ferna continued talking.

"Back at my cottage, it remained night for as long as I've been there, with nowhere to escape. How can I ever forget these horrible memories and heal my pain? That cottage was everything to me, even though I'm free now, I miss my home."

Nedos held his hand out and called over the raven as it landed gracefully onto his leather armband. His gun metal armor shined with movement, and it had a deep engraved scratch across the center of his chest area. Armored boots up to his knees resembled that of the guards but had spikes on the rim at the front of his foot. Nedos began giving the raven orders.

"Go into the nearest part of the forest closest to the castle. Gather everything from Ferna's cottage at the X-Graves and position them gently," he said.

Ferna looked at Nedos, puzzled. "If it is alright with you, would you like to live with us, beside the castle?" I asked.

Ferna thought about it for a moment, then looked over at me. I smiled with delight, and she agreed to the proposition. I couldn't believe so much was happening and changing for the better. I almost began to feel complete joy.

The guardian of the dead that watches over the X-Graves broke through a slit in the air with a tied net full of spices and herbs from Ferna's kitchen. The raven was fluttering around it, directing where to place each item before they headed back. Not too long after, I could see everything from Ferna's house spread across the open area in the forest. Nedos came to the middle of everything and held his hands out toward a tree. He snapped it from the roots, disconnecting it from the ground, dismantling and dividing the wood into pieces while it was mid-air.

I watched him as he worked his magic, stacking piles of wood onto another. As Nedos manipulated the tree's wood around us, I could see the wood continuing its process even as Nedos stopped his hand signals. The trees around us started breaking and separating into wood to be used for Ferna's cottage. As the process continued, the area for her cottage began to open up.

"The cottage will be replicated exactly how you remember it," Nedos said as he turned to Ferna.

"It should be finished within the next phase of the sundial," He pointed toward the cemented stone sundial standing on a bed of purple flowers.

I watched as Rylo and Ceju were conversing with each other and interrupted their conversation.

"You guys know this isn't the end, right?" I wrapped my arms around both of them, holding them close to me, trying to distract myself from my true feelings.

I thought back at the times we shared together as our skins melted into each other while reminiscing.

"Rylo, you're more than welcome to stay here if you like. You too, Ceju."

"No thank you. I think now that I'm in my true form, I should check up on a couple of things," Ceju replied.

"I wouldn't mind having company along the way if you aren't too busy. Want to join me?" He said while looking at Rylo.

"Most certainly, that sounds splendid," He responded.

Iscana summoned a portal for them to travel through. Watching as they entered, Ceju winked at me with his star eye, and in that moment, I knew I would never lose contact with him. Seeing the both of them leaving together was like a part of me being ripped away. Them being around made me feel comfortable. I tried not to fill my mind with memories and focused on the task at hand: to defeat Nedos.

CHAPTER 16

Echoes of the Past

iving in Wormwood Castle now with Nedos as his Queen has been challenging. I try not to think about the suffering I'm about to endure. Every day here has become a routine, each one feeling exactly the same as the last. Ferna seems to have settled fine at her new cottage near the castle. I head over to her place often to talk and bake goods with her. One of our favorite things to make together is mini pies filled with sweet blueberries.

Blueberries were her favorite, and they have been one of mine ever since I first tasted one of her pies. She is such an artist when it comes to baking. Everything is done with such precision and perfection. I lose track of time when I'm with Ferna. A feeling of home overcomes me; we have so much in common. We were both cast away by our loved ones, and I know how she feels. Ferna holds a special place in my heart and always will.

She keeps her windows open, and the sweet aroma of baked goods constantly spreads through the air. Sometimes, it's like she's calling me specifically to come over. I asked if she was a witch one day out of curiosity. Ferna explained to me that she doesn't believe in any of that, and she doesn't have any magic powers like the rest of us, but she believes in the power of prayer.

I start to remember when I was leaving her cottage the first time we met, and she prayed over me. It was all new to me, and I had never experienced anything like it. To me, it felt like magic, but Ferna took no credit and gave it all to a higher power. She pointed to the cross symbol hanging over her door and explained it to me. The cross represents forgiveness; it signifies both a painful defeat but also an ultimate triumph.

Her cottage is now easier for me to find, although it's a close walking distance from the castle. At first, she didn't mind the changing from the sun's rotation to the moon, but after a couple of days, she expressed to me that she didn't feel as if she were home and didn't enjoy the sun over her house. I thought maybe she'd just become accustomed to the dark nights spent trapped at the cottage in the X-Graves. I brought the matter to Nedos, and he placed the same spell over her cottage as he once did long ago.

I am somehow starting to feel for Nedos, and viewing him in such a different light. How could someone so evil change so quickly like this? I was becoming more understanding of Nedos and this whole situation. The empathy I held for him continued to grow. I can sense there was a time when he was different, long before all of this happened.

He couldn't have always been so wicked in his ways. He's beginning to show me such patience and softness, allowing me to sleep in a separate room until I feel comfortable in the same room with him. Even though the room I sleep in is inside his room, I do respect the barrier and him not forcing or guilting me into being in the same room. I think I slept wrong while being here because my upper back behind my neck felt strange for a while, as if I'd slept on a rock.

Iscana is still here. She's keeping a close eye; she still doesn't fully trust the situation with me being at Wormwood Castle. She's been living at the castle long enough, so leaving really isn't an issue or as appealing. I'm thankful to have such a protective, loyal friend by my side. She occupies a dome-shaped room that resembles a greenhouse by the left wing of the castle.

One rainy night, I was heading downstairs to the main kitchen to have a drink of water. I made my way through the dark halls, lit by a small candlestick guiding my path. Pouring water to the top of a clay cup, I drank it all, then filled the cup again to take back with me. Heading towards a window to watch as the rain fell melodically, I noticed Nedos sitting in a dark corner of the room with his head looking down, facing the window. His shadow illuminated and flickered along with the flame of the candle sitting on the small table beside him.

I slowly walked over to him, tiptoeing and trying to be as quiet as I could, holding my breath with each step closer. Glancing over behind him, I see that he's fallen asleep with an old picture in his hand. It's the same picture I found hidden away in the crawl space, all burned up around the edges. I didn't think he would have any connection to the picture until now as I watched it gripped in his hand.

I started pondering whether he could be related to the old man in the wheelchair. As I slowly turned around, my hair breezed across my face, with a few strands intertwined with my eyelashes. Flipping my hair away from my face caused the water in my hand to drip onto the floor. Turning around cautiously, I made sure Nedos didn't wake up and see me so close to him. I stopped and swiped my warm, fuzzy, knitted socks— Ferna made them for me one night at her cottage— over the spilled water. The pressure I applied was enough to make a creak in the floorboards, waking Nedos up.

"Show yourself, who's there?" he got up, looking in my direction.

I turned around with a frightened look, as if I'd been caught doing something I wasn't supposed to. Looking at him in the darkness brought back every fear and negative emotion I felt towards him. It was like he was the same monster from before, just in disguise. His red eyes glowed in the night like lasers pointing into my soul. I froze for a moment, and then explained myself.

"I was thirsty and couldn't sleep from the sounds of the rain," I said to him.

"Come sit with me here for a moment," he said calmly, almost half asleep.

I went over to him as he scooted over in his chair and made a slight space, almost big enough for me to sit in. Our bodies touched while we were snuggled together on the chair, watching as the pouring rain continued to pound against the window. The view of the night seemed different from when the sun was out. There was a certain kind of enchantment that was unshakable.

I noticed Nedos beginning to reveal the picture he was holding in his hand. Making any sudden movement that would cause him to think I'd seen this before was not what I wanted. Acting lost, as if it were my first time seeing the photo, I touched the burned edges while he passed his fingers over the picture. He began to talk while focusing on the patterns of rainfall.

"I don't expect you to remember, but this is us, My Queen."

Looking more confused than I was acting, I looked over at him and glanced back at the photo. There's no way this can be us. I mean, that's not me; she looks a lot like me, but he's honestly losing his mind, along with everyone else who thinks I'm this Queen.

"You are the reincarnation of Queen Hexia, my darling, can you not feel her powers within you?" he said while holding onto my arm.

"I've been searching for you for countless moons. One night long ago, I became very ill and began to age rapidly, not knowing what was becoming of me. I suspected the cook was poisoning my food."

"You began searching for a cure for my sickness after getting rid of every cook in the castle. A few seasons went by, and you returned with a potion that allowed me to regain my strength and young body again until the rise of the next full moon," he continued.

"You spoke to me of stories you heard on your journey of people mentioning immortality if they consumed the flesh of a mermaid."

I began to panic as soon as I heard him mentioning eating mermaids. I know they weren't the nicest of creatures, but that just sounded repulsive and strange. For one thing, I'd become close to a certain mermaid, and just the thought of someone consuming her made me sick to my stomach.

"After I drank the potion, I disappeared with a crew of fishermen in search of the mermaid who would grant me eternal life."

Looking up in shock, I just listened and kept eye contact with him as he told his story. I could feel his hand rest against my thigh, with the picture still in hand.

"We got to an island that was known for mermaid sightings and slept on the beach that night, hoping to attract the mermaids."

"That same night, I woke up to a mermaid crawling towards me on the sand. She became so fixated with me and began to fall in love. I was gifted a substantial-sized mirror with a mermaid on it that I would be able to use to call upon her wherever I was."

"I placed the mirror safely onto the ship when no one was around. We all spent a number of days and nights on the island while I was trying to gain the mermaid's trust."

"When the fishermen would fall asleep late at night, I would go into my room in the ship to the mirror and call out for her. I watched as she pulsed rapidly through the waters, heading my way. We talked about many things and had many nights under the stars, but it was all a part of my selfish plan."

"I tricked her into thinking I was in love with her in order to lure her into my trap. Days flew by as we grew closer, and time continued running out," he continued.

"This pocket watch here in the picture is the same exact watch you have with you now, my Queen. The same exact watch you enchanted and gave me to head out on my journey with, to help lead me back to you if I were to get lost."

My hands began shaking, shaking from the realization that everything he was saying to me could possibly be true. I did find that watch right on the island, around where I first noticed Merlissa. I didn't say anything while trying to hide my nerves from showing, convincing myself that this was just a lie being told for some reason.

"Unfortunately, the watch got lost on the island one night. I stood there waiting under the stars for one last night before I could murder the mermaid who fell for me, as the full moon grew closer."

"A younger mermaid arrived instead of Merlissa, and the fishermen trapped her. Any mermaid would be good enough to cause immortality, so I ordered the mermaid dead."

"I didn't speak of the mermaid granting the gift of eternal life to the fishermen in fear of them wanting to consume some of her flesh as well, so I ate the mermaid alone while the others were asleep in secret."

"Wanting to leave before anyone noticed the horror that had been done, I boarded onto the ship, and we all left the island, leaving behind the mermaid's remains."

"Well, we thought everyone boarded onto the ship, but one of the fishermen was left behind on the island. By the time we realized his absence, we were already too far gone to help. I could see groups of mermaids swimming around towards the island. It was too risky to head back, so we just kept going," Nedos continued.

"Poor man. I can't begin to imagine what those mermaids might've done to him after realizing one of their own kind had been murdered on that same island," he said with such guilt and remorse.

"I tore up that whole ship from top to bottom, every single day, looking for the pocket watch you'd given me to lead me back home to you. But leaving in such a rush must've been another thing left behind."

"The guilt I carried for centuries and the pain of being alive without you... I was certain you were dead because you hadn't eaten the mermaid's immortal flesh. Sadness consumed my heart and soon overflowed with evil and hatred towards any and everyone. I began to lose hope in everything, that is, until I crossed paths with you again."

"From the moment my eyes caught a close glimpse of you, I knew it had to be you, Queen Hexia, reincarnated."

"I know you can feel it, tell me you can feel this connection," he said while trying to get something out of me.

"I don't know what I'm feeling right now, I can't explain it, but I do feel something," I said while trying not to seem so scared.

Nedos held me close to him and dropped the picture on the ground. He held his hand over my head while pressing slowly against his chest. I could feel his heart beating and noticed mine synchronizing with his. For a moment, we just embraced each other and relaxed with a strange comfort.

"So much time went by lost at sea. The fishermen began dying one by one around me, leaving no one alive but myself. Eventually, I found my way back to the castle, but there was no sight of you."

"I felt you must've gone looking for me. I've beat myself up every day for losing you, but now that I have you in my arms again, I promise I will never lose you, my Queen."

"When I saw you with that pocket watch in your possession, all my doubts melted away, and I was certain it was you!"

For a moment, I felt safe in his arms, forgetting where I was. The love from his heart rapidly pulsed through his body, vibrating into mine. A strong connection began forming all of a sudden, but I tried to shake it off. Thinking this could be a trap of some sort, I couldn't let my guard down.

"I'm really tired now. Do you think we can continue this in the morning?" I asked him.

He just looked into my eyes and rubbed his palm over the side of my cheek, then kissed me right where his hand was. As we both walked silently to our rooms, I turned around and hugged Nedos without realizing it, like an impulse reaction. I entered his room with him, then entered the door leading to my room as we said goodnight. In my room, I began to stare at the candles spread across the mantle. The flames danced chaotically in the night. Lying in bed alone and scared, I focused on the flames of one of the candles and watched as it stood still.

The candles stood neatly all in a row of purple, gray, and black solid colors. I watched as the other flames danced in the night. With nothing more to do, I stared at another flame, commanding it in my head to stand still. As I slowly drifted off to sleep from focusing on the flames, I continued making the flames stop flickering until they all stood perfectly still in the dark.

I woke up feeling extra refreshed in the middle of the night and tried to fall back asleep. The candles still stood straight up like a line of soldiers ready for battle. No melted wax seemed to have formed, keeping the candles looking brand new, still as if they'd just been lit. While sitting up and grabbing a sip of water from beside my bed, I recalled a dream.

I remember having a vivid dream of being outside the castle, sitting by a lake, watching towards the sky as a massive blue ice dragon soared past the castle. It was a hot summer day with the scorching sun out, but at the same time, cold snow mixed into the weather. The dragon kept circling the castle as I watched every movement it made. It almost looked as if it were trying to get my attention specifically. I felt it was trying to communicate with me.

As I lay underneath the covers trying to fall back asleep, I felt a slight tugging at the covers, which were opening by my feet. I pulled the covers over my head to see what it was and saw the Red and Green fairies. They quietly led me to the other side of my room, where a secret door was hidden in the wallpaper. We headed through the passage and exited outside the castle. They led me to a tree deep in the forest that reached high into the sky.

Upon entering inside, a lift appeared, forming into the wood of the tree. I stood inside of the tree's base as it lifted us all the way to the top. The pressure rose, and I became lightheaded for a moment while continuing to raise so high up. A warm sensation started expelling from my nose; I wiped it and realized it was blood starting to drip from my nostril. After cleaning myself and looking around, I could see beautiful fairies flutter in the air in all types of colors, flying brightly through the skies. For a moment, I wiped my eyes, believing I was still asleep.

CHAPTER 17

Fountain of Tears

The fairies had their own world of tunnels and doors floating in the air. All miniature in size, I wondered exactly why they had brought me here. The Red fairy went to a small door covered in rose petals. I watched as she rummaged inside the tiny space, which probably felt normal-sized to her. She vanished and returned in the same breath, a tiny, sparkling potion in a clear, tear-shaped bottle now in her hand.

"Welcome to Cloud Fairy," I hear repeating over and over in my head.

"Drink this," she communicated telepathically.

I tilted the tiny bottle, sticking out my tongue to catch the single droplet that fell. Shortly after, a sharp pain began to form on both sides of my back. I screamed in terror as something started ripping out from inside my skin. My legs shook and trembled while I struggled to hold myself up. Unable to handle the pain, I fell into a fetal position, hitting the ground at the top of the tree from which we had come.

I watched from the corner of my eye as the Green fairy, the Red fairy, and the Pink fairy gathered the other colorful fairies. Together, they came to surround me. It felt as if glass was ripping through my shoulder blades as it protruded more with every moment. The fairies began to sing a rhythmic melody that sounded like ringing bells. I slowly felt myself regain strength, and the pain was sucked away by their songs. I sat upright on the ground, finally able to make sense of my surroundings with a clear mind.

I smiled, noticing how many fairies were around me. The sight of the Red, Green, and now the Pink fairies flying happily, no longer trapped inside the mirror, was a huge sigh of relief. I took a deep, painless breath and got closer to the Red fairy.

"What did I just pour into my mouth?"

"Look behind you," she responded telepathically.

I turned my head, shocked to notice I had crystal-clear wings sprouting from my back. I could still feel blood dripping from the sides, but the pain was gone. Moving and stretching my arms, I could feel my bones cracking. I kept moving to make my back feel comfortable again.

"Follow us to the Fountain of Tears," I heard the Green fairy's voice say in my head.

I watched as they all headed off toward a lavender-clouded area. I lifted myself easily off the ground, feeling the wings on my back rapidly moving, causing a buzzing sound and a vibrating sensation down my spine. Following them through the clouds, we soon arrived at the center of an empty fountain. It felt like the fading heartbeat of the fairies—more than a decoration, but a living testament.

"This fountain is the reason we brought you here; the water is drying up rapidly. We haven't been able to bring fresh supplies ever since the portal to Starfall started closing up."

"Portal to Starfall, the human realm? I've heard of that place," I said, confused. "What exactly do you do in Starfall to get this fountain water?"

"We gather droplets from humans, both adult and baby tears, and bring them to our fountain. Those tears are what keep us alive and the fountain flowing with life. The three of us—Red, Green, and Pink—were created to sustain this cycle. Without the Fountain of Tears, our whole existence is in jeopardy. The mixture of the tears from the innocent and the tears of the broken combined gives us our magical essence. Starfall is a mournful, strange place, and we must never be seen there."

"We haven't been able to travel through the Starfall portal because we were bound to the mirrors. It has simply been minimized from lack of use," the Green fairy responded.

"Once the fountain is full enough and we continue refilling it as we normally would, the portal to Starfall will stay completely open. If the fountain doesn't have enough tears and the portal remains inactive for too long, it will slowly begin to close and vanish forever, along with all of us."

The Pink fairy handed me a small thorn removed from a rose in her petal-filled room.

"Prick your finger and drip your blood onto a butterfly, then eat it whole. This will become your barrier, and you'll become smaller and invisible while in Starfall."

We flew through the clouds and got to an area with specific butterflies all resembling one another. The butterflies all gracefully danced in the sky, unaware that it would be the end for one of them. I asked the fairy which one I should take.

"The butterfly will choose you. Prick your finger with the thorn and hold out your hand," I heard echo in my head.

I did just that, and my hand started to tremble from the small piercing of my finger. A butterfly landed on the beaded droplet of blood sitting at the tip of my finger. I watched closely as it began to suck the blood from my wound, taking the pain away at the same time. The butterfly's white wings slowly began to fill with my blood, turning a deep crimson red.

"Now, eat it quickly!"

I shoved the butterfly in my mouth before I could stop myself and chomped down fast, feeling the squirt of my blood bursting inside my mouth. I started noticing the fairies seemed more detailed in size in front of me. Looking at my arms, I could see through them; my whole body seemed transparent. Noticing I was the same size as the fairies, I wrapped my arms around both the Red and Green fairies, giving them a hug. It seemed we were about ready to gather some human tears.

"We ask for your help because we know we can trust you, and we're unable to pass through to get to Starfall until the portal opens up wider."

"We trust you can find a way. Here is the bottle for the tears."

The Green fairy handed me a petite bottle wrapped in a golden leaf tied with a string around it.

"Hold this under the tears of the humans and fill it up. Bring it back here to the Fountain of Tears, and the portal will grow larger. From there, we can take over."

"Our lives depend on you."

Thinking of the only person I knew who could summon portals, Iscana, I told the fairies not to worry. I headed down the lift in the tree from the skies and back toward Wormwood Castle. Going to Iscana's room in the left wing of the castle, I flew in through an open window. Iscana was pacing back and forth. I called out her name, trying to catch her attention.

"Iscana, I need your help."

"Astra, is that really you?" she asked.

"Yes, the fairies are in trouble, and they need help, otherwise their whole species will go extinct."

"What are you talking about, Astra?"

"I have to get to a portal connecting to Starfall, the human realm, and gather their tears, then bring them back to the fairies so their portal will open up. It's kind of a long story."

"Do you think you can open a portal there?" I asked.

"I can open the portal for you, not a problem, but please be careful and hurry back. I'll make sure the portal stays open for you. There's much we need to talk about when you return."

Iscana began to draw a symbol on the ground around herself, and a bright yellow light emitted. As she stepped away from it, the light got darker, becoming opaque.

"Go and be careful. You'll be able to see the portal's light stretching out towards the sky, just as you do now. Just stay focused out there. If my skin wasn't such a distraction to look at, I would go with you."

I entered into the portal's flashing lights, which blinded my eyes. Winds pushed against my wings, tossing me in every direction. As I finally got control of myself, I turned to see if I could locate the portal's light. Now that I could see the way back, it was time to find some human tears.

While traveling through Starfall alone, I entered a house with a young man playing a musical instrument —something I'd never seen before. I stared at him for a while, drawn to the music he played as if I were in a trance. His fingers carefully pressed down onto black and white keys inside a wooden box while he sat on a bench close to it. I admired the sound and then started flying around inside the house, looking for a crying human, child or adult.

No tears in this house, so I began to head back outside. I noticed an old, beaten-up house with very dimly lit lights. As I got close, I could see a woman serving cold plates of food onto a small, rectangular wooden table. There were young children sitting around the table with sad looks on their faces. One chair didn't have a child sitting in it, but there was food served in front of the chair. The woman serving the food just threw it on the table each time, not caring if it spilled over.

I flew around inside this house, and my head began to pound. This place started to bring feelings I'd never felt before. I didn't know why, but I began to feel sadness, as if old memories were flashing before my eyes. As I made my way out the back of the house, I saw a small playground in a park nearby. A single, whimpering cry from the distance drew my attention closer.

I continued on in the park, looking for whoever was crying, and stopped by a playground where kids were playing frantically in the sun's harsh rays. I could hear the cries of a child nearby, but they were out of sight. Flying through a dim tunnel around a play area that began to vibrate and echo with cries.

Inside was a small child crying, holding on to her bloody, scraped knee. I pulled out the gold leaf-wrapped tear bottle and gathered enough tears from the child to fill it up. Her unruly, curled hair reminded me of my own, and I felt as if I saw myself in this child. As I was leaving, I saw a very small dandelion in its seed stage, and I bit onto the stem, removing it from the ground. I brought it over to the child in the colored tunnel, struggling while carrying it.

Her crying stopped as she noticed the dandelion gently floating toward her and landing on her scraped knee. She blew onto the dandelion, causing the seeds to scatter throughout the air, pushing me along with it. Once I got control of myself, I started to head back toward the portal's light, then got distracted.

CHAPTER 18

Magic Me Well

The energy from a small shop down below in the village catches my attention. I fly there before I head back to the portal just to get a glimpse inside. I see a woman performing hand movements over candles and placing them on the shelves. She sprinkles glitter over some of them and repeats different hand movements. I watch carefully as she carves symbols into the candles with precision. There's a strong smell coming from within that shop that somewhat feels familiar.

I fly into the crack underneath the door to try and understand why this smell feels like a lost memory to me. Flying around carefully, trying not to knock anything over, I see a bookshelf with books written in a different language. All of them are covered with dust and have strange symbols on them. Some have stars on them while others have moons. Cobwebs hang in each cornered area with small spiders intertwined.

Magic Me Well, the title of one of the books I could understand, is sitting on the counter. A picture of a woman tossing plants into a cauldron is on the cover of the book. The woman who was carving symbols into the candle looks over her shoulder halfway in my direction and grins, turning back as if she knew I was there and didn't seem to view me as a threat. The fairies made me invisible to the human world. There's no way she could actually see me.

I watch her head toward the book on the counter and open it up. She turns through the pages one after another, skimming the words along each page, reading carefully as she squints her eyes to focus. The riffing of the pages fills the room as she starts to pick up speed until stopping suddenly.

A small child knocks on the door with a frightened look, crumbling what seems to be a pouch filled with coins in her hand. She waits in anticipation for the woman to come to the door.

"Come in, child," the woman says as she holds the door open.

The small child walks with the woman toward the back of the shop. A burning stick of incense smoke leads the way into a beaded doorway with the image of a large eye in the center of it. They both go into the room behind the beads as I follow. A table in the center of the dark room is covered with hand-painted cards spread out in a neat pattern. Two chairs are next to the table, one on each side.

A thick wooden stick, lying on one of the chairs, is picked up by the woman as she sits down. She directs the small child to take a seat across from her. I watch as the child hands over the small cloth pouch full of coins, and the woman counts them while sitting at the table. The bubbling sounds of the small black cauldrons on the shelf beside them fill the room. Dead rabbits hang over a large cauldron, dripping blood from their necks into it while hanging by their feet. The woman grabs both of the child's hands over the table and calls out for her ancestors to join them in the room.

The woman grabs the wooden stick and slams it aggressively into the floor three times. Afterward, she places the wooden stick against the wall and starts waving her hands across the cards. She swipes them off the table into her hands and starts shuffling them. The young child sits watching as she bites her fingernails, tapping her foot repeatedly.

Black soot begins forming in the room, flying in the air gently. Within it, still lines of smoke circle the area as if there wasn't any air in the room. Small flashes of bright blue lights, as if lightning was striking the room, caught my attention in multiple areas. I can feel as if there are many eyes watching in the room. After the cards have been shuffled, the woman spreads them back across the table, but facedown this time.

"Pick a card, my dear, whichever one your heart desires," she says.

The child goes for a card at the far left, then hesitates for a moment, and reaches for a card off-center of the spread. She lifts up the card and looks at the image for a moment before revealing it to the woman. An image of a heart pierced by three long swords on the card is placed down over the spread.

"It's getting late. I really must be going now."

She leads the child out of the room toward a shelf with bottled water in different shaped bottles, some slightly tinted various colors. The woman grabs a light blue tinted water bottle and hands it to the girl.

"Take this water and fill a bath when home alone. Light a candle and pour the bottled water into the bath. Soak in the bath until you feel a tingle in your right foot."

"This will rid the negativity from inside of you completely. But make sure no one in your home sees this bottle. Keep it hidden until the time comes when you use it."

As the woman walks to the door with the child, she gives her one last thing. She goes up the wooden staircase in the shop; crystals on the walls pulse with a glow as she brings back a small stone.

"Hold this stone and make a wish, then throw it into the river wrapped around a piece of your hair. Soon you will have your wish," she tells her.

A darkened shadow moves inside the stone. I know it's a bad thing for the young girl to do. I can't allow myself to let her continue with this process. I exit the shop with the young girl. Looking behind me, I watch as the woman watches us, almost making direct eye contact with me. For a moment, it's as if I am stuck, frozen, watching as the woman looks deeply at me.

Once I break from her gaze, I look around, but the young girl is nowhere to be found. Upon entering back into the portal's light, I return to Iscana's room. She isn't there, and I head to the tree in the forest that leads up to Cloud Fairy. As I'm heading up in the lift, I start to dig around my body frantically for the bottle of tears. I don't feel it tied to my waist like it was.

I exit the lift and see the fairies all greet me eagerly. The Red and Green fairy get in front of the others and ask for the bottle of tears. Before I can even explain, the Green fairy giggles while reaching into my hair and grabbing the hidden tears.

"That's the first time I've seen it there," the Red fairy replies.

"Oh, yeah, it was the safest place I could think of, yeah," I say nervously, thinking to myself how lucky I am for not losing it.

I follow the fairies to the Fountain of Tears and watch as they pour the tears into it. It comes out as a thick, melted gold. As soon as the first drip goes into the fountain, it begins to liven up, and the fountain's golden color begins to spread throughout it. The fountain is now full enough for the fairies to fit through the portal and keep themselves safe from perishing.

"Thank you, thank you, thank you!" the fairies all say in unison.

"Take this rose thorn and prick your finger once you get down to the ground. Drip the blood down your back onto your wings, and they will begin to retract as you return to your normal size."

"We can't thank you enough," the Red fairy mentions.

"It's an honor. You really helped me when I had no clue what was happening. I will never forget the kindness you've sprouted into my life."

"If you ever need us, just close your eyes and visualize our bright lights approaching. You'll always be able to call on us."

I turn toward the lift, heading back down from the tree. When I get down close enough to the ground, I fly back to Wormwood Castle. I get to Iscana's room, and the portal is gone, but I still don't see her. I prick the thorn into my finger and squeeze the warm blood onto the wings on my back. The feeling feels so reviving and soothing as the wings retract back into my skin, closing up the open wounds.

I can see all around me; everything begins to look normal sized. My body is back to the way it was, and I figure now would be a good time to go to sleep. Transforming into a fairy really took a toll on me, or maybe it's because I haven't slept a full night in a long time. Either way, I know I need to rest. I sneak back into the door in my room where the fairies led me in the castle. The candles at the fireplace still stand without flickering the same way I left them. Pulling the covers over my head, I fall asleep.

CHAPTER 19

An Unforgivable Betrayal

Awakened by the smell of burning wood from the fireplace, I sat in bed looking out the window. The peaceful scenery of trees all around began changing colors with the season. Mixtures of green, yellow, orange, and red bled harmoniously together, creating a wonder to soak in. I glanced out the window for a while before deciding to get up. After freshening up, I mixed tree sap with mint leaves and rubbed it into my mouth. I spat out a small amount, leaving the majority to soak in and marinate. As I headed though the door to Nedos' room, I could see him sleeping still.

Quietly, I got onto the bed next to him and scooted closer to his face. His thick mustache moved with each breath exhaled. Killing him in his sleep right now would be so simple if he weren't immortal; he didn't even feel me near. I pondered the idea, but the peaceful look on his face as he slept pulled me in.

Kissing him on the lips, I woke him up to a surprised look on his face.

"Good morning. Hope you slept well," I said to him, not really understanding why.

I felt a different outlook on life this morning; for a moment, I felt complete. After helping the fairies and knowing everything with them was alright, I didn't hold much anger towards Nedos. I knew he had caused a lot of problems for everyone, including myself. Yet, I couldn't help this sudden attraction I felt towards him. Nedos gently brushed my hair with his fingers, pushing back strands behind my ear.

"Good morning, my Queen. Yes, I did. I hope you did the same."

"Oh, I most certainly did, thank you. Go get yourself together; I'll see you downstairs."

I headed downstairs and entered the kitchen. The smell of freshly baked bread hit me as I got closer. As I entered, a freshly made, steaming loaf of bread sat by the window. I knew exactly who this was from. A note on the side of it read:

"Enjoy the fresh baked bread.

Stop by the cottage when you can.

I have a gift for you."

— Ferna

Folding the note into a small square shape, I placed it into my pocket. The clothing made me itch from its snagging fabrics. I wasn't used to this royal garment that Nedos insisted on me wearing. Purple really wasn't my color, but I would wear it just for the sake of pleasing him.

As Nedos came downstairs, he held a wooden stick in his hand, lighting it towards his mouth, puffing and creating smoke. He used the fire to light the few candles on the table where I sat. Putting the stick to the side, he made it stand as a torch in the corner by the window. He used his magic to gather berries from a nearby bush outside the castle, watching as they slowly floated in through the window.

"Don't worry, these aren't poisonous," he laughed as he mentioned it.

I started cutting the bread Ferna made as he crushed the berries with a wooden bowl and stick. I watched as he created a nice blueberry spread, perfect to top the warm bread in front of us. He spread the mixture on two slices of bread and handed me one. For some reason, a slither of doubt emerged inside. Suddenly, the fear began to creep back into my heart: could I truly trust this man?

Without fully thinking it through, I took a big bite while keeping eye contact with him, smiling and feeling the berries drip down the side of my mouth. He laughed at my messy face while taking a bite of his own and wiping the berry from my face with his finger. I thanked him while blushing and continued eating it. That simple gesture felt so loving, something I'd never felt before. Is this feeling real?

I felt so deeply connected to him and stopped fighting the urge to resist it. After we both finished eating, he mentioned he would be going away for some time to gather more lavender to plant around the castle to uphold its magical barrier. I didn't know why a barrier was necessary—everything seemed to be going perfectly—but I didn't ask any questions and watched as he called out to the raven. It went to the ground and began expanding its wings and growing in size, large enough for Nedos to hitch a ride on.

"See you soon, my lovely Queen Hexia," he said as he blew a kiss towards me, heading off into the sky.

I decided to head towards Ferna's cottage while eating another slice of her wonderful bread with the blueberries on top. It was so good I couldn't resist having another serving. Curious about what Ferna had to gift me, I hurried along the path to her. Still chewing the piece of bread, I got closer to her cottage.

I began to feel dizzy as my vision went in and out of a haze. I reached Ferna's door and knocked with the little bit of strength I had left, gripping onto the bread in the other hand. I fell to the ground. I could see her legs as she dragged me into her cottage. My ears started a deafening ringing and then went into complete silence.

My vision continued to go in and out as I watched Ferna panic and rummage through her belongings. She pulled out a silver cross pendant and placed it over me, then poured out some water from a vial and splashed it over my body. I could feel each drop of water as it hit my body. She opened a black book, holding it open in one hand.

"I command all evil spirits to leave this body at once!" Ferna yelled out. She said every word with great authority in her voice. I watched as a dark shadow expelled from my body, with my sight slowly regaining its focus.

"Go back from where you came, you aren't welcome here."

The shadow began to vanish into the air, flowing out the door towards the forest. Ferna started mixing some herbs together and making a warm pot of tea. I watched as the veil left behind by the figure inside of me went off into the distance until completely out of sight. Ferna walked towards me and placed a warm cloth around the back of my neck, then grabbed the hot beverage.

"Here, drink this. Carefully, it's really hot." She handed me a small cup filled halfway while sitting me upright.

"What was that? What just happened?" I asked after drinking a few sips.

"Death was knocking at your door while you were knocking on mine. It was sent to you; it wasn't your time."

Ferna noticed the blueberry spread on my hands and noticed it on the bread I brought in as well. She picked up what remained of the bread and held it up to look at it closer. Her eyes opened wide, raising her eyebrows as she took a slight step backward. Dropping the bread back onto the ground, she turned to me with swiftness.

"Who gave you this? Who told you it was okay to eat this?"

I knew she wouldn't be happy with what I was about to tell her. Looking around for a moment, I nervously told her it was Nedos. Shaking my head in disbelief, I couldn't look her in the eyes. A feeling of heat spread from my chest up towards my face as the rage built up inside of me. My hands began tightening, clenching into fists, knuckles growing pale from the pressure.

"I can't believe he would try to kill you. That deceitful, horrible man! I will never forget this."

"These are the poisonous blueberries," she continued.

Has everything he said to me about our past together been a lie? Did he not really love me after all? Am I really his queen reincarnated? So many questions raced through my mind. I didn't know what to believe anymore.

"We have to get you to a safe place until we can return and put a stop to this once and for all," Ferna said.

"Come with me to Wormwood Castle before we leave; we have to find Iscana. And there's one more thing I want to do."

"Don't worry, Nedos headed out to gather lavender for the castle's protective barrier," I replied, assuring her we would be alright.

It all started to make sense to me why the barrier was needed now: He was preparing for a battle. I removed the ring Nedos gave me and threw it into a bush by the dungeon entrance. As Ferna and I entered the castle looking for Iscana, I was drawn to the room where I found the dragon statue underneath the floorboards. We entered the room, walking carefully around the opening in the floor towards the mermaid mirror. As I stood in front of the mirror, holding it in my hands, hoping to come in contact with someone, I called out.

"Is anyone there? Merlissa, Are you there?"

I waited for a brief moment and called out again, hoping the time we met wouldn't have been the last. I was unsure if this mirror was really used to connect with the mermaids. Why do I still believe the stories Nedos told? How foolish could I really be? I called out to the mirror one last time while Ferna's puzzled look pierced into the mirror behind me.

"Merlissa, Mermaids, Can anyone hear me?" Swirling shades of blue started forming into the shape of water from inside the mirror.

"Astra, it's you! How is this possible? I'm so glad to see you," Merlissa appeared in the mirror's reflection.

"You won't believe this, but I'm at Wormwood Castle, where Nedos, the man who murdered and consumed your sister's flesh, lives."

"He told me a story of hunting a mermaid to consume and be granted eternal life. He tricked one into falling in love with him and was going to kill her, but another mermaid arrived the night of her trap and ate her instead."

"No, that can't be true," Merlissa replied.

"That isn't possible; my sisters killed him, and I saw his remains left behind on the beach where we would meet in secret."

"That wasn't him; a fisherman was left behind accidentally, but now I'm realizing maybe it was all a part of his plan," I said while putting it all together.

"Listen, Merlissa, I need all the help I can get. Nedos tricked me into believing I was his Queen reincarnated. He replaced some of my memories and even showed me fake pictures of myself. On top of it all, he poisoned me while eating early this morning. If it wasn't for Ferna here, I would probably be dead."

Ferna waved hello to Merlissa while standing behind me, watching as we spoke. Questioning what was real and what was not, I didn't really know what to think. If the mermaid story was true, what else was? Something had to be done about this.

"I'm going to leave, but I'm taking this mirror along with me. I'll be in contact with you soon; it's really good seeing you, friend." I said goodbye as we both watched Merlissa fade away, with the mirror returning back to our reflections.

Placing the mirror carefully in my pocket, I went over to the pocket watch laying on the fireplace in my room. Holding onto it, I started to feel the magic energy within it. Is this really enchanted with my magic from long ago? I started feeling my heart beat racing, beating faster with each tick from the watch pulsing through my chest. Did I really give this to Nedos to help him find his way back towards me? My brain started playing tricks on me, and without thinking too hard, I tossed it into the fire.

Watching as the pocket watch sat in the flames, I stared at it with a vengeful look, ready for anything that was headed our way. As Ferna and I made our way out of the room, we continued searching and calling through the castle. A glowing light from underneath a locked door brought my curiosity towards it. I pushed into the side of the door with the sai weapon and kept pushing until it unlocked. The room's walls were filled with lilac-colored crystals, clear enough to see a faint reflection of myself in it.

A hand-drawn map was sitting on a desk in the center of the room next to a feather quill dipped into a cup of black ink. Circles were drawn over certain areas on the map while other areas were crossed out. It seemed as if Nedos was following something. I tapped my finger onto the map for a moment; a part of the ink transferred to my finger.

"This part was recently done," I turned to Ferna.

As we went to exit the room, I grazed my hand against the crystals on the walls. I started to see an image consume my sight of what seemed to be an angel with massive purple wings and flowing long hair. She floated gently still in place while two bright lights glowed above her head. I shared the vision with Ferna, but it didn't make any sense to her either.

We couldn't seem to find Iscana anywhere. Trying not to think of the worst, I began to fear for her life.

"Oh, I almost forgot to give you this gift." Ferna handed me a cross-shaped necklace.

I remembered all the crosses I'd come across since meeting Ferna. The symbol had grown on me and felt like a safe place whenever it was around. Especially after seeing it remove death from inside me, I was absolutely excited to have my very own by my side. Gripping the necklace in my hand, I admired it for a moment. The silver metal of the cross was heavy with love and peace. Tying it around my neck, I gave Ferna a great hug afterwards.

"Thank you so much, Ferna, I truly appreciate this gift."

Staying close by each other, we scanned the halls of the castle, calling out for Iscana. No sight of her anywhere. Still, we carried on. I noticed the guards standing outside from the back of the castle, all as if they were listening to commands. Some of the guards were leading the others, all yelling loudly. Heris burst through the top of the castle, looking down at us.

"Astra, come this way, hurry," he yelled in our direction.

I looked up, realizing who it was as he removed his metal helmet. Ferna and I headed up the long, spiraled flight of stairs towards him. Heris explained to us that the castle was going to be soon filled with guards looking to kill anyone wandering inside and that they were all outside preparing for an attack. Nedos had ordered them all to go for blood.

"Nedos is on his way back; you mustn't be here when he returns," Heris said.

"I ran into Iscana walking outside towards the forest near the castle. She told me to tell you she is coming back and not to worry about her."

"Thank you, we'll head in that direction then," I said to him while hearing the metal clanking of armor echoing from downstairs.

"The guards are already inside; you two must hurry."

He led us to a painting of Nedos sitting on a throne with a golden crown over his head. Pressing onto the side of the picture, it sprung open. Inside was a small room. Buttons lined along the walls inside with symbols on each. Heris pointed to a red button and told us to press it once he closed the painting behind us, then hit the blue button immediately after.

Without saying another word, he closed the painting, leaving both Ferna and myself inside the dark room, illuminated by the small, lit buttons on the wall. I stood in front of the red button, ready to press it. Hearing the metal armor of the guards seeming closer, I pushed hard on the red button. Ferna pushed the blue button right after, and we both stood back towards the wall as all the buttons lit up, flashing and pulsing one at a time rapidly.

The room began spinning around slowly as it clicked. Once the clicking stopped and the room stood still, the lights on the buttons stopped flashing. Only the red and blue buttons remained lit. We both pushed through where we entered. A transparent revolving door stood in front of us. I could see a woman with long brown legs and high white ears on the top of her head. She stopped the revolving door, holding it still, and told us to come with her.

"Heris sent me to guide you safely to the forest. I'm Niara, the guardian of all animals and creatures residing in these parts."

I gazed at her intense beauty. Her dark skin glowed with sparkles of glitter within it. Flowing white strands of hair draped over her shoulders as tall white and pink rabbit-like ears sprouted from up top of her head. Red and black ladybugs sat scattered around her hair, almost in a decorative pattern. Her human body mixed with rabbit features made her a sight hard to look away from.

"Please follow me; I will lead you to your friends. This way you can all join in the fight towards defeating Nedos," Niara said.

As we followed behind her, I couldn't help but watch her instead of our surroundings. Her fluffy circular rabbit tail and white fur rising up from her legs midway caught most of my attention.

CHAPTER 20

Spiritwood Grove

While Ferna and I continued following Niara, we passed through an area in the forest covered in mushrooms. I could not help but notice how joyful she was while leading the way. She pranced through the mushrooms, twirling around them and doing flips. Her slim, curvy figure was able to swiftly move through the area as if it were a rehearsed dance. I held on to Ferna's hand as we both tried to keep up with her. Nothing in this area felt familiar to me; I did not recall even seeing one mushroom in our parts of the forest near Wormwood Castle.

"Hey Niara, wait for us! You're going too fast!" I yelled.

"You two have to do better than that," Niara responded as she began swinging from vines hanging off trees.

Every tree around us felt darkened with a certain kind of energy. Sap oozed all around the base of the trees, causing the ground to get stickier with each step. I looked around and realized it was not stopping but getting worse. Ferna jumped onto a mushroom big enough to hold her and continued hopping from one to the next, heading toward Niara. She sat up in a tree, watching us as we tried to navigate through the mess below.

"This does not seem too difficult a task," I said aloud.

Following behind Ferna, I hopped onto one mushroom at a time, carefully avoiding the sticky sap on the ground below. I held onto a vine to steady my balance. I tossed a hanging vine over to Ferna to make sure she did not accidentally slip. As she tried to catch the vine, she trembled and missed it while jumping onto the next mushroom. The mushrooms began glowing a bright orange color as the forest around us darkened, pulling us deeper inside.

Niara watched us from up in the tree, looking quite impressed at the distance we had covered so far. Each tree began tossing its branches chaotically as if to avoid intruders from entering. We both watched as she maneuvered through them with ease. I knew neither Ferna nor myself had the agility to mimic what she did. Holding out my hand, I focused and drew the diamond shape into my palm, letting out a freezing ice mist that froze the trees' branches. In front of us, the branches immediately began melting, dripping rapid drops of freezing water onto our backs.

"Thanks for the help," I yelled to Niara.

She didn't seem to have heard me and continued swinging smoothly through the trees. I pulled out the sai weapons Ferna gave me and quickly handed them to her.

"Use these if anything comes your way unexpectedly." I held my hand out and continued freezing the tree branches. Ferna chopped some, allowing us to fit through certain areas and helping us to get by safely.

A tree sat in the center of the forest, surrounded by a shallow body of water. Niara walked through the water as it splashed against her feet and stood there, waiting for us to meet her. As both Ferna and I reached Niara, she raised her hand to the top of the tree. It had lights of little fireflies flying all around it. The leaves on the tree were transparent and we could see straight through them.

She pulled a leather whip from her side and latched it onto a thick branch in the middle of the tree. Pulling down with her whole body, she shook the tree until a couple of leaves began to fall down to us. Niara handed us each a leaf while rubbing one all over her body. It produced a slime-like substance that was absorbing quickly into her skin.

"A little goes a long way with this leaf. Here, go ahead and rub this onto your skin," she said. "In order for us to pass this next area, we have to cover ourselves in this tree's scent."

Ferna rolled up the sleeves to her lace dress and tried not to ruin it while rubbing the leaf carefully into her arms. She rubbed it onto her legs as well and gave the leaf back to Niara. I did the same onto my arms and legs and looked toward Niara for more direction.

"Watch this," she said.

Niara whistled loudly while placing two fingers into her mouth. Her whiskers by her tiny pink nose sparkled with light as a group of green antelopes came heading in our direction. They all kneeled down to her as she spoke another language to them. When she spoke, the whole forest around us stood still. The air stopped blowing, as if it knew she was near.

The antelopes stood up straight, and two of them walked toward me and Ferna. I held my hand out and allowed the animal to smell the scent on my arm, coated with the transparent leaves from the firefly-filled tree. Strangely, the animals resembled the green fox I fought at the X-Graves when trying to find Iscana's parents. Both antelopes kneeled down before us gracefully while we rubbed the tops of their heads.

"Get on top of them and hold onto their horns tightly; they're going to bring us through the next area," Niara said while getting onto one herself.

The horns on the antelope she got on were larger than the rest. It must be the oldest of the bunch. I could feel the heartbeat of the antelope as I grabbed a hold of its horns. They all walked toward each other, standing in a line facing the dark forest ahead. The other antelopes stood on the outside of us, keeping us protected in the middle. Ferna and I were on each side of Niara as she pointed off into the forest. She spoke in the foreign language again, and the antelopes began racing through the dark. The area around us glowed briefly as we passed through.

Falling all around were petrified blossoms and glowing motes. The antelopes dodged through each one as they fell, all making it down the path safely. I saw the others ahead of us, all illuminating the way. The eyes of the antelopes glowed a neon green, as I noticed when Niara quickly turned around while on her antelope to check on me.

As the falling of everything began to lessen and stop completely, I felt the ground below begin to shrug and crumble. A long vibration went through the antelope's body, jolting through mine as we passed through the area. Long trees started to jut up from the ground, as if growing rapidly for the very first time.

The trees sprung up toward the sky and shot back down, almost as if they were being used as a weapon to attack us. The emptiness around us soon began to fill up with trees going in and out of the ground, trying to hit us, but the antelopes' swiftness was too smart for the trees. They seemed to have mastered the area here as well, not showing any type of fear.

As the trees began to lessen with intensity, we all headed onto a large tree stump with multiple rings glowing into it. It began to bring back a familiar feeling I could not explain. While all on top of it, the tree stump rose up into the air, high enough for us to see Wormwood Castle from a distance.

"There's the castle," Ferna said.

I could not believe we were so far away from the castle at this point.

"Niara, do you know why we had to come so far away from the castle?" I asked.

"Yes, Nedos placed a magic spell over the castle when he returned and sent all the guards on a task to eliminate anyone in the area who was not one of his army," Niara responded. "He could track your magic near the castle. That tracking would alert the guards, who would find you sooner than you would expect."

"What about our friends? How do we know they're safe then? How do we know we're not doing all of this for nothing?" I asked.

"Your friends are safe. Heris gave them strict instructions not to leave their portal door and enter back into the forest until it's opened from the other side."

"We are going to have to open their door to let them out. The door around them is in an area in the forest that cannot detect magic. Nedos won't be able to track them there."

Niara mentioned as soon as they would step a couple of feet towards the castle, it would be a trap. Making sure everyone is together before heading to Wormwood Castle is crucial, because we'd need her help to do so.

"I can't be in two places at once, now can I?" Niara said while looking around as the tree stump began lowering us down.

Her voice as she spoke to us was so soft and calming, almost like a lullaby. I could listen to her speak word after word and just be intertwined in her words. The light seemed to bend around her, softening her edges until she felt as if a forgotten memory. There was an ethereal beauty to her that remained impossible to grasp.

Niara began to guide the rest of the antelopes off the tree stump, and she pulled out her leather whip. Flicking the whip toward the ground while sitting high up on the antelope, she began disrupting the dirt, causing it to rise and crumble in the air with each strike. Transparent strings revealed themselves from underneath. She kept hitting the ground with her whip until every string came to the surface. Grabbing each one in her hand and holding them all together, she pulled it up and down, fanning it quickly in the air.

The strings began to form a solid structure. A path enlarged above us, heading into the distance. I could see other animals below the area ahead of us. All the animals were a green, glowing shade that matched the antelopes we rode on. Before we got onto the path ahead, I asked Niara a random question, "Is this path really trustworthy? It doesn't seem too stable to me."

"I'm not here to deceive anyone or let anyone reach their demise. Trust me, my friend." Niara reached out her hand while stepping on the path, leading the way. We got behind her, and the antelopes walked carefully down the narrow clear path.

The weight of all of us on the path frightened me. Thinking that we were too heavy to make it, I closed my eyes, feeling the wind as I was being carried over slowly. Ferna was making some kind of chain in her hands, I noticed when I opened my eyes. She was connecting links of metal to one another, creating a long, very thin metal chain. "Is it another necklace?" I asked her.

I began to see pumpkins floating in the air around us, floating onto clouds of fire. Below us were tons of animals living amongst each other in harmony, all green and glowing. I saw some foxes in the area that reminded me of the one I fought at the X-Graves.

"Niara, those foxes there, are they all under your control?"

"Yes, I am the mother to all animals of this forest. They all glow with life because of me. A long time ago, Nedos destroyed the whole forest beyond Wormwood Castle, including every bit of wildlife living within it. After a long winter's hibernation underground, I rose up to find everything destroyed."

"Crying out to the forest, I begged for help. That's when this orb of light came to me. It was glowing bright green, just as the animals you see before you. It enveloped my body and allowed me to awaken their spirits."

"I walked around the area for days, reviving every creature that once lived and protected them in this area here, beneath the clear wires you saw earlier. That's the only sure way I know to protect them. Only one has escaped my keeping, strangely enough—it's one of those foxes that you mentioned."

"Crazy thing is, I saw one of those exact foxes at the X-Graves. I actually had to fight it for a moment, as if it were a guard in the area, protecting it," I told her.

"Oh, please don't hold it against me. It's in the animals' nature to defend themselves against anyone who isn't an animal or a hybrid animal creature. They associate human bodies with Nedos, unfortunately. The only strange part about it is how it ends up all the way over at the X-Graves."

"Eventually, I ended up creating this trap and living forest, Spiritwood Grove, to protect the creatures residing here. They don't deserve what happened to them, and they definitely don't deserve it happening again. If only Nedos knew there were so many magical creatures residing here, he would be furious. The orb that came to me was as if a life source of its own," Niara said as she revealed a small necklace from underneath her clothing.

The necklace pulsed a bright green glow as she pulled it out into the open air. As she placed it back between her and her clothing, the light dimmed.

"I have only memories of how this place once was. There was a time where everything was peaceful, and we didn't have to live in fear and hiding. My life has changed completely, but just knowing that the heart of the forest lies in the animals brings me to go on another day."

"Without them, this place is nothing. A handful of my children were poisoned by Nedos. One night, they went to gather berries from nearby Wormwood Castle and were found lifeless on the ground. That was the last time anyone ventured out of the area. I absolutely loathe him. He is the reason for all of this suffering."

"I'm sorry for everything, Niara, I really am. Nedos definitely has another thing coming to him. He will get what he deserves."

"He poisoned me with those blueberries as well. Tasty as they were, I almost died. I would've been dead if it weren't for Ferna here. She saved me before it was too late."

I showed Niara the cross around my neck Ferna gave me. "This cross is a smaller version of what she actually used, but its feeling is like no other. I feel like a brand new person with this on."

We finally reached the other side of the clear path where the antelopes gracefully walked along. The animals below were unaware of us walking above them; their calmness remained undisturbed. I felt for them, but was at least happy they were able to continue living, even if it were as a forest spirit.

CHAPTER 21

Sanctuary's Vow

The trees attacking us as we passed through the area were only a mechanism for protection. The dead remains of animals are buried beneath the trees, fused within the seeds that grew. Niara made it so they protected the area with the last of their soul power. They live on through the trees and the green orb that gave them life.

"The Tree of Life, where we are heading, is full of green orbs," Niara explained.

"I've heard many stories of that tree; some say it was just a myth. I can't believe it's true," Ferna said, holding her hand over her heart.

"What exactly does the Tree of Life do?" I asked.

"The Tree of Life is said to revive anyone with the exchange of life. So, in order to give life, it must take life. I have never seen it used before, but just being near it is energizing. I think we're going to need all the energy we can get," Niara said.

"Let's rest here for a moment. It is more than safe to let our guard down." I began to get comfortable on the ground below.

As I sat there with Niara and Ferna, I thought about the Tree of Life and its powers. What if there was a way to trick it into reviving someone without killing and transferring its life force? I pondered for a moment, trying to understand it. I looked over at the others and realized they'd fallen asleep. My curiosity caused me to get up and venture ahead without their knowing. It could be my last venture alone.

Was I really that compelled to risk my life rather than wait with the others? Something was pulling me closer, as if a magnet was attached to metal. I saw a tall piece of cloth hanging from a wooden stick. It resembled a ghost with big, dark black eyes and a scary-looking mouth drawn on it. It looked as if it was created as a warning to keep something or someone out.

Walking into the fields ahead, I felt a tug against my wrist, pulling me back.

"We mustn't go this way, Astra," Niara said.

As we headed back to the Tree of Life, we joined Ferna once again. Sitting underneath the tree, I could feel my body being charged with energy and strength, as Niara mentioned. I needed a lot of charging; it seemed like the journey never ends. Niara sat with us under the tree, watching and making sure I didn't venture off this time.

I ended up snoozing off for a moment until I was awakened by a creaking sound. The ground underneath the tree opened up. Niara pulled on a latch with her whip attached to it, which was hung over a branch for extra leverage. As she pulled it open, a dirt-covered tunnel paved with white pebbles scattered around the ground as a road was revealed.

"Come, I want to show you guys something before we head over to Wormwood Castle."

"Niara, I don't think we have time for this."

"Don't worry, your friends are safe. As long as they stay put and wait for us to open their portal, they're being protected, Astra, you have my word."

We followed behind her through the underground passage. The roots from the Tree of Life spread all throughout around us. Thick, strong roots mixed with small, thin roots everywhere. Niara whistled, and the roots began flowing with light, guiding the way through the tunnel. The roots were glowing a green light, just like the orbs around the tree and the one hanging around her neck.

I could feel a warmth getting nearer as we pushed along the way. Ferna's eyes widened in excitement as I looked back at her, as if she was prepared for something I didn't know. We got to a dead end, and I looked around, thinking this was a joke. Niara began clawing at the wall ahead, digging a passage through the wall of dirt that blocked our way. The wall was the only side not covered in the tree's roots. As she continued digging, a shine of light burst through the dirt wall. I began to help her, but it didn't seem to make a difference. She had these long, sharp claws that made her digging seem effortless.

We stood at the top of the new entrance, looking down. I watched in amazement and pure shock. A whole world of creatures that were hybrids lived down below the soil of the Tree of Life. Niara grabbed onto the wall of dirt, gripping her claws into it, and slid down towards the ground. I knew I couldn't do the same, and the height was too much to risk the attempt.

"Wow, did you see her slide down the wall like that? She's so amazing," Ferna said.

Niara was below us in the distance as we watched her being greeted by a group of hybrids such as herself. Everyone was mixed with a certain kind of animal. It was a safe haven, for sure. The sense of tranquility was strong. A small river flowed across the ground below, and the area wasn't blocked off or felt restricted.

Everything felt open and had small blue mushrooms illuminating the area in certain spots. The roots of the tree spread out through the area, giving it a faint, dim light, enough to get around comfortably.

Still dark underneath, I could see the glow from Niara's orb necklace, making her stand out.

"Listen, listen everyone, Niara has arrived!" A grand voice echoed through the area, causing everyone's attention to focus on her.

Hybrid bunnies were seen gathering around Niara, everyone joyful and celebrating her return. "Everyone listen, I brought someone special here to meet you. She's up there," she said while pointing up towards us.

I smiled and waved down below so that they could see me. Ferna waved along with me. Our waving caused the dirt from beneath us to loosen, and we felt the pull of the dirt falling towards the ground. Ferna pulled me back before it dropped us both down to the ground below.

"That was close, thank you, Ferna," I said while catching my breath.

"These are two very important people. I'm leading them to their friends. Their mission is to defeat the wicked Nedos. Soon, we will all be free from living in the shadows."

They all burst into a unified cheer. As they began to celebrate, I couldn't have thought any less of us. Yes, we definitely were going to defeat Nedos, somehow. I knew it had to be done. I wouldn't fall for his tricks again. I wondered for a moment if he was alright. Believing he was pure evil, I couldn't force myself to think so. He did remove the curse from Iscana. I didn't understand why he would do such a thing if he were completely bad. Either way, he tried to kill me; there's no going back from that.

The hybrids wanted to meet us, so they created a ladder out of twisted vines tied together tightly. It was made almost instantly as they all worked together. Niara took the ladder made of vines into her mouth and climbed back up the wall towards us. She dug a slight dent into the walls on each side, wrapping the vine around the strong, thick roots of the Tree of Life. A firm tug against it to make sure it was safe for us to get on, and we made our way down. One after another, as Niara watched from above, making sure the vines stayed intact.

Making our way down below, Niara clawed onto the wall, sliding down again. Surrounded by all the beautiful creatures around us, I never felt such a presence. There were so many wonderful faces full of hope and bright energy. I was pleased to have come this far. Their fates were now in my hands. I had another reason to defeat Nedos now, adding on to my long list.

"Hello, I'm Nii. It's my pleasure to meet you."

He grabbed onto my hands, excited, shaking both my hands between his with glee. The fur around his palms tickled me but was soft to the touch. He is a hybrid bunny, like Niara. His fur was dark brown, almost matching his dark brown skin tone. His ears were shorter than Niara's and had white inside. He grabbed onto Ferna's hands next, introducing himself to her. I noticed there were plenty of different types of bunny hybrid people. They all were in different sizes and colors, all different from the rest.

"Welcome to our small oasis. We're pleased to have you here. Please have dinner with us before you head out on your journey. It will bring you good luck."

"We will begin to prepare a meal. Please let us show you the area, and don't hesitate to ask for anything at all you may want to take along with you," Nii said.

Walking with Niara through the area, with her being our guide, I noticed how wonderful everyone was. Small children were playing and hopping around joyfully along the path. Everyone was very positive, although they were confined to this underground space. They had their own farm section that grew crops for them to eat without having to leave in search of food.

I held onto the side of a house built of clay and noticed my hand print left behind on it. The hybrids in the area all had a red string tied around their ankles. I was curious to know what it meant, but I didn't want to offend anyone if it were something that bonded them. I watched as Nii and Niara spoke to each other as they pointed out different areas for Ferna and I to look at.

"Niara, what exactly keeps you all thriving down here? How did you all survive down here for such a long time?"

"If you must know, I'll tell you. I was created by Nedos some time ago as a failed experiment. I didn't obey his commands and was set for execution by the guards on the next new moon."

"I sat waiting in the dungeons for my life to end, along with some others, until a small fluttering light of red and green came towards my gate. It flew around the lock and freed me from the grips of Nedos' fate."

"I escaped the dungeon along with another on my side: Nii. He was there in the dungeon chamber beside me. The lights allowed both of us to escape, guiding us along the way. We made it out of the castle and headed to the forest. Deep within it, we created our own sanctuary together. Everyone down here is a descendant of the two of us. We weren't able to perish after so many centuries. I believe it could be because we were created to thrive alongside Nedos. He would've been the only one able to take our lives from us."

"Since we escaped, death hasn't been able to find us. Nedos twisted off one of my claws, ripping it from the nail bed just to force my obedience. Something inside me felt more than a servant. Although he gave me life, I feel powers stronger than he could ever imagine."

"The universe guided us here. It helped us to survive. And right when I thought all hope was gone is when I was set free. Sid here was created after me as a replacement. But, just as I felt, he had a certain resistance to him. When we were created, our names were N-I & N-II. I came up with my name while secluded in the dungeons, wishing to be viewed as a living, breathing being, not only a failed experiment. Nii felt it was easier to keep his original name in a way and just be called Nii instead of N-II."

"Yes," Nii said, "not only did it feel easier to adjust to, but it was something I never wanted to forget. Although I despise Nedos, I'm still thankful for being created. I use my name as a constant reminder not to give up and never to forget how much I've overcome and been through in life—to fight with all my might, as a warrior."

Their words touched my heart. I would have never guessed they were created by the hands of such wickedness.

"Is everything with you alright?" Ferna asked me while pulling me aside.

"Of course, I'm fine. Don't worry, it's nothing."

We all continued to walk around the massive underground area they built. I could tell the two were madly in love and bonded by such a closeness. I'm sure they've been through a lot, but it must be a wonderful feeling to have someone who understands you and stands by your side. And it's just a bonus that they share the same body type.

I tried to mention the fairies to Niara to let her know what those colored lights were that freed them from the dungeon that day, but I got sidetracked. There was a dirt wall that was filled with tiny glass windows. The inside of each was a small, confined sleeping space. A few were occupied with the hybrids as they were either sleeping or just relaxing. A hole in front of the wall surrounded by small pebbles outlining it was an entrance inside.

"This is where we sleep. The tree's roots throughout the wall protect us, so we built this area," Niara said.

It was very comfortable looking. Blue glowing mushrooms were seen in each area as a light source. The faint glow of the colors was a relaxing moment to behold. I felt as if I could go for a nap there right about now. A few more entrances on the ground showed up as we came across them.

The two of them brought us to a pond where green spirit fishes swam through. Koi fish, larger than I've ever laid eyes on, gulped up for food when Niara came closer.

"These are the Koi fish that used to reside near Wormwood Castle. One of them that had a blue spot on it turned into a dragon—a large, iced one. Nedos, jealous of its majestic body and magic abilities, froze the dragon in stone. He lured it into the castle, and from there, it was never seen again."

CHAPTER 22

Promise Secured

othing could have stopped Niara from showing us around the area. Nii was absolutely proud of everything they had created together. This was all the product of their hard work and life together. I asked Niara if she had any idea when dinner would begin. We walked over to an open hole in the ground where three youngsters popped out. They were all wearing masks over their faces made of black mud, running around and trying to scare others in the area.

Nii grabbed one of them by the hand and began wiping the mud off their face.

"Terrorizing one another isn't a nice thing to be doing now, is it?" he said.

"Go find the others, get cleaned up, and meet us at the eating circle. We're going to have a farewell meal with our guests here. You should be on your best behavior."

The young one obliged and ran to the others to get ready for dinner. When Nii was finished speaking, I told him and Niara about the dragon statue I discovered from Wormwood Castle. At first, they looked shocked and didn't truly believe me. Ferna joined in and backed me up.

"It's true, the dragon was underneath the floorboards," Ferna said.

"I wonder if the dragon I saved a while ago has any connection to this," I said aloud.

"I was walking down a blood-stained river that led to a dragon that was wounded badly. Its blood mixed into the river as I saved a fish. When I got to the dragon, I touched it a little and it caused my hand to change to this blue shade," I said while showing my arm.

"It's true, this is the work of the Ancient Frost dragon. But how? It's been sealed behind stone in Wormwood Castle. How could you possibly have run into it dying at the side of a river? Could there have been others?" Niara asked.

"There easily could have been. As we know, Nedos is notorious for slaying any life whose magic seems greater than his. I wouldn't be surprised if it were true," Ferna added.

"Well, either way, I'm glad you did what you did to help Astra. That blue hand is a constant reminder of your noble actions. We truly appreciate you. Come, let's all go to the eating circle. Then we can tell everyone of the great things Astra has done."

"Please, it really isn't that big of a deal."

There we all sat around a bulky wooden log raised over the ground on top of hardened pieces of leaves stacked on one another. As we all sat on the ground in a circle, the two hybrid women who prepared the food came and placed the meals in the middle.

Large amounts of fresh fruit and leaves of all kinds were mixed together. The mixture of fresh carrots and cabbage was boiled to a soft, steamy texture. Dandelion flowers and greens were mixed in as well, and there were various sized pieces of the roots from the Tree of Life.

When I saw and noticed the roots, it clicked in my head. That's how they're all surviving so long without even realizing it. The roots from the tree had to have been keeping them alive and safe for all this time. I picked up a steamed root and placed it in front of me. Ferna wrapped it in a steamed piece of cabbage and broke it in half. We shared it together, both chewing and forcing it down. The taste was unbearable, but knowing it was from that tree made the struggle worth it.

Everyone around us ate harmoniously as they shared with one another and passed different portions around the table. Niara continued to eat while telling us she hadn't been down here in quite some time. A large explosion disrupted the place, and the hybrids began to scatter and hide into their holes, going to their safe places. I looked around to see where Nii went and noticed him not too far away.

Nii pulled out a bow and arrow from behind a barrel filled with old metal objects. As we all stood guard by the table, we prepared for what seemed like an invasion.

"How could this happen? I shouldn't have brought you here," Niara said.

Niara focused on the ground below. It began trembling and shaking, coming toward us. The dust and debris from the explosion began to disappear, leaving behind a faint shadow slowly revealing itself.

It was guards sent by Nedos. A group of them stood there watching as we looked confused, staring at them. Nii shot an arrow in their direction and told us to escape through the hole in the ground with the others. Leaving this fight wasn't an option. I told Ferna to get ready as she pulled out the sai weapons she once entrusted me with. They began glowing a bright red at the blades, and her purple eyes ignited with intensity.

Before the guards could get closer to us, I expelled an ice rain from my palm, stopping their movement. "You aren't welcome here!" I yelled out to them. One of the guards in the back began walking to the front center of them all. I noticed it was Heris. He wasn't wearing his helmet, and his eyes were completely black and lifeless. He seemed as if he were under the control of a dark force. Nedos had to be the one behind this. He's hypnotized somehow. I tried to freeze everyone in place, but before I could do so, Heris used his fire staff to block and melt my attack, rendering it ineffective.

The guards began to get closer. Niara began to kneel onto the ground with her head bowed down. The ladybugs from her hair began to fly off into the air one by one, each forming into an exact replica of herself. They all stood up from the ground at the same time. I couldn't tell which one was the original Niara. A guard launched a sharp metal object toward us.

One of Niara's clones tossed her whip into the air, catching it and whipping it back toward the guards, knocking one to the ground. We all began to fight. Niara's clones were doing the majority of the fighting as they all swiftly leaped through the air, some even jumping on and over the guards. The whips were used to strangle and confine them. Ferna was head-to-head with one of the guards as she got back into the fighting spirit. You could see a slight joy in her face, as if she was delighted to have an opportunity to fight once again.

"How could you betray us, Heris!" Niara yelled at him.

"No, don't hurt him. He's under Nedos' control, he's not himself—I can sense it," I told Niara.

"Heris, please, snap out of it and remember who you are. Remember who we are."

The other guards were all bound by Niara's clones. One of them ran out toward the mess where they entered with the explosion, and Nii went out behind him. I held onto Heris' staff, trying to stop him from using it against us. Without knowing it, I could see the ice from my hand slowly consuming the staff as I stared into his eyes. For a moment, it was almost fully covered in my ice. Heris broke free and lit a stream of fire in front of us. It was large and tall, making a barrier between us. "Just go, go now before he makes me do something bad to you. Please," Heris begged us.

"Let's go, we have to go now. His fire power is no match for us, especially while under the control of Nedos," Ferna said while pulling me toward the small hole in the ground. Niara leaped toward us, kneeling back to the ground and absorbing her clones back into the ladybugs that gently landed back onto her hair. She led the way toward a hole that was just big enough for us to fit in. Before we went inside, she asked for Nii.

"Where did Nii go?"

"He went to get one of the guards that escaped."

"How foolish of him, why would he do such a thing?"

"Let's go, hurry before Heris snaps back under Nedos' control."

As we crawled into the dark hole in the ground, Niara waited to go last, watching as we crawled inside.

"Keep going, girls. I'm right behind you. Just going to pull this boulder over the hole so we're not easily found."

She used her whip to wrap around and pull a boulder over toward the hole. As it began rolling in our direction, we all started crawling into the hole. When the boulder covered the hole, the darkness began to fully surround us.

"Where is this leading us?" I asked while crawling in the front, leading the way.

I could see a faint glow of Niara's green orb necklace lighting the way from behind me.

"Just keep going along the path, Astra. This is going to lead us to safety."

Crawling became climbing, and I grabbed onto roots heading upwards, gripping onto them tightly. I could hear the chatter of the others up ahead, frantic. As I arose from underground, a fresh breeze of air punched me in the face. It was dark around us.

"We have to head to Iscana's portal now before it's too late," I mentioned.

We all began heading in the direction Niara led us toward. She glanced back behind her with a sad, concerned look on her face. I knew she was thinking about Nii and his safety. She had all her children here to take care of, and I felt the panic and pain she did.

"Almost there, everyone, don't lose sight of each other," she said as she swiftly moved through the forest.

Ferna and I were catching up better with her this time around, becoming more agile than we were before. From a distance, I could begin to see a door forming. Niara stopped, and we all caught our breath around the door. We walked to the other side of the door and I saw a clone of Niara standing in a dormant position, protecting it. She knelt to the ground while it absorbed into a ladybug, flying gently back onto her hair.

A silver door covered in rusted patina and vines stood before us. She opened the door slowly, and Iscana walked out with Ceju and Rylo by her side. I ran to them, jumping into their arms all at once. Before I could say anything to them, Niara begged Iscana to protect her children at a safe place. She told them her home had been destroyed and didn't know what else to do. Niara's main concern was fueled with protection.

"What's going on? Are you all alright?" Iscana asked, worried but still aware of every surrounding here in the forest.

Iscana closed the door from which they came through and made it vanish completely. She summoned a white door framed with gold writing. When she opened the door, it was a large field full of flowers and plants. The sun shone down brightly but wasn't too hot. The breeze in the air had a slight chill to it. White mountains covered in snow stood in the distance. They all entered inside the door as Niara looked from the other side.

"Be comfortable knowing everyone is safe here."

"I'll be back, everyone. As I always do, don't worry about me. Please be at peace. We will be reunited soon, I promise," she said with tears building up in her eyes.

The sound of a waterfall pounding against the water turned my attention inside the door. I could already see some of the hybrids jumping into the gleaming waters and enjoying the freedom felt from being confined underground for so long.

"I love you all, take care of each other. See you soon," Niara said while blowing them kisses.

"Thank you, Iscana," she thanked her again.

Iscana closed the door after Niara finished speaking, making the door vanish out of sight instantly. I told Ceju, Rylo, and Iscana eventually about everything that happened between me and Nedos and how he tricked me into believing false memories of him. I briefed them on what they missed while introducing them to Niara. They weren't shocked to find out Nedos once trapped Niara in the dungeon as well.

"Nedos invaded our home, somehow he knew where we were hidden. For so long we've been safely tucked away from his spiteful hand. Until we brought Astra and Ferna to visit, that's when we were ambushed. We left the guards there."

"Yes, Heris, the reptile we met that was guarding you in the underwater cave, Iscana. He was under some kind of mind control," I said.

"He led a group of guards to where we were. Strange enough, he was able to break out of the mind control for a brief moment. He placed a fire barrier between us and told us to escape before he ended up hurting us. My ice powers weren't able to overpower him, especially while under Nedos' control," I explained quickly.

"Iscana, how did you know I was in danger? I went back to Wormwood Castle with Ferna looking for you, and you were nowhere to be found," I asked.

"Your fairy friends visited me while you were in Starfall and told me they knew Nedos would try to poison you when you arrived back. He knew that you

232

left to help the fairies, and that enraged him even more."

"The fairies?" Niara said out loud.

"I'm almost certain it was the fairies that rescued you both, Niara," I said.

She looked down and mentioned that she was worried about Nii. She explained that he didn't have any magical powers to protect himself as she did.

"When Nedos created him, he made him to be powerless as to not compete with him. The only thing wrong with Nii is that once he found out he was an experiment, it was his turning point. One day he was walking in the dungeon and noticed me there. Our distinct similarities made him obsessed. We had an instant connection. He tried to release me from the dungeon, and Nedos locked him down there with me shortly after."

"Nedos wants to be the only mystical being. His goal is to kill everyone with power, each and every one of us included," Niara continued.

CHAPTER 23

The Awning's Flame

Standing in the stillness of the forest, the worry began to fade from Niara's face, turning into anger. I found a small note, scrolled up and tied with a red string, on the floor. It had been carried on the wind. I chased it for a while until Iscana stepped on it, keeping it from flying away. Picking up the note, I unraveled it and saw it was written in charcoal ashes. There was a drawing of a small map of some sort. Nothing on it seemed to make sense to me. I passed it around to the others to see if maybe anything stood out to them as significant.

"This is the X-Graves," Ceju said. "Look here—that resembles the gate to the X-Graves, and those three lines above it could be the pixelated beast."

"Let me see that again." Ceju handed me the note as I scratched my head, trying to see what he saw. It didn't seem like that could be a possibility. Why would this just be floating through the forest like this?

"It could be a trap. What if this is all part of Nedos' plan to have us all trapped inside the X-Graves? That would definitely be an easy way to get rid of us all."

"True, but what if it's something else?" I began to think of other possibilities.

"Wait, let me see this," Niara grabbed the note.

"That's Nii's claw mark on the back of this," she said while comparing it to her own claw, noticing it was an exact match.

"Nii must have written this note. He's in danger. They're taking him to the X-Graves; he has to be captured. I know it."

I couldn't believe what I was hearing. After all she'd been through, now this. I couldn't understand why they would want to bring him to the X-Graves. I just hoped it wasn't another trap.

"Ceju, can you sense Nii from his note and try to locate him with your eye, please?" I asked while handing him back the note.

Holding Niara close to me, I comforted her as she slowly began to worry the worst was about to happen.

"They're at the X-Graves entrance now, holding him in chains bound to his feet and arms. We should wait a while before going there. I think it would be best if we catch the guards by surprise."

"Heris is there, leading the way. I don't know what they have planned, but we have to get there and stop them before it's too late."

"Okay, let's think for a second. Niara, you can come with me to the X-Graves when we get there. Ferna, I think it's best you stay put and wait for us at the entrance. It's too risky for you. Ceju, I know you can't enter, so you'll keep Ferna company."

"Iscana and Rylo, do you mind coming along with us? I could really use your powers down there."

"My ice magic is useless against Heris' fire staff. I don't have any other ideas."

They both nodded their heads in agreement. I could feel a slight vibration in the ground. The flutter of the trees began to strengthen as if someone was coming nearby. In the distance, more guards from Wormwood Castle could be seen. They scanned through the forest, chopping down branches with their enchanted swords, killing the trees used as protection.

"This is a good time for us to get to the X-Graves and away from here."

I looked around for the black ribbon that would summon the unknown creature of death to bring us to the X-Graves gate, but it was too far away, toward the area where the guards were coming from.

"Let's go this way, hurry!" Iscana opened up a darkened portal door, holding it open as we all entered.

Transported to the outskirts of the X-Graves, we climbed the small mountain leading us to the gates. They must already have gone inside. Heris and the guards were nowhere in sight. I couldn't believe we were on another rescue mission. Nedos was really starting to become a thorn in my side. When I got my hands on him, he would surely pay.

"Ceju, can you check and see any updates on Nii and Heris? We can catch them by surprise."

"They're walking down a path lit by small mushrooms."

"Okay, let's rush there." I ran to the gate's entrance and tried to open it with the running water fountain, as I did last time. The gate slowly opened as the pixelated beast began to read from the book.

"We don't have much time, but as long as Iscana is with us, we can travel through her summoned doors, making our way through the X-Graves much easier."

As the four of us entered into the X-Graves, the sounds of the growling and the gates began to get louder with each step until the gates closed completely. I asked Iscana to summon a door to the lit passageway. We all entered inside swiftly and hid behind a massive wax pile left behind from the wax giant.

I could see Heris leading the guards and Nii toward an awning that appeared out of nowhere. Heris waved his staff in circles around it for a moment, making the awning ignite in flames. The inside looked as if it were a darkened chamber of fire ready to consume Nii.

Niara yelled out before Heris finished waving his staff, distracting his focus and causing the inside of the awning to disappear. My heart sank to my stomach as they all turned around toward our direction.

"If you want to destroy him, you'll have to go through us first!" Niara said while standing firmly, ready to fight.

Stretching her limbs, getting ready to do what she does best, she looked over at us and dropped down to the floor, quickly turning the ladybugs on her hair into clones of herself. The green orb on her necklace began to glow as she started talking to them in another language. I could tell the difference between them now, as she was the only one with the orb necklace.

"Heris, give him back! You don't have to do this!" I yelled out toward him.

"Foolish girl! When will you understand this realm is completely mine?" he responded.

For a moment, I forgot it was Heris speaking. It sounded heavily like Nedos, as if he was beginning to speak through him as a vessel.

"Let him go! Both of them! You have no right to do this and claim the lives of the innocent!"

"Then come and exchange your life for theirs if it's so important to you," Heris said while his eyes glowed red.

I slowly started walking toward him, almost in a trance, unable to control myself. Rylo pulled me back and held me behind him.

"You'll have to try harder than that!" he yelled toward Heris.

"Don't hurt him, please! He doesn't know what he's doing. He's under Nedos' control," I said.

Rylo created a protective barrier around me so I wouldn't be so easily mind-controlled by Nedos working through Heris. Surrounded by the transparent indigo stars forming around me, I began to feel myself snap back to reality. I held out my hand and drew the diamond shape into my palm. I conjured up a pair of ice horses to join the battle.

Heris summoned two fire horses to battle the two ice horses I sent out. They vanished almost instantly. Realizing once more my ice magic was no match for him, I turned to Iscana. She let out a loud, shrieking scream toward the guards, causing them all to begin to fall to the ground. Niara's clones leaped over them. Some were holding down the guards while the others tried to fight Heris, attacking him from a distance with their whips.

I held onto my cross necklace for a moment and just hoped for something good to come out of this. Iscana began to point out a bright green light glowing brighter in the distance. Niara turned toward the light and stared at it longer than she should. Heris knocked her to the ground, unconscious, with his staff. Her clones all returned back to the ladybug form and returned to her hair.

"What have you done! Heris, stop it! I know you're inside there somewhere! Please stop this madness!"

A shining green light brightened in front of us. It was the same green fox that I battled the first time coming here. It didn't seem to be bothered by me and was focused more on Niara, who was lying on the ground. The fox raised its peacock-feather tails and aimed it toward Heris.

"Wait, don't hurt him, please!" I yelled.

The fox began to attack Heris at all angles, causing him to lose focus of Nii. Iscana went through a portal she summoned and grabbed Nii, bringing him back to our side. Rylo stood by Niara and made sure she was protected as he placed a barrier over her. The guards began to slowly get up from the ground. I started to panic as Heris fought the green fox, hoping neither one of them would get badly injured.

The green fox pierced through an unprotected opening in Heris' armor by his shoulder, which allowed his arms to bend easily. Its peacock-tail feathers shook violently in the air as it prepared for an attack. The feathers became extra bright as it stabbed into Heris' shoulder again. It pinned Heris to the ground. The other guards, hesitant to attack, stayed back and didn't pass to our side, afraid the fox would attack them.

"Stop it, please!" I yelled out to the fox, but it didn't respond to me.

"Wake up, Niara, quickly! Hurry!"

Nii rushed over to her and began helping while listening to her heartbeat, making sure she was still alive. I pulsed an ice block small enough to fit in my palm and tossed it to Nii.

"Place this on her skin, hurry!"

The coldness of the ice woke Niara up almost instantly. Before she could realize what was happening around her, it was too late. The fox had pierced through Heris' arm completely. His amputated arm lay on the ground, dripping in a puddle of his green blood. Shocked at the sight, I turned around, feeling as if I was going to be sick.

Niara noticed her fox and called to it in her language. The fox stopped in its tracks and made its way smoothly toward Niara, as if it were floating on a cloud effortlessly. Niara petted the fox for a moment while pressing their faces against each other, bonding. The guards began standing up without anyone holding them back. She made sure that they knew not to come close or they would get hurt, just as their leader did.

I ran toward Heris as he lay on the ground bleeding. I talked to him to make sure he was alright and to see if he was back to his normal state. Then and there, he spoke with pain.

"Don't worry about me, my Queen."

As Heris spoke while I held onto his arm, I could feel his body begin to shake. I felt the worst was about to happen. Looking over at his arm that was cut off, I could slowly see something moving from inside him. A green vine mold began growing out of him, slowly but surely turning into a full-grown arm, just as he had before. The color and texture of his arm began to resume to normal as he moved it, making sure. He got up and did a light stretch. Walking up to Niara and the green fox, I didn't know what he was going to do.

"Heris, you were being mind-controlled by Nedos, please don't take it personally."

He went down to kneel and thanked the fox. He kissed the feet of the fox and stood there for a moment. Iscana examined his arm that lay on the ground. As she removed the armor from it, she noticed there was a white light shining from underneath his skin.

"You guys, come see this," she yelled our way.

Heris looked closer at the light shining within his arm. Confused, he cut through it with the bottom of his staff and popped out a sphere of light.

"This must be what Nedos used to control me. I don't remember how it happened."

"That green fox saved my life. Thank you eternally. Guards, I want you to know these people are not enemies; Nedos is the real enemy. Queen Hexia will rule over the land and take over Wormwood Castle," he said while pointing toward me with his new hand, uncovered by the armor.

"Thank you, Niara. I knew I could trust you helping Astra unite with her friends. Your ability always surprised me. Yours as well, Nii, it's great seeing you both again."

We all gathered around as the thundering growling of the pixelated beast caught our attention.

"We can't stay here much longer, otherwise we'll be trapped here for good."

Iscana opened up a portal door leading back to the entrance of the X-Graves. The guards entered first as we followed behind them, including Niara's green fox. When we exited Iscana's door, she removed it as we all headed out of the X-Graves. Ferna sat there patiently with Ceju. They got up, coming toward us once they noticed we had returned. The guards' defense was down and they were no longer a threat.

"Why would Nedos feel the need to trap my fox here at the X-Graves?" Niara spoke to Nii.

It didn't make any sense to either one of us. Before we decide to go to Wormwood Castle and take over, I think it would be best that we all rest and fully prepare for what's about to happen. Nedos will not be easy to overcome. His powers only exceed in strength.

CHAPTER 24

Hourglass Trial

The small garden snakes wrapped around the sharp points of the gate to the X-Graves began to fall to the ground, turning black and melting. The floor around us began filling up with the black liquid that the snakes turned into. The skies and everything around us slowly started to be consumed by the darkness. Iscana opened a portal for us to enter, but as soon as it appeared, it vanished. She tried again, but her magic was unable to work. The only thing we could think of was cautiously moving through the area, trying to find a way back.

Rylo's jewel, set in his forehead, gave a glowing light to help in the darkness. It made a substantial difference. Niara was easy to find as her orb necklace glowed brightly. The green fox's light illuminated against her body, and as I watched in their direction, it was the brightest visible thing.

"Oh, I don't think we're at the X-Graves anymore; this place feels mighty different. Everyone, be on your defense, something strange is amiss."

A pixelated projection of Nedos appeared in the darkened skies above us. I looked around and noticed multiple games and carnival rides beginning to form. It was almost as if we were transported to a haunted playground. People walked around us, seeming half-dead and covered in blood. I tried not to look too scared, as Nedos watched us from above.

"You all think you've escaped my grasp? Well, think again. I control this area of the X-Graves, and with you standing at the gate, I was able to bring you here."

"Nedos, let us go. We don't want any trouble with you. Why can't you just leave us alone?"

"Can't you see? With you all alive, my powers are just a portion of their greatness. Until I am the only magical being, I will stop at nothing. You all have a big surprise in store for you. This time, no magic will be able to penetrate this area. You will have nothing but your own strength to help you."

"As you can see, I've brought you to the Carnival of the Living Dead. The zombies here will walk amongst you, drooling over your every move, waiting on your downfall," Nedos continued.

"There is a ticket booth at the end of this carnival. In order to escape, you have to redeem eight tickets total. The tickets will be given just as any carnival would—by winning a certain game. I feel the need to tell you, although this might sound fun, there is a time limit. You have until this hourglass reaches the last grain of sand. Once it is complete, the zombies' thirst and hunger for flesh and blood will completely overwhelm their bodies, leaving you all as a living meal."

"A trial simulated before you can return back to your pathetic lives, that is, if you survive!" Nedos laughed manically.

He flipped the hourglass over, and the sand began to slowly drop. The timer had already started. I watched as Nedos faded away into the darkness of the sky above. The hourglass glowed bright, as if it were resembling the moon up above. As we walked through the carnival area, I could see the number of zombies multiplying continuously.

"Alright, we have to play by his rules if we want to get out of here; we don't have any other choice," I said to everyone.

"Maybe we should split up."

"It sounds like a great plan, but it might not be the safest."

"We only need to gather eight tickets to redeem. That shouldn't be so hard."

"We'll meet at the ticket booth at the end of the carnival. Just pay attention to the hourglass above."

"Let's split up in groups: Ceju and Rylo; Niara and Nii with the green fox; Ferna and myself; Iscana and Heris. Since there are ten of us, two guards can join each pair."

We all headed out in different directions. I went with Ferna towards an isolated ring toss area. The lights all lit up when we got closer to the game. The music sounded broken and all out of tune, slow and creepy with each moment. I tried to figure out how to start the game to retrieve the rings that were set behind a metal gate. The two guards with us stood behind us, making sure no zombies tried to sneak attack. They all seemed to walk past us, unbothered.

The game didn't start until I walked inside a red circle of blood in the center of the game. While in the circle, I could see the floor below me start hissing, releasing a smoke. The gate with the rings inside opened, but I wasn't able to grab anything. I was bound inside the blood circle. Ferna grabbed the rings in her hand and tried to throw them, but they wouldn't reach, as if an invisible barrier was in front of the game. She tried again, but nothing. Ferna passed me a ring and asked me to see if it would work if I threw one. Once in my hand, the ring started to drip in blood, making it hard to get a firm grip. A total of six rings were in Ferna's hands.

"Match three rings in a row and this game will be finished. Sounds simple enough," Ferna said with an uncertain look on her face.

I threw the first ring that Ferna handed me, and it hit one of the poles standing between the old, beat-up and dirty stuffed animals hanging on the wall. Their cotton insides were spread all around. The ring slipped off the pole as soon as it made contact, due to all the blood on it. The ring of blood I was standing in began to slowly rise up.

Ferna handed me another ring. I tried wiping the blood that began to drip off it onto my clothing, but it continued to bleed and drip as if it were alive. I threw this one a bit further, not aiming at the pole, but instead aiming at the deformed animals on the wall. It ricocheted off one of the animals and fell right through one of the poles, stopping its bleeding and glowing a bright red color.

Two rings thrown, only four remaining. I only needed to get two more in a row, and we would have this. My nerves tried to overcome me. I tried not to panic and think of it as just a game, but the blood slowly rising inside the circle made me wary. The blood didn't spread outside the circle and began getting higher. I gave a toss of another ring that Ferna handed me.

As soon as I touched each ring, the blood began pouring out drastically. Ferna handed me the next ring, and the entire section that had the poles lined up started to be covered in flames, with each metal pole beginning to move up and down. Trying not to lose focus, I threw the ring and missed completely. The next ring I threw, not even thinking about it, spun around the pole, going through it successfully.

Two rings remained in Ferna's hand, and I only needed one more shot to win the ticket and be freed from this blood-filled circle. I didn't think my life would be at risk trying to play this game. The blood reached past my waist. I could feel it getting into my belly button and getting higher with each passing moment.

"Focus, Astra! You have to focus!" Ferna yelled out.

I held the next ring Ferna passed to me. She pushed her hand into the blood-filled cylinder I was entrapped inside of. I reached my hand, trying to feel where the ring was. I tossed it to the middle area where it was needed, and it hit the pole. Slowly, it spun around it and slipped away, as if pulled by a magnetic force.

Surprised, I gave one last terrified look to Ferna as the blood began to reach above my shoulders, rising up higher. I held my breath as it began to cover my mouth, slowly reaching my nose. Ferna handed me the last ring. In a panic, she dropped it on the ground. It rolled on the ground as if it was running away from us. I watched as Ferna scurried around trying to catch it. She jumped mid-air and slid across the concrete ground. Grabbing the ring, she ran back to me. I saw her coming over with what was left of my sight.

Holding my breath underneath the blood, I began to panic. I couldn't hold my breath any longer and feared this was the end. Ferna handed me the last ring as I watched through blood-covered eyes, making it difficult to see. I could feel my lungs begin to give up. Unable to focus, I just threw the ring in any direction, completely giving up.

It bounced around and magically landed in the middle, connecting all three, which released me from the blood circle, causing me to fall onto the floor with all the blood spread around me. Ferna came to pick me up off the ground. I threw up blood that I had swallowed from being submerged. I didn't know that Nedos would make this game into a fight for our lives. It seemed to be controlled somehow, as if we weren't meant to win.

"A dark, levitating, black-hooded figure was there, and it guided the last ring onto the pole," Ferna told me as I tried to catch my breath.

"What?! Something helped us?"

"It seems so, but we should go and try to find the others," Ferna responded.

A ticket machine on the side of the game, covered in dust and spiderwebs, lit up and made a rustic noise as if it were breaking down. It spat out two metal tickets with razor-sharp edges. I placed them in my other pocket, the one that didn't have the mermaid mirror. I pulled out the mirror to make sure it was still intact and placed it back in my pocket. On the ticket was an image that looked to have been cut off.

When we took a closer look at the stuffed animals, I realized they weren't actually fake, but real animals killed, mutilated, and stuffed with cotton. Nedos is one sick monster. How could he do such a thing to these beautiful creatures?

"Nedos isn't playing fair, that's for sure."

Ferna took the bottom of her long braided hair and wiped the blood off my face, which absorbed into her silver silky strands. A thick curtain of smoke and dust emerged into the air nearby. In a panic, we ran through the zombies in our area. They slowly began to notice us a bit more than they did before, making eye contact and turning their heads, but not pursuing us. The hourglass up above still had a lot of sand in the top half, giving us enough time to keep our composure.

A locked gate prevented us from entering where we saw Niara and Nii trying to beat a moving target game. I looked in the distance and saw Nii using a crossbow to hit targets passing by. He was tied to a chain by both his legs while standing on top of a sharp spinning disc. I called out to Niara, but she didn't seem to hear me. The two guards with them were unable to see us, even though they were looking right at us. The green fox was the only one behind the gate that noticed our presence.

We watched as the movement of the disc Nii was standing on slowly began. It spun as he tried to hit the targets moving by. The targets were all made of small pieces of metal, but projected into moving holograms of his children. The ringleader of the area, who was responsible for keeping the dead attractions mobile and running, watched as we hung onto the gate trying to get their attention. As targets began to be hit by Nii, a green light would appear underneath the gate. Four targets total needed to be hit in order to release him, open the gate, and retrieve the tickets. Another target was hit with no problem.

Nii hesitated to hit the targets as the platform he stood on began spinning faster, tangling his legs in chains. I could tell the targets were only holograms, but I felt as if Nii thought they were really physically there. I yelled out that they weren't real, but my attempt was useless. As I watched Nii get wrapped in chains, a black-hooded figure stood behind one of the holograms, making it noticeable that it wasn't really his children.

While the hologram began to glitch, Nii hit the last two needed while his body was tightly constricted. The gate unlocked, and the chains fell from his body. Niara went to check on him. The chains dug deep into his skin, causing sores to appear, slowly getting bruised and red. He lay on the ground in pain for a moment. I heard the mechanical chatter of the nearby ticket machine turning on and spitting out two metal tickets, just as sharp as the ones I received.

The green fox stood up, watching as the black-hooded figure moved across the path ahead, leading through a zombie-filled area with a tank full of water. I watched as it disappeared into the water and went toward that direction.

"Niara, I have the tickets. Grab Nii and meet us at the ticket booth. I'm going to go look for the others."

I helped Niara put Nii onto the back of the green fox and gave Niara a big hug. Looking around, I could notice more zombies gathering. The smell of the blood on my body was like a magnet, attracting their senses. They could sense that Nii was hurt, watching him as he lay on the green fox. I realized the sand capsule in the sky was getting closer to running out.

"That red arrow surrounded by the lights, it's the exit. We'll meet you there," I told Niara.

She headed in the direction, holding on to Nii carefully as they maneuvered through the zombies. The two guards stood by each of her sides, using their bodies as shields, just in case the zombies attacked. Their swords stood clean and untouched, not wanting to cause any havoc from killing the zombies without them attacking.

I looked around the area and behind the target game Nii was at and followed along the way to the tank filled with water. Rylo sat in a small chair above the water as Ceju tried to hit the small button to drop him into the water. With every attempt made, Ceju began to hold his heart. The platform he was standing on was sending electric shocks up through his body, causing his aim to be completely off.

Slowly, human skeleton remains were appearing within the murky water tank. I ran closer with Ferna towards them, hearing something hit the ground. Looking behind me, I noticed Ferna face-planted on the dirt, trying to get up. I went back and helped her up, both running side-by-side. The ball wasn't able to hit the button. It repelled away from it like it was magically protected.

I looked at the bucket of balls sitting beside Ceju as he threw them painfully, one at a time. Rylo had grown in fear, watching the skeletons begin to come alive in the waters below, reaching up towards him, trying to grab him. Someone was going to be hurt. I couldn't bear this torture much longer. I glanced back into the bucket to realize only one ball remained.

"Ceju, don't throw it yet. Hold on to it."

He held onto the small ball and tried to keep a firm grip while being pulsed with electricity. The longer he held onto the ball, the more skeletons began to form in the water. I didn't want this last throw to end with a loss. We needed those tickets fast in order to escape this nightmare. Slowly, I started seeing the black-hooded figure levitating around the button, flashing in and out of sight with each electric zap that pulsed through Ceju.

"Ceju, this is your last chance! Hit the target!"

He threw the ball towards the target, and the black-hooded figure guided it to the button, allowing Ceju to be released from the electric torture. Rylo fell into the tank of skeletons as he panicked to escape. Sharp bones dug deep into his skin, causing blood to seep out into the water. I looked around for anything to help bring him out and grabbed a hold of a thick metal chain.

Getting to the top of the tank, I threw in the chain, pulling Rylo up while kicking off the skeletons attached to his body and clawing into his skin. Their eyes burned with a fire under the water, making each glance at them a terror. After removing Rylo from the water, the old ticket machine nearby began making a loud clank noise. I heard the metal tickets being dropped onto the ground. The two guards that stood by handed me both the metal tickets.

Ferna ripped a piece of her dress off the bottom and wrapped a piece around one of Rylo's deep wounds on his leg. After tying him up, both Ceju and Rylo seemed very weak and unable to move on. Ferna and I helped them get to their feet and told the two guards to help them get to the exit. I pointed over to the red-lit arrow where Niara went with Nii.

"Make sure you all get there safely. Niara and Nii are there already. We will be right behind you. We just need to find Iscana and Heris."

They went off in the direction, leaving Ferna and me alone. The two guards with us went along with them. One guard on each side of them helped carry them over to the ticket redemption area. A coldness within my bones began to stir up.

As Ferna and I carefully ran through the zombies side-by-side, I could hear as if someone called my name. I turned around while running and couldn't see anyone. Feeling a metal pole, I banged my face into it. My lip was slightly split from the impact, spitting my blood onto the ground as it slowly filled up in my mouth. I held my lip for a moment, looking around.

"I could swear I heard someone yelling my name," I said to Ferna.

Looking around confused, a brightly colored, dingy house began to grow behind the pole I banged into. I looked up at the distance it reached up into the air, growing large until it stopped. I began to hear my name again. Staring at the house, I felt like I should enter. My body fought against my will, making it difficult to move.

"Astra, please save us!" I heard one last time before heading into the house.

Taking a look inside before fully entering, I began to notice rows and walls full of mirrors. This was going to be some sort of maze, and I wouldn't let Nedos get the best of us. He wasn't playing fair, and neither should we. I asked Ferna if she could unwind a thick piece of material from her clothing. She unraveled a piece, keeping it attached to her as I tied it onto my waist.

"Stay out here, and whatever you do, don't let the fabric break off. I'm going to use it as a guide to find the way back out. It's too dangerous for us both to enter. Nedos isn't playing fair."

Ferna stood in front of the entrance to the house of mirrors, holding one of the sai weapons in her hand while leading the fabric in the other. When entering the house of mirrors, I began to feel confused. In the reflection behind me, I saw different ways of me being killed. One showed me falling into a pit of snakes, being slowly eaten alive, while the next showed me running through a rocky area as a wall of needles slammed me between them. I lay out on the ground, covered in blood, as wild animals drank my blood.

Trying to move through the mirrors without getting too close to them, I could hear my name being called again. I ran closer to where I heard my name. The mirror straight ahead of me had both Iscana and Heris trapped inside with their two guards. A darkness in the mirror surrounded them as if they were just floating in mid-air. The mirror began fully darkening. Everything around me became dark, without mirrors. I felt something behind me, turning around slowly.

There was an old, hunched-over woman sitting behind a circular table covered in a red cloth. There was another seat in front of her. As I walked towards the table, she held her hand out to the chair, insisting that I sit. I looked down at the table, and there was a spinning wheel all filled with black spaces. She stopped the wheel from spinning with her hands. Her blue veins pulsed atop her hands with each breath I took.

When she stopped the wheel, I noticed just one of the spaces was colored red. Without saying anything, she handed me a black marble, then spun the wheel. I didn't say anything as I stared back at her for a moment. How could I possibly get out of this situation?

I watched the spinning wheel go around multiple times, never getting slower. The red space was difficult to keep track of. I threw the black marble as if I knew what I was doing. My soul's intuition kicked in, causing me to throw it without realizing. Watching as the marble spun around in circles, I looked up at the old woman, who was grinning at me.

As the wheel began to slow down, I could see it landed onto the one red space. The old woman looked into my eyes and handed me a book bound in leather. I opened it, revealing the single, chilling word: *WITCH*. I looked back at her and saw her walking with an older woman; they turned away from me, smiling. The room around me began to fill back with the mirrors slowly, and the book vanished from my hands along with the women and the table. Iscana and the others walked through the mirror with no difficulty.

We gathered around, looking for a way out. "Hold on to each other and stick together," I said. I grabbed onto the fabric around my waist. Following it carefully, I began to hurry with the others. A rip happened without me noticing. I stared at the fabric that lay on the ground as I pulled it into my hand. Without saying anything about it, I remained calm and reassured everyone.

"Everyone hold hands and stay close behind me; we're almost out of here," I said, while trying not to panic.

A black-hooded figure caught my attention in a mirror that we had passed. I went in front of it and looked at it carefully. It didn't show the reflection of any one of us, nor even a glimpse of anyone dying. I touched the side of the mirror, and it swung open like a door, revealing the path where we came from. The piece of Ferna's fabric was lying on the ground. I picked it up and followed it, which led us all out.

The house of mirrors immediately fell back into the ground, allowing us to be fully surrounded by the zombies. The metal pole I banged into started to vibrate and make loud noises. At the top, from a slight opening, fell out the last two metal tickets needed to escape. I grabbed them and placed them in my pocket.

The zombies began to salivate over us profoundly in a frenzy. The time was running out, and we had to be quick. Niara arrived on her green fox and took Iscana and Ferna on her back as we all ran towards the bright red-lit arrow pointing to the ticket booth. Zombies began following behind us all at once.

The guards stood protecting us as I redeemed our tickets to escape. Getting closer, the sounds of the zombies growling became louder, and for the first time, caused me to be afraid of them. Placing the tickets on a statue holding out a metal tray, I set them down carefully. The weight from the metal tickets pushed the statue down into the ground as it slowly made everything around us fade away with nothing but Nedos' face in the sky, surrounded by darkness once again.

CHAPTER 25

Crystal Prison

Nedos finally released us from his dark, twisted games, and the blood and wounds on us all began to disappear. We quickly hurried away from the area of the X-Graves, stepping into a portal Iscana summoned before us. We all rushed inside and were transported to a crop field. As we came back to our senses, an extended barrier was placed around us by Rylo. I thought of the horror we had overcome and how we could try to defeat Nedos—all of us working together.

Heris noticed a magnetic pull on my body. He reached for my upper back, removing a beetle that had landed on me.

"There's something inside you, I can feel it."

"What are you talking about? That's not possible."

Everyone looked at my back closer, trying to see what Heris meant. I took the mermaid mirror and held it up to view the area.

"There, you feel that ridge? Feel it."

Heris guided my finger over the area, and I could feel a small, round bead embedded into my skin. It moved slightly as I pressed into it. I could tell it wasn't a part of my body—almost as if it were hard metal or glass.

"Hold still. This will only be uncomfortable for a moment, I promise," Heris said as he got a better grip on my skin.

"Hold on, wait," I said, taking one last deep breath. "Okay, I'm ready."

Heris dug his claw into the top layer of my skin. As he dug, the small object popped out. I felt immediate relief in the area, almost as if his claw hadn't just pierced my skin. Niara picked up the small object and handed it to me. It looked similar to the one found in Heris' arm—the one Nedos used to control him. I couldn't believe what I was seeing.

"I don't know how this is even possible. When could this have happened?"

"Could have been when you were staying at Wormwood Castle," Iscana said.

I had no memory of it happening. Then again, I didn't seem to remember much recently. I held the small, round object in my hand, watching it slowly pulsing with light.

"It's a tracker. I've seen Nedos use these on us soldiers many times before," Heris explained.

"So that's how he was able to locate our hidden oasis?" Niara asked.

"Yes, and I'm sure that's what led him to us at the X-Graves. Well, no more playing dirty."

"We should formulate a plan to stop him." I stomped on the circular object, crushing it on the ground.

A purple-winged creature emerged from the crushed tracker. The wings pressed up against the barrier Rylo had created, causing the whole area to fill with a bright purple tint.

"Thank you for releasing me. It was my destiny to track anyone whose body I entered for the longest time. Nedos trapped me inside that crystal marble and used me to his own advantage with large lilac crystals."

A woman with long purple hair and magnificent feathered wings began slowly floating down to the ground, noticing we weren't a threat. She had two antennae at the top of her head emerging through her hair; the tips filled with a radiant light. The wings on her back flattened against her. Her bright white eyes were completely whitened, without any visible pupils.

"My name is Violet. I never expected to be released from that prison Nedos placed me in. He killed many of the powerful creatures and beings long ago, trapping some of us and using us to his advantage."

"This place we're standing in isn't safe. Nedos knows we're here. We must hurry out of the area before he realizes I'm free," She said while looking off into the distant fields around us.

"Don't you worry, Violet, I was once trapped inside one of Nedos' crystal marbles as well. Believe me, he should be more afraid of us now that we are united and freed. Pleased to meet you. I'm Iscana." She introduced the rest of us by name.

"Let's get out of here."

Iscana summoned a portal within the barrier once more, allowing us all to enter. I waited and watched around as the others entered, then saw dark, shadow-looking creatures arriving through the tall crops. I felt their magic attacking the barrier and causing a disruption. Everyone was inside the portal but me, Violet, and Iscana. The barrier around us broke, and Iscana lost focus, causing the portal to vanish.

We were suddenly surrounded by tons of shadow-looking creatures of the night. I held up my hand and pressed the small black heart on my wrist, causing me to leave my body lying on the ground. Iscana shrieked loudly at the creatures, making them all shudder with the supersonic vibrations. I flew around the air with Violet, looking for their entry point. Violet flew faster into a whirlwind, trapping most of them inside the tornado of sand and crops.

I located the entrance through a hole in the ground where they were coming from. Iscana summoned a portal around the hole, causing the remaining creatures to immediately get trapped inside. I saw my body being dragged away by one of the creatures. Violet created a violent gust of wind by flapping her wings toward the creature, but it didn't do a thing. We followed the creature into the crop fields where it hid with my body.

Iscana stayed behind, making sure the portal in front of the hole continued to trap the creatures from attacking us. I didn't see any signs of where this thing could be hiding with my body. I shouldn't have thought this was a good idea.

Flying through the crops, I could see Nedos in the distance. He was accompanied by his army, sending out guards as they chopped down every crop, moving closer toward us.

"Bring her here!" Nedos commanded.

"Stop him!" I yelled out.

I saw the creature crawling out from a crop that was already removed, dragging my body by the foot. Violet had two long pieces of silver in her hands and struck it down like lightning. I watched as it pierced the ground below with a thundering sound. The creature dropped my body and scurried toward Nedos' direction. Flying down into my body as fast as I could, I got up and ran back toward where Iscana was.

"Violet, get down here, hurry!"

She flew down close to the ground with me and began flying next to me as we both heard loud snapping and crackling all around us. The crops all began bursting into flames. Nedos, enraged, sent out a fire to consume the whole area. Smoke filled the air, making it hard to breathe and see clearly. I started to stumble from inhaling the smoke. The crops were filled with different plants I'd never seen before, and I didn't know what inhaling them could do to me. I felt Violet carry me while flying toward Iscana.

"Hurry! Nedos and his army are behind us!"

Iscana turned away from the portal by the hole and summoned a portal for us to escape in. We got in with just a moment to spare before Nedos saw us or got a hold of us. As we reunited with the others, we told them what just happened. Iscana brought us to a massive red bridge that had a collection of shipwrecks underneath it. This area seemed very secluded, as if no one had been here for a very long time. As we all stood atop the bridge, we came to an opening in the bridge's structure.

"Follow me down here," she said.

We followed behind her as we all climbed down the ladder into the bridge. Inside was a set of very old chairs covered in dusty cushions. An area rug covered most of the floor. The spaces between the floorboards were enough to feel the breeze from the water below us. Rylo went to the cushions and started dusting them off, getting ready to sit down. There was a table full of seashells in the corner of the room. A circular wooden window in front of the table looked out toward the open water. The glow of Niara's green fox became a night light for us.

"What is this place?" Rylo asked Iscana.

He looked around, grabbing onto the hanging fish nets on the ceiling, examining things around him. The moisture in the air made breathing so refreshing, as if smelling mint leaves in the area.

"This is my hideout from when I was younger. I would come here to escape from it all. Back then, things were more peaceful."

"Creatures of all kinds would mingle and get along; no one lived in fear. That all changed once Nedos became immortal. He used his powers shortly after to gain control of everyone and destroy anything or anyone who intimidated his powers."

"Luckily, my beauty saved me—enough to not be dead, but to be trapped in that marble you found," she said while looking at Rylo.

"Nedos always did have a thing for beautiful creatures."

"I came here on a stormy night to get away from my parents' request for me to attend magic classes. I knew it was a waste of time. The only magic I felt truly connected to was the one I felt naturally; learning magic is a forced thing. The humans that came here really were the ones who studied that kind of magic, and I didn't want to be associated with them, even if it meant confining my abilities and disobeying my parents. Over time, I created this area, bringing certain objects along with me each time I came."

"While looking out the window I created, the storm began to disrupt the waters. I noticed a sort of whirlpool forming on the surface of the water and went down to get a closer look."

"Getting closer, I noticed a group of mermaids frolicking and playing in the water that created the whirl. I called out to them to get their attention."

"They were so sweet to me. Occasionally, I would find these seashells left behind around the bridge. I knew it was the mermaids leaving them as gifts. I had never been able to see such beautiful items up so close, taken from the depths of the ocean."

"I would sit by the water with my feet hanging into it, getting wet and splashing until one of them would notice I was there. For years, we would greet each other."

We all listened closely as we sat near each other in the chairs. Heris stood with the guards by the ladder we came down from, just in case we were being followed. I insisted that they sit down with us, knowing the tracker had been removed from my body, but he didn't want to let his guard down.

"I fought to keep this hideout hidden for so long. I almost forgot about this place."

"One night, I came here and saw it all. A ship with a crew of fishermen came by, and ever since then, things just got worse. The ships that came by after that were all stopped and attacked by this bridge. I haven't seen the mermaids since. Only shipwrecks. As if they were causing a blockage to the path. I wasn't sure why, but they've changed."

I held my hand over my face as I listened to her story. Everything slowly started coming together.

"I believe that ship you saw leaving was Nedos' ship," I told her.

"That was Nedos. He told me a story of how he went on a search for mermaid flesh in order to become immortal. He killed one, causing them to turn viciously evil."

"How can you be sure anything he says is true, Astra? He's not one to be trusted!"

"I completely agree with you, but look at this."

I pulled out the mermaid mirror I took from the red decorated room in the castle. As I looked into the mirror, everyone watched me in complete confusion.

"Merlissa. Mermaids. Anyone. Can you hear me?" I called out into the mirror.

"Mermina, that's her name, I remember now. The mermaid I would play catch the sea turtle with was Mermina, the youngest of the mermaids," Iscana said.

The waters in the mirror began to change colors, forming a magical show of blues intertwining until finally someone appeared.

"Merlissa, you won't believe the journey we've been on since I last spoke with you."

"Everyone, this is Merlissa." I turned the mirror so everyone could meet our underwater ally.

"Wait, I remember you," Merlissa said as I passed the mirror in front of Iscana.

"You're the girl who used to play with my sister at the bottom of the bridge. How can I forget such a unique face?"

"Yes, it's me. How are you? So good to see you. How's your sister, Mermina? That's her name, right?"

Merlissa stood in silence for a moment. "Yes, that was her name. Unfortunately, she was murdered by Nedos. Her death caused my sisters to never trust humans again, which led to the buildup of shipwrecks in this path, never to allow another human into our world."

Iscana looked over to me, finally realizing everything I spoke that I'd heard from Nedos had been terrifyingly true. I didn't know what to say to break the tension in the room. Everyone stood in silence.

"Merlissa, gather your sisters and get ready. Our plan is to attack Nedos all together at Wormwood Castle. He won't expect us to attempt such a dangerous mission."

"What he doesn't know is that with all of us together, our magic outnumbers him."

"Be prepared for battle. I will reach out to you when the time comes for an attack. We all have been waiting for this moment for too long."

As we all said goodbye to Merlissa, I placed the mirror back into my pocket and began to explain to the others. "I believe we will be able to defeat him if we all work together. Finding each other doesn't seem like a coincidence; it's as if the universe brought us all together for this exact reason: to defeat Nedos and return things to how they once were."

Slowly, I began to remember parts of my life in Starfall after Iscana and Merlissa mentioned it. I saw myself as a young child living in an overfilled orphanage. No one paid attention to me, and I was neglected for so many years. One night, I followed the red and green lights that led me through a portal opening in mid-air. I would come back every so often, thinking it was a dream but knowing deep down it was something more.

I began to grow, and as I got older, I stayed longer in the portal, never wanting to go back to the orphanage. I knew I had a connection to Starfall since I went to collect the tears for the fairies, but I never would have guessed I lived there for part of my life. Now that I remembered, I had to know more.

"All this talk of humans—I was once one too," Violet said quietly.

"I remember after moving in with my father, he showed me around the area and pointed toward one shop, forbidding me to enter it. Without any reasoning or anything, it sparked my curiosity, and I entered the shop one day by myself."

"The shop was lit with candles and had a very dim light. In the window was a glass bowl filled to the top with money next to a circular crystal ball on a fabric covered with crescent moons. I looked around for the shop owner or anyone, but I couldn't see anyone. Although it was just me, I didn't feel alone."

"Walking through the aisles of the shop, I came across candles with symbols engraved into them, bracelets with amulets hanging off them, and many dried herbs pinned to the walls. A wooden staircase led to a little area upstairs. It was filled with crystals."

"Voices began coming from all around me, telling me to reach my hand out toward it. I felt a strong urge to resist but wasn't able to pull away from the crystals. I got pulled into them and turned into this new form that you see before you."

"I tried going home that night, but no one was able to see me, as if I didn't exist. I left hints and gifts around my father's house, but he only thought it was an evil spirit, and he put up a ward, making me unable to get closer."

"I went back to the shop right after, hoping I would find someone able to change me back, and there was a strange man standing outside. He promised to return me to my body if I agreed to help him, but he went against his word and kept me as his own tracking device, trapped in the lilac crystals. Had he not used me to track you, Astra, I would never have found my freedom. Even though I'm not my true self and my father is long gone by now, at least I can live a life free from Nedos."

We all watched in shock as Violet told us the sad truth of her life. I couldn't believe Nedos had gone so far with his wickedness.

"This is crazy, Violet. I'm so sorry this happened to you. I feel like I visited that same shop when I was in Starfall helping out the fairies."

"Only there was a woman inside, and she was doing things with a young child. I should have stopped it earlier, but it was too late."

"I was going to follow the girl and stop her from following the woman's directions, but she put me in a trance, and by the time I broke free, the girl was gone."

"We have to destroy that shop and put an end to the suffering of the humans in that area! Who knows how many people have been lured in by their traps?" Violet yelled and slammed her fist against the wall furiously.

"I agree with you completely. We should head over to Starfall and get rid of that place, especially since Nedos has something to do with it."

CHAPTER 26

Passage Confirmed

I close my eyes and envision the red and green fairies, summoning them for their guidance. They emerge through my hair, one from each side.

"Those lights are awfully familiar," Niara said, looking closer.

"Wait a second," the fairies flew closer to her.

"These are the lights that saved us from Nedos' dungeon and helped us escape. You see this?" She said, looking wildly at Nii.

Nii began to smile as if he knew a magical force was behind their survival all along. The fairies began to flutter. I asked the fairies if they could tell me more about my previous life now that I remembered where I came from.

"Why did you bring me here? I'm thankful for having escaped the dreadful fate of the orphanage, but I don't understand."

I could hear them answer telepathically in my head, "You were always chosen for greatness. We waited long, trying to locate your soul to return and be ready to take over." Take over? What could they be talking about? I still didn't fully understand them.

"We introduced you slowly as you grew, making it easier for you to deal with the changes once you got older. That's probably why some things felt familiar to you."

"You belong here in the magic realm of Genesis Veil. You always have..."

The fairies have been slowly gathering us all and helping us get together to this point, as if they'd planned this all to happen exactly how it should. They knew that with enough magic, Nedos would be able to be defeated for certain.

I asked the fairies if they knew anything about the shop from Starfall that I entered—the same one responsible for Violet's entrapment.

"That shop is filled with dark, powerful magic forces. It would be wise not to venture there."

Both fairies fluttered around in the bridge hideout where we were all comfortably gathered. We needed to come up with some type of plan to destroy Nedos. He won't expect us to return to the castle. After all he'd put us through at the X-Graves, I think we were all a bit hesitant. The fairies told me that Nedos couldn't control our minds and alter the area around us anymore; he only could do that at the X-Graves.

I didn't want to put anyone at risk and asked who wanted to come along to defeat Nedos. Not one person wanted to stay behind. Everyone had a fire inside them to destroy him. The black ribbon for the guardian of the dead showed up, tied to a corner of the wall as a decoration.

"Iscana, where did you find this ribbon?" Ceju asked her.

"It was tied down below on a pole by the bottom of the bridge. I thought it was pretty, so I brought it up here."

"This ribbon will summon the guardian of the dead. It transports to the X-Graves but can also read your mind and take you elsewhere if you think strongly about it."

"Yes, we've used this as a means of transportation multiple times," I added.

"May we take this ribbon just in case we need it? We can never be too sure when fighting Nedos, and having backup transportation could come in handy."

"I completely agree, please take it," Iscana replied.

As Ceju began to remove the black ribbon from the knot it was tied into, I didn't know what to do. For a moment, I felt stuck, scared that if we continued with defeating Nedos, something bad would happen.

Ceju placed the ribbon on his wrist and began to tie it firmly. Ferna helped adjust the ribbon and made sure it was comfortable on him and easy to remove. The fairies told me one last thing, now that I was ready and we were all finally together to defeat Nedos: Go to the lighthouse with everyone, headed east. There will be a Sword of Majesty hidden inside. In order to find the sword, we have to prove ourselves worthy of it.

"Once we locate this sword, then we will go to Starfall and see what this shop is all about," Iscana mentioned. She seemed just as furious as Violet was about the shop being a place of evil doings controlled by Nedos.

When we got to the lighthouse, there was a pile of stones scattered around the bottom of the area. Each pile looked meticulously placed and neatly laid out. Some were stacked on top of each other, with the stones getting smaller as the stack got higher up. This didn't seem natural; someone had to have done this. I don't think the fairies could have.

We walked around the lighthouse and saw the entrance was completely blocked with cemented bricks. Two beams of light from the top of the lighthouse flashed down toward the ground in front of us. Inside the lights, the ground burned with heat, causing it to melt. The lighthouse looked to be defending its weapon inside. I jumped out of the light's burning ray and held out my hand, drawing the diamond shape onto my palm. I thought of a freezing ice mist to stop the burning in the ground, but as soon as one area froze, another ignited.

The light of the lighthouse seemed to be coming for us. Rylo placed a large barrier over us while Violet flew around over the top of the lighthouse to view what was causing the attack from inside. As Violet fluttered around the top, dodging through the lights, she yelled out toward us.

"There's a small, furry animal controlling the lights!"

She broke into one of the windows, impacting the glass with her head in a spinning movement. Once she broke through the glass, everything around us stopped burning up. I heard a loud rummaging through the lighthouse, not knowing what was going on.

"Iscana, can you open a portal to the top of the lighthouse now?" I asked her.

She opened a portal heading inside while Ceju, Rylo, Nii, and myself entered behind her. The others stood behind guarding the area. Niara and her clones circled around the lighthouse, with Heris and his guards in front. We couldn't be too safe or sure of anything. Nedos would surely attack at any moment if he had the chance.

Ceju began to repair the glass windows, returning all the shattered pieces around us back into place, cleaning the area. Ceju placed a barrier around us as we walked together, looking for the weapon the fairies sent us to retrieve. The Sword of Majesty will be able to help aid us in defeating Nedos.

Violet flew through the inside of the lighthouse alone, looking out for the animal who tried to burn us alive. We walked toward a panel of electronic switches on the ground. So many different colors and levers—I didn't know what would happen if we moved one. For all I knew, it could possibly start up the lighthouse flame light and hurt the others below. I was very cautious not to touch anything as we walked by.

A tiny chair sat next to it, almost big enough to fit a small child. Corners were filled with dried leaves, fruits and nuts, making a mess in this rustic place. I held my hand out and drew the diamond shape into my palm, freezing the electronic area in front of the chair to make sure nothing would happen unexpectedly.

Violet spotted movement under a pile of leaves against a wall. She sent out a gust of wind with her wings, blowing away the leaves and revealing what seemed to be a young raccoon hiding, crawling into itself. As it trembled in fear, I asked Rylo to remove the barrier around us.

Walking closer to it, I called out, "You don't have to be afraid of us, little one."

It didn't move, and for a moment, I convinced myself it wasn't alive and breathing. I grabbed a stick on the ground and poked it gently. The raccoon turned around, grabbed the stick, and flung it across the room. It froze in the corner as it watched us.

"We didn't come here to harm you, just to look for a secret weapon. Do you know anything about it?" I asked.

The raccoon looked over at the frozen switchboard and began to speak.

"I know nothing of any weapons. I was recently placed here by force and blackmail," it said.

As we looked around for the weapon, I could hear the raccoon speaking to Ceju.

"A raven kept a close watch on me, occasionally bringing me fruits and nuts to survive on. I was told to destroy any intruders, otherwise my father would be killed," the young raccoon said.

"Your father helped us a while back. He gave me this eye here in exchange for my own eye. It helps as a door to visions."

"I can check on him and see if he's alright," Ceju said, holding his hand over his other eye, causing a vision into the father's life.

"He seems to be perfectly fine, still in his tent at Desert Driftia. I don't know what mind games Nedos is playing on you, but do not believe what he says."

"No, I don't trust you. How can I be sure that you really know my father? What proof do you have?"

I didn't know what to tell the young raccoon to reassure him everything was okay and that he could trust us.

"Do you think this is him?" I said to Ceju.

Ceju shook his head, pointing to his ears, hinting that one of them wasn't white like Nexus had mentioned. I noticed a star fruit lying on the ground near the pile of fruits and nuts. I went closer to make sure it was what I thought it was.

"Did you eat this one?" I asked the young raccoon.

Looking at the half-eaten star fruit, I picked up a whole one in my hand and showed it to Ceju and Rylo.

"Do you two remember these?"

"Yes, that's the fruit that allowed us to breathe underwater to save Iscana. But what is it doing here?" Rylo said.

I thought it was strange to see it here as well. I picked up the star fruit and held it in my pocket, feeling it might be of good use.

"Do you know of any hidden weapons here?" I asked the raccoon.

He watched me in silence, not saying anymore as if he didn't trust us. We led the way down toward the bottom of the lighthouse to the exit that was blocked. Going down a wooden lift that has to be pulled with a rope to get to the lower level, we went down in pairs. Violet stood up and pulled the rope, allowing us all to get lowered safely, then flew down toward us. Iscana had a sudden realization.

"There's a portal hidden somewhere around here—I can feel it."

Iscana let out a loud shrieking scream toward the space where she thought a portal was hidden. The air in front of us began to spread aside as if parting open. A breeze of air flushed by us. The portal seemed to be placed here by the fairies. It felt like this is what they sent us here to look for. This is where the Sword of Majesty was hidden. It had to be.

CHAPTER 27

Spiritual Dance

Before stepping into the portal, I was able to see inside of it. A castle, almost identical to Wormwood Castle, was visible behind a sprawling field dotted with many people.

"Violet, would you mind staying behind? If we're not back before the sun begins to set, could you fly out to the others and let them know where we are? Only if we don't return in time, of course."

"Yes, not a problem. You go ahead and please, be safe. All of you." Violet said, wrapping her wings around us in a warm hug.

We all entered the portal as Violet stood guard, floating mid-air angelically. The young raccoon came along with us. Upon entering, I watched the portal we came through slowly fade into the nearby tree. Iscana approached the tree and examined it closely.

"This portal is the same as the one we entered; it isn't visible and is hidden from the rest, but it's still here. I can reveal the exit portal when the time comes for us to leave. My guess is the Sword of Majesty has to be around here somewhere."

Sitting together on a bench underneath the tree, we began to brainstorm ways to bypass the guards and people in the area without being seen. The young raccoon was sitting on the ground by us, next to a plant. We came up with an idea: perhaps we could call over the closest guard and trick him into giving us his armor. At least then one of us would be able to infiltrate the castle.

Everyone hid themselves as the young raccoon lured the guard into our area. Ceju swiftly knocked him to the ground. We removed his armor, revealing his strange, green-tinted skin, and I passed the armor to Iscana. She felt most certain she would be able to locate the sword. If it was inside another hidden portal, we all would be useless. I helped her get into the guard's oversized armor. The golden metal she was inside clearly didn't fit her; it moved more than it should.

The guard we stole the armor from was unconscious and lying on the ground. We dragged him into the plants around the tree, which were large enough to hide him. A higher-ranking guard noticed Iscana in her armor, standing apart from the other guards, and came over toward us. She quickly closed the face helmet, hiding her face. When the guard came close, we all tried to act as normal as possible not to draw any more attention. He instructed Iscana to enter the castle with the others, and she went quickly inside, leaving us behind. I knew she would be alright.

The guard began to question us. He had no idea we had traveled through the portal hidden in the tree, and I did all the talking so we wouldn't get caught in any lies, appearing more suspicious than we actually were. The guard noticed the black ribbon tied around Ceju's wrist and looked as if he knew exactly what it was. Before I could draw the diamond shape into my palm and freeze him in place, I noticed both my wrists had metal bracelets on them that hadn't been there before. Ceju and Rylo looked down at their wrists and saw they had the bracelets as well.

"What's going on? What is this?" I asked.

"You three don't belong here," the guard said, as he made us follow behind him almost magnetically.

I tried to use my ice magic but was unable to as long as these shackles were around my wrists. The reality of our captivity refused to sink in. I looked behind and watched as the young raccoon poked its head from the undergrowth. Somehow, I began to put my hope and trust in this small animal that didn't even seem to trust us one bit. As we followed behind the guard, he brought us over to an area where he tossed us some old, raggedy clothes.

"Put these over yourselves and be quick."

He tossed them at us, and we put the dusty old clothes over ourselves. We turned a couple of corners, still outside the castle. I began to notice others the same clothes sitting on the ground with the same bracelets binding their wrists. Were these people magical beings, just like us?

The guard directed us to sit on the ground in a circular spot drawn into the grass. Everyone sat still with their heads bowed down, not moving. Ceju and Rylo sat in the circles and placed their heads down.

I sat closest to the back of everyone since I was the last to sit. I quickly turned my head, looking behind me, and noticed a very tall gate with barbed wire on top—impossible to escape through. I somehow forced myself out of the circle and walked over to the gate. While getting closer to it, I could see a long rope reaching up into the sky, going out of sight higher than the gate.

Another guard noticed I wasn't where I was supposed to be because the colored cloth I was wearing over myself wasn't the same color as the dark blue cloths of the people entrapped in this area. A long line formed where everyone mindlessly waited, one after the other, trying to climb the rope. As the guard came up to me, he laughed and mentioned I could join in the line as he continued laughing. I cut into the middle of the line instead of going all the way to the back. No one seemed to care, as if they were all dazed or mind-controlled in some way. I began to watch as the others climbed the rope, trying to take notes and learn by the time it was my turn.

Then, as if I didn't expect it, people began falling from the rope in the sky. I felt the vibration as their bodies slammed against the ground, killing them instantly. Their lifeless bodies were dragged away one at a time, leaving no room for their bodies to be piled up. Guards waited and watched menacingly for the next person to fall so they could drag them into the nearby ditch. I knew there was no other way to escape this fate unless I spoke up. It was all just a setup—a way for us to think we were making a choice in fighting for our freedom.

I walked out from the line toward one of the head guards watching over the area. It was a woman with green skin, eyes, and hair. Her armor was the same as the other guards. She looked like a part of nature itself. I could feel her eyes trying to pierce into my mind and soul, trying to control me. I fought back her powers and spoke up for everyone.

"What is this setup you place before us? There's no way anyone would be able to make it to the top of that rope and back down alive. Why are you fooling us all?"

She looked at me with a devious grin and seemed surprised I had spoken to her in that tone. But at the same time, she looked impressed by my bravery. Dirty ropes hung around her neck as if they were whips that were covered in mud and dirt, smearing all over her green-tinted skin. I could tell they were used to whip and beat the people trapped here, as their clothing was covered with lines of mud.

Everyone in the line that was formed, ready to climb the rope into the sky, stood in silence as I protested for a fair chance at freedom. The green guard woman agreed to lower the rope by half, but that seemed like another trick. Since the rope was so high into the sky, cutting the distance in half would really make no difference.

"No one has been able to make it to that distance of what you say is half. Why are you so afraid of one of us succeeding?" I said.

She looked at me, squinting her eyes, trying to get a better view of me.

"Fine. That tree right there will be the guide for the rope. Guards, make a rope as high as that tree!" she demanded, pointing to the tree in the distance where the portal was.

The tree was high up, but I knew it was the best option we had. Climbing the distance of the tree didn't seem as outrageous as climbing into infinity. She continued to laugh at my bravery and watched as the guards used their magic to remove the rope and add another with the height of the tree.

"Does this look better for you? Of course, it does. And let's say someone would fall from it, they'd just simply break their legs... Maybe," she said happily.

I didn't say another word and walked back to the middle of the line where I once stood. I could hear the others in line whispering to each other about me, as if I wasn't on their side trying to help them. A few got close to the top of the rope, giving me a glimpse of hope that it would be possible to reach. As they fell, some landed on their necks, killing them instantly, while others broke an arm or a leg, making them unable to move.

"There's no way out of this one, you weak-minded child," she said toward my direction.

I stared her down, not breaking eye contact or even blinking, as I got closer to her, standing in front of the rope, waiting for my chance to climb it. She felt intimidated by my powers flowing from within me and stepped in front of me, blocking me from trying to climb the rope. She placed both of her hands on my shoulders, digging her nails into my skin. Suddenly, we weren't outside in the open anymore but in a narrow hall with light beige walls, as if covered in dried mud.

Looking around, I could see others behind her wearing the same colored cloth as I had on. Ceju and Rylo were in the crowd behind her as well. She put out her hands in front of me as if wanting me to place my hands in hers. Without noticing, we started doing hand gestures with our hands intertwined. The sound from the clapping of our hands hitting each other created an echoed melody. My hands were following along out of nowhere and actually keeping up. It felt second nature to me, as if I knew exactly what I was doing, like a muscle memory that had been unlocked.

The others from behind her started to spread out around the narrow-walled area and all began doing the hand movements in unison, making the echoed sounds louder, causing nothing to be in my mind other than the sounds. I couldn't even hear my own thoughts or heartbeat. Everyone moved as if in a dance to the rhythm of the clapping. I separated from the green guard woman and went about heading to others in the area.

A woman came up to me as our hands guided each other's. She had a very familiar face, but I couldn't remember her. I asked her telepathically what we were doing and what this was all about as I looked into her soft eyes, confused. Her thoughts entered into my mind as I heard her voice.

"Don't you remember? This is the spiritual dance of the witches."

After hearing that in my head, I was suddenly reassured everything would be alright. Something took over my body shortly after. Every bit of fear inside me vanished completely. I became as free as a bird soaring through the skies, dancing swiftly through the narrow space around the others. A sense of gathering others towards my energy and side came over me.

My energy, confidence, and dance began changing, moving along with the sounds from the clapping hand movements. The woman who spoke to me stood behind my area as I ventured into the green woman guard's side, watching her very closely as I skipped through, giving her a side eye.

They all gathered around me, making their clapping hand movements with one another. I moved one by one with my dancing and clapping and focused my energy, causing them to head toward my side of the narrow hall. More and more of them began to head over toward my area until all of them were under my spell. Once I realized there were no more people left standing on the green guard woman's side, I could see her standing there alone, looking defeated.

The area around us began to fade away, and we were back outside around where the rope was set up. I could see the bracelets around our wrists all began to disappear as we watched in shock. Ceju and Rylo came over toward my side as the green guard woman spoke.

"Who are you exactly, and what are you doing here?" she asked.

"I'm Astra, and these are my friends. We've come here to locate a certain item, but now we'll be leaving with more than that. We're taking every prisoner along with us."

She didn't seem to have any other option but to allow us to have our way. The guards all stood in fear as they watched everyone snap back into reality that was once bound under their control. They were all capable of using magic. I could feel it just by the fear they projected.

CHAPTER 28

The Sword of Majesty

Walking back over to the tree portal where we came from, I called out to the young raccoon to see if it was still there. I noticed that the guard who had been unconscious was no longer hidden under the leaves. The young raccoon pulled through the leaves below and revealed a body of water. To me, it looked like the plants were just overwatered, but the raccoon's head stuck out, suggesting it was deeper than it seemed as it jumped inside.

"Eat the star fruit and follow me," he instructed.

I ripped off the tattered cloth from my body, reached into my pocket, and ate the star fruit in one bite. I stepped into the grassy area below the tree, feeling nothing underfoot. I allowed myself to fully jump in. Before doing so, I told Ceju and Rylo to wait here for me and keep a lookout for Iscana.

The young raccoon and I headed underwater, swimming through the area beneath the castle above us. Every detail was in sharp focus as if we were behind glass. The raccoon pointed to a chest sitting centered in a bubble of air. As we swam inside the bubble, everything around us looked as if it were covered with wax. The aquatic haze cleared completely, revealing a dry atmosphere.

The wax was multi-colored. Some areas of the wax had small flames sitting on top of it, but the heat wasn't causing the wax to change form or melt. The air inside the wax bubble felt as fresh as if we were standing in a field full of nature.

I held out my hand toward the chest, and it opened as if it would only open for me. A tingling sensation ran through my palm. Inside the chest was a long rope with knots tied into it as grips. I watched as the young raccoon made his way down the rope quickly, without a second thought.

I followed him carefully. The area below was covered in colorful magic crystals; some were so brightly colored I couldn't look at them for long. I followed the raccoon in a straight path. Gems and jewels scattered around the area gleamed with light, reflecting rainbow colors onto our skin. The young raccoon led me to the Sword of Majesty, sitting atop a glass statue. Inside the statue, a light glowed orange from within.

"Why are you deciding to help us? I thought you didn't trust us," I asked, confused.

I was certain the raccoon finally trusted us after seeing that we freed the others from certain death and allowed them all to regain their magic abilities.

"You've proven yourself to be the true owner of this sword. We've all been expecting you," he said.

"Legend says that the one who is able to remove the sword and harness its powers will be the one who will rule Genesis Veil."

I grasped the sword and pulled it from the glass statue. It felt light as a feather, and I swung it without thinking about its weight. The glass statue came to life and whispered in my ear:

"Soon you will be awakened, Queen Hexia. We are pleased to meet you once again."

"Once again?" I questioned.

I didn't recall ever meeting a glass statue like this. As I paused to think, I realized this statue was almost identical to the ones I'd seen in the past: the ones in the maze of the X-Graves and the one in the secret garden area of Wormwood Castle. I didn't think I could speak to them, though.

Out of nowhere, I saw the path we walked down starting to fill up with different colored glass statues.

They all began to hold out their hands, revealing a colored marble in each. Nothing was mentioned, and I couldn't see the way out anymore. I looked around and asked the young raccoon if he understood what was happening.

"This is the way out. You have to solve this last test to exit," he said.

I looked at each marble carefully and picked one up from the dark-gray colored glass statue. The marble had white smoke swirling inside of it. I didn't know what to do with it, but as soon as I grabbed it, the room began to slowly fill with smoke.

Afraid to activate any of the other marbles, I just glanced over at them, trying to see what was inside before touching them, but I couldn't make out much through the smoke. I went back to the statue where I had removed the Sword of Majesty and sat below it. The young raccoon seemed unaffected by the smoke, as he just stood surrounded by it.

The familiar dark, levitating, black-hooded figure appeared, staring at the statue. It started guiding my hands into drawing a shape in the dirt: two diamonds, one on top of the other, connecting into one symbol. In the middle of it all, I stopped for a moment and looked up to notice the space around us felt infinitely larger than when we entered.

I looked down at my hand, thinking maybe I could use my ice powers to help in this situation. But then something struck me. The splinter I got in my hand from the old wooden door leading to Ferna's cottage at the X-Graves suddenly looked more noticeable, its tip no longer deeply embedded. I picked at it and tried to remove it. After the third attempt, I got it out, and watched as the small splinter of wood began growing larger.

The wood resembled the O-Wood I used to reveal the orange fur candle back at Wormwood Castle. I wondered if this was the same as the O-Wood. I snapped it in half and placed one piece on each side of the statue where I took the marble from. It slowly removed the smoke from around us and melted down to the ground in the form of glowing, sparkling water.

The black-hooded figure was nowhere to be found, leaving me wondering if it really happened or was a figment of my imagination. I noticed the symbol drawn into the ground started to shake the area around it, causing the ground right below it to open up. An orange glowing light emerged from the symbol and flew rapidly around the room. It went into the Sword of Majesty and made it change from a silver metal color to a glowing orange.

The young raccoon came up to me and pulled on my dress. I looked down at him and watched as his eyes grew big as he smiled. We both walked toward the way we came, stepping in the melted sparkling water from the glass statue. It began to create an ice path leading us through the area.

The glass statues all began to clap together, cheering for us as we walked away, heading back up the rope that slowly revealed itself again. As we headed back up the rope, their bright colors started to fade, turning back into the darkness. Holding onto the orange glowing sword and climbing was easier than I expected. The sword gave me a physical strength I hadn't felt before. Climbing this rope with only one hand made me wonder what else I would be able to do.

While we were both swimming back toward the tree, I could see images of small white birds flying underwater alongside us. I was sure I was seeing things, but one of them got closer to me, and I felt its wet feathers brushing against my skin. They all swam around us on both sides, guiding the way. Their yellow and red beaks stood out as they snapped them, creating small air bubbles.

As we got back to the tree where we entered and came out from under the water through the grass, we saw Rylo, Iscana, and Ceju waiting for us.

"I see you found what I was looking for, Astra," Iscana mentioned.

"We found the Sword of Majesty the fairies spoke about," I said, dripping with water as I showed it to them.

Iscana was still in the gold armor from the guard we stole it from. She decided to keep it on since she felt a bit stronger with it. I passed the sword to Ceju so he could get a better look at it, but as soon as he grabbed it, it fell toward the ground. It was as if it was too heavy for him. I handed it over to Rylo to see if the same thing would happen, and sure enough, it did.

"The Sword of Majesty is bound only to its keeper. No one else will be able to use its powers," the young raccoon mentioned.

"Your ear—it's white," Ceju said.

I turned to him and noticed it was white now that we had come from underwater. Confused and excited, I bit my lip, certain that we had found Nexus' son. The water had cleansed the dirt from the raccoon; he must have been sitting in that lighthouse longer than we thought. Ceju started to pull out the drawing given to us by Nexus.

As he handed it over to him, he began to explain: "Your father, Nexus, is alive and well and has been looking for you. He gave us this image to give to you."

"What was his name? Vex?" I said, unsure.

"Yes, Vex. Does that sound familiar to you?" Ceju said to him.

His hands began to shake as he stared at the drawing, running his claws across it. He told us how he drew this image when he was living with his parents before Nedos took over and captured him.

"There's magic inside you. Your father said you were old enough to be able to harness the magic within you."

"Magic?" Vex said, as he scratched behind his ears vigorously.

Iscana let out a loud, shrieking scream toward the portal in the tree, revealing it and allowing it to function once again. I gathered all of the prisoners who were outside in the castle area. They all began to remove the dirty cloth garments over their bodies, revealing pristine outfits underneath.

"Iscana, did you find anything of interest while searching for the sword in the castle?" I asked her before we headed out.

"Well, there was one room I couldn't get inside, even with my portal. It was covered in orange wax."

I guided the now-freed prisoners into the portal, letting them know to follow Vex, who would lead them back to their freedom away from this place. As everyone entered, I went back to the green guard woman, who sat on the ground, defeated and scared, with the other guards.

"You don't look the same as you did before," I said to her.

The energy in her eyes had changed, as if she was fully stripped of her powers. I asked if she was all right and if she wanted to join us and leave this place behind. She mentioned that she wouldn't be of any use to us now that she had no more magic.

"You can still live a life, a life worth living. Life is a precious gift," I told her, while the other guards, all with the same green skin, eyes, and hair, relaxed slightly.

While she refused to come along with us, she began to gag on the air, almost as if about to regurgitate. Out came a seed the size of my palm. She handed me the seed with tears streaming down her face.

"We were all under Nedos' control. The deal was that we wouldn't perish if we kept hold of the magic beings as prisoners here at Aetheria Castle in Stillhold. When everything resumes to normal, plant this seed and save our race of the Viridiani Tribe, my Queen."

The green guard woman and her people began to fade into the ground, reforming back into the dirt and grass from where they originated, leaving their armor behind. I called over Rylo and Ceju to take some armor along with us, and they got inside the armor, making them resemble Iscana's gold armor, as if all three of them were royal knights. As we got inside the portal back to the lighthouse, we saw Violet flying above it.

"Right on time. I was so close to gathering the others," she said.

Once we got to the bottom of the lighthouse, garlic cloves hung all around the exit area inside. Vex was hesitant to go near them. He told us the smell drove him crazy and was absolutely toxic to him. A group of the magical prisoners we freed began using their magic, breaking down the wall to the outside of the lighthouse.

I saw Niara and her clone shadows standing with the guards, ready to attack through the cloud of debris it created. The glow from her green fox spirit animal allowed me to notice her quickly.

"Don't attack! It's us!" I said through the smoke caused by the rumble.

Vex told us how he'd been trapped there by a man with glowing red eyes and metallic armor. I knew immediately it was Nedos. Iscana opened a portal outside of the lighthouse and told everyone who was saved to stay put there and hold on until we defeat Nedos; then they all can return to living their lives, just as she did with Niara's children.

CHAPTER 29

Starfall Infiltration

To make this work, we had to be as discreet as possible and blend in with the humans. Ferna and I were the only ones whose appearance wouldn't immediately draw stares. I asked her if she would be willing to come along.

"You can't just go with the two of you," Violet protested.

"How will you bring that place to the ground?"

"I'm coming with you," she added, looking down.

"Don't you remember? No one in Starfall can even see me, not even if I wanted them to."

It was settled then. I thought it would be best if everyone else stayed at Iscana's hideout. It felt safe and was a good place for everyone to rest and regroup before we headed off to defeat Nedos. Iscana opened a portal there while we all relaxed for a moment. Vex mentioned he could come along with us too, since raccoons are common in Starfall and he wouldn't stand out.

"Before you head out, let me make something for you." Ceju pulled out a shard of glass from his pouch and created a back strap for the Sword of Majesty.

I slid the sword into the strap and wrapped it across my body, where it lay flat against my back. The material covered the sword's orange glow, making it easier for us to travel without drawing attention.

"Thank you, Ceju!" I said, adjusting the straps until they were comfortable.

"Iscana, could you open a portal, like you did when I went to collect tears for the fairies?"

She opened a portal, and I jumped through with Vex, Ferna, and Violet. As we reached the other side in Starfall, I saw the portal reaching up toward the sky, just as it had before—easily found.

"Okay, Violet, do you remember where the shop is located?"

"I'm certain I still do," she said, looking around at the place she once called home.

Having Violet fly us would've been much easier, but we couldn't risk being seen floating in the air. We followed behind Violet as she slowly flew through the area until she stopped at a house. The house had a metal gate in front with two stone angels flanking it.

"This is where I used to live," Violet pointed out.

"My family is long gone now, but this place brings back so many memories."

We continued, following Violet as she flew past the house after only a brief stop.

"Almost there!" Violet called out behind her as we approached the shop.

I could see the brimstone of the shop ahead begin to glow a bright green. The warmth of the area overcame my body, and sweat dripped down my face. Vex ran ahead of us toward the shop and looked in through the front windows. He then scrambled up the walls onto the roof and dropped down into the smoky chimney.

Getting closer, I heard the front door being unlocked and realized it was Vex. He opened the door and ran around the shop, sniffing through candles and dropping things along the way as he looked for items to take with him.

"Shhh, be careful. We don't want to bring any attention to ourselves here."

I picked up the candles he'd dropped and placed them back. Noticing the beaded doorway toward the back, I moved in that direction. A low fire pulsed underneath a cauldron in the corner of the room. Wondering if it had been recently lit, I looked around to make sure no one else was there.

"What brings you here?" A voice called out.

The candles in the room began to ignite one by one, casting multiple shadows. Slowly, the shadows on the wall began to resemble evil beings while the voice continued to speak.

"Who are you? Speak now."

"I'm Astra, and I'm looking for the shop owner. I have a few questions for her," I replied.

"The shop is under a spell that can never be broken. Nothing you are thinking of doing can destroy this place."

I wondered how it knew my intentions, since I was trying to be as coy as possible. Feeling the shadows start to hover around me, I saw them peeling off the walls and entering the physical space.

"Make your intentions clear now, or you will perish."

"I came here to destroy this shop. Is that what you want to hear?"

The shadows began flying around Violet and me, spinning rapidly and causing the room to darken. I felt my body slowly lifting off the ground, levitating, and losing control. With all my strength, I reached toward my palm and slowly drew the diamond shape, expelling a rain of ice from my hands. This caused them to stop.

"Witch, witch, witch, witch," the voice began to whisper louder as I regained control of my body.

Ferna held out her cross pendant in front of her, turning around the room to make sure nothing caught us off guard. It was the same cross that had saved my life once before. I pulled the cross necklace she had given me from underneath my dress, letting it hang in plain view.

The shadows fused back into the walls, watching and following us through the room. I walked over to the rabbits feet hanging against the wall; they began to gently float and dance in the air. Most of the feet were from small baby rabbits, but toward the back were larger legs that looked too big to be a rabbit's. As I looked closer, I was grabbed by a dark, shadow hand that choked me by the neck.

Violet tried to remove the hand, but her body was transparent, rendering her unable to help. I slowly grasped for air, trying to grab the sword hanging from my back. Before I could touch it, Vex jumped out from the corner with a jar of salt in his mouth, sprinkling it over the hand as he ran past.

I got away from that area and grabbed my sword, keeping it close in my hands, ready to attack. Its orange glowing light made the nearby shadows vanish, spreading them into only the darkest corners. Vex had made a mess with the salt throughout the area; I could clearly see the trail he created.

"Come out of this area now!" Vex yelled. He stood outside the doorway, waiting for us to follow.

He poured the salt heavily on the ground in front of the entry. The books on the shelves in the room began to lift and float in the air. Each one opened, shooting out magical flies that filled the area with a buzzing loud enough to drive anyone insane. I hid behind the candle area. Violet swung her massive wings, creating a whirlwind that trapped the flies inside. The buzzing of the flies vibrated in my head, beginning to become louder.

"Astra, are you alright?" Ferna asked as I tried not to make a big deal out of it.

"Yes, don't worry about me. We have to find a way to destroy this place," I said, holding my hand over my mouth.

The books began to let out a dark mist, creating shadow monsters that formed, each holding an open jar in its hands.

"Stay back, creatures of the night! Your powers are useless against us," Ferna said, holding out the cross.

A book flew across the room and hit Ferna in the face, causing her to fall and knocking her cross pendant to the other side of the room. I gripped the Sword of Majesty tightly and started swinging it aimlessly in their direction. The majority of them were taken down by the sword, but they continued to regrow, reforming through the others holding their jars open.

I turned around, watching as Violet tried to help Ferna back on her feet. I felt a cold breeze over my shoulder as the shadowed monsters breathed behind me. The shadows began to pin them both to the wall, sucking their energy out. I could see the light and color of their complexions fading, turning them a pale blue tint.

Vex, standing atop a hanging chandelier full of lit candles, held out his hand and screamed at the shadows, "STOP!!!"

He made one of the shelves of candles slam into the group of shadows holding Ferna and Violet. I looked up at him, confused, not knowing if it was him or not.

"Try that again, Vex! I think that was you. Your father said there's magic in your blood. Believe in yourself!" I yelled.

He held out his hand and repelled a flying book that was heading toward him, trying to knock him to the ground. His hidden telekinesis powers were revealed at that very moment. I could see his white ear stand up as he used the power.

"We have to destroy all the shadows with the jars at once, otherwise they'll keep multiplying," I said, standing in front of Ferna and Violet.

Ferna took out her sai weapons and got ready to defend herself. Vex used his telekinesis to retrieve the cross that was knocked out of Ferna's hand and slid it across the room toward her. Ferna grabbed it and handed Violet the cross. Violet flew around the room with the cross, pushing the shadows into one corner as they avoided the salt on the ground. Books continued to zoom through the air as Vex repelled them away from us.

I released a wall of ice, blocking the shadows in the corner. Ferna ran closer to the books, with Violet standing behind her, guarding her side with her wings spread out. Ferna read from the book opened on the counter for a moment, and suddenly the books began to fall to the ground one at a time. I looked up to see if Vex was doing anything to make them fall, and saw him over by the crystals above the staircase in the corner. Smashing sounds grew louder as he slammed all the crystals against each other, causing them to shatter all over the shop.

"These crystals were the source of control," Vex explained.

"Somehow they were allowing the magic to pulse through this store. I saw these same crystals in Wormwood Castle a long time ago. I figured it had to be important."

Ferna took one of her sai weapons and stabbed it repeatedly through the ground, causing the shop to begin to quake. The writing on the weapon started to glow bright red, and her purple eyes intensified. Watching her stand there, looking down at the ground with her braids floating in the air, she told us to escape outside.

I looked for Vex to head out the door while Violet held it open, still holding the cross Ferna gave her. Vex jumped onto the counter, grabbing the opened book and taking it with him as we waited for Ferna. She left her sai weapon pierced into the ground as she headed towards the open door. Vex held out his hand, drawing the sai weapon from the ground and bringing it back to Ferna. The store crumbled and smoked all around as the door closed. Violet held out her wings over us to protect us from any fallen debris.

Bricks and stones fell, creating a loud commotion. People in Starfall slowly began to gather, but it was as if no one could see us underneath Violet's wings. Her invisibility was shielding us from their sight. Some men in dark clothing gathered close to the fallen shop, placed black candles in front of it, and directed everyone to stay back.

As they lit the candles, I saw the same shadow monsters coming out of the flames and scanning the area for us. We rushed toward the portal to the lighthouse, but stopped in front of a woman wearing all white. Her dress was covered in dirt at the bottom as it dragged on the ground while she walked. Her face was covered with a white lace fabric, and she took a puff from a gold pipe. Trying not to breathe, even though my eyes seemed to have made contact with hers, she blew the smoke directly at us, breaking through Violet's invisibility.

We pushed past her, continuing toward the portal's light. The smoke lingered on our bodies as we ran, leaving a visible trail behind us. The dark shadow monsters followed the trail, giving us no room for error or stopping.

After getting into the portal back to Iscana's hideout with the others, I yelled out to Iscana, "Close the portal now! Hurry!"

"There were shadow creatures chasing us," I said.

"Thankfully, we were able to destroy the shop, but a woman in all white noticed us while we were under Violet's cover."

Vex placed the book he took from the shop on the table as he skimmed through it with Ferna, looking for anything useful.

CHAPTER 30

The Final Stand

I keep having this uncontrollable urge to trace the diamond shape into the palm of my hand with my index finger. For some reason, I continue doing this throughout the day, but without pressing into my palm. It's as if I'm preparing myself. Something doesn't feel right. We all head to Wormwood Castle's dungeon area, to Iscana's secret weapon and armor room.

As Iscana opens the room, everything inside is covered in a sizzling, dripping, slime-like substance, with smoke still expelled from it. It looks as if it recently happened. Every bit of armor was completely destroyed with some type of acid. I watched as Iscana tried to figure out how something like this could happen. She's kept this room a secret for so long she couldn't comprehend how anyone could've possibly found out about it. A black-spotted garden snake starts to slither through the cracks of the walls.

Ferna tells us we should head to her cottage for one last piece of armor. We get there and the whole place is ransacked and completely destroyed. You can see the pain in Ferna's eyes as she sees yet another home of hers gone in an instant. She carves out small wooden crosses from the broken wedges of wood lying around and ties them tightly together with wire, crisscrossing the two pieces. She hangs them around the necks of everyone.

"The Almighty one will protect you."

A loud crack of thunder split the sky. The darkness around Wormwood Castle was surrounded by a ring of magenta smoke. It started to spin around like a tornado. As we approached the entrance, I noticed the lavender flowers by the side of the castle. I tried to crush them underneath my boots, but they were protected by magic, which caused the tornado barrier to spin faster in rage. Nedos was showing his true self as the coward he was; hiding from battle.

I yell out to him from down below, "I, Queen Hexia, order you to come out and fight!"

The ring of magenta smoke spinning around the castle made an arched opening, allowing us to walk inside. I tell Ferna to wait for us in the forest, as it was too dangerous for her. When we entered the archway opening, the smoke closed behind us, trapping us within the castle area.

"Get ready for anything. You don't know what to expect from him."

I turn to Iscana and quickly ask her if she could summon a door for the mermaids to come through. She looked around for a body of water nearby and made a coral-covered door by the swimming pool on the left side of the castle. I could see the door forming underneath the water as air bubbles rose to the surface. Vex heads off into the castle without saying a word, vanishing quickly. I pulled out the mermaids' mirror and called out to them. "Merlissa, anyone there?" No one responded.

"Mermaids, we're going to avenge your sister's death. The man who consumed her flesh is among us," I said as I gently placed the mirror on the ground nearby the planted area.

Nedos steps out on the balcony above us and begins to laugh menacingly.

"You all are right where I want you. Once again, I have you all in the palm of my hands, trapped."

Confused, I called out to him, "Come down, Nedos, and face your death!"

"This realm has had enough of your evil ways spreading around it," I yelled.

Nedos began pointing his hands toward the gargoyles guarding the castle. One by one, they broke from their stone shape and began to move, flying down toward us like dive-bombing predators, throwing gouts of fire-covered stones from their mouths. Rylo begins to drag one while descending from the air by whipping his hair and holding onto one, snagging its stone leg with a lightning fast grip. The creature thrashed, its claws scraping sparks from the castle wall, but Rylo anchored himself, using his strength and weight to slam the monstrous statue into the courtyard ground leaving a deep crater where it was shattered.

Violet didn't engage in the fight directly. She becomes a blur of motion as she flies through the air around them, generating a cyclone of pressured air, trapping some inside. They struggled against the unseen force, their cemented wings useless against the dizzying spin. The wind ripped the fiery stones from their mouths before flinging them high against the castle walls, where they crumbled to dust.

Nii was a master of ranged defense. His bow launched rapid arrows, not at the creature's bodies but at their exposed joints and eyes. One of his arrows hit a gargoyle in the shoulder right where the stone met the wing, making it seize up and sending the creature out of control. Beside him, Niara began multiplying with her clones which were focused on disruption, darting through the chaos to distract the remaining gargoyles.

I drew the diamond shape into my palm, and a wave of bitter cold erupted from me. I sent out an ice rain, hundreds of razor-sharp shards skewered a gargoyle mid air. The creature froze instantly, a jagged block of ice in the air fell rapidly and exploded once hitting the ground. I tried spreading the frost to another, but they were too swift, dodging the encroaching ice. Nedos watching from above looking genuinely infuriated.

"All this time, you think you'll be smarter than this? Surrender now while you have the chance," Nedos yells.

He calls to a statue where the orange-fur candle once was and summons it alive. I can see the statue moving from afar, entering through the ring of smoke. As it entered, the Red and Green fairies snuck behind it. While the statue came to life, I can start to see its cat-like facial features that weren't noticeable before. It was the body of a man with the face of a cat. It was standing there blankly, waiting for a command from Nedos.

Instantly, before Nedos can utter a word, Ceju launches a dark, glistening projectile at the statue. It struck the chest, thousands of beetles, poured from the black sticky substance, swarming the colossal statue. They didn't just crawl; they burrowed, consuming the stone and then the underlying, human-like flesh rapidly. The statue dissolved into a heap of dust, an unbelievably potent and sickening display of Ceju's new power. Something I'd never seen before. Ever since he turned back to his true form, he hasn't really shown me anything. Then again, ever since he changed to himself is when we were separated. I was amazed at the small yet powerful attack he used on that statue.

Nedos barely registered the statue's demise before Vex, who had sneaked through the castle's shadows, launched himself from the balcony railing. Vex didn't just jump onto Nedos; he landed with his full weight, digging his sharp claws into his neck and shoulder. Nedos howled a rare sound of pain and slammed Vex backward against the stone wall. Vex hissed, disentangling himself and running off toward the nearest shadow, a bleeding wound stained Nedos' fine robes.

"I see you've all gathered against me. I'm impressed," Nedos spat, pressing a hand to his wound while frantically scanning the shadows for Vex.

A loud chilling marching and synchronized clatter of armor from the guards of Nedos' castle began to form. They emerged from the castle in a perfect line, their armor unscathed in perfect condition as if they'd never seen battle. Heris and his guards stood in front of the others, trying to convince them not to attack and that they were fighting on the wrong side, as they should be with us. They all seemed to be under Nedos' mind control and began to attack.

Heris didn't hesitate, springing into defense. Niara's clones jumped around using a snatch-and-grab tactic, dodging the heavy swings of the guard's great swords while skillfully disarming them, tossing their weapons to the side. Nii moved with a warrior's grace, his bow being used as a close weapon. He used the sharp reinforced ends of the bow to strike and pierce through the gaps in the guards armor, standing shoulder to shoulder with Niara, defending her with fierce efficiency.

Rylo and Ceju slammed into the main line of the guards, their sheer ferocity a chaotic counterpoint to the enemy's rigid formation. Rylo fought like a mountain, trading heavy blows, while Ceju moved low, unleashing streams of specialized insects that targeted the chinks in the guards armor. Then Iscana dispensed a desperate, earsplitting shriek. A high pitched frequency that shattered glass windows of the castle and made the mind controlled guards clutch their helmets, their coordination breaking as they fell down to their knees in pain. Seeing the momentary advantage, I slammed my diamond etched palm to the ground.

Jagged, crystalline shards of ice erupted from below, forming a tight, inescapable prison around the screaming guards, locking them into a frozen tight circle. Nedos, driven into a rage by the tactical loss, threw a small, black object toward the ground. A cloud of sickly white smoke billowed, and through it, the spectral form of the woman we encountered in Starfall wearing all white materialized, as a silent furious ghost. She raised her hands, and before she vanished, she finished her summons: a horde of inky black shadow monsters poured from the smoke and headed in our direction.

Niara with her back turned to the immediate danger, closed her eyes and gripped onto her orb necklace. The wind around us didn't just blow, it roared. Leaves, dust, and debris were caught in a strong, spiraling gust that intensified around her. Emerald imprints of animal spirits began to emerge. A towering bear, a lightning quick wolf, a massive charging boar and a myriad of other animal spirits formed around her, ready to fight alongside us.

"You won't be able to outsmart us! We have stronger magic on our side, stronger than you expected us to be!" Niara yells toward Nedos as the shadow monsters close the distance.

"Still alive, I see. Don't worry, that won't be for too long," Nedos replied, a cold smile twisting his lips.

The green animal spirits didn't wait. The ghostly wolf snapped and devoured a shadow monster whole. The bear swiped and tore two apart then consumed the shadows as if it were nothing more than a simple meal.

As the last shadow monster disappeared, Niara's green fox which had been standing by her side protecting her began to glow brighter, empowered by the effortless victory.

"You think you've won? You think this is the end?" Nedos yelled, his voice strained with anger.

"BEHOLD! My latest creation. Yours truly: XARA!"

"Wait, what are you saying?"

Nedos mentioned how he brainwashed Xara into doing his dirty work and leading me to him. Although my own memories of my past life still seem blurry, I didn't care as long as I had my friends by my side. I would make sure now he wouldn't take any more innocent lives.

"Leave Xara alone and give her to us now."

"As you wish." Nedos tosses Xara toward us from the balcony, and she begins morphing into a massive scaled snake-like creature mid-air.

"She was too easy to manipulate, even easier than you, Queen Hexia," he says as he lets out another wicked laugh.

"I placed an enchantment on her food one night, causing her to eat the very food I told her not to eat, knowing she'd do the complete opposite. What she thought was a box of baked goods really was a box of venomous, poisonous snakes. I warn you not to get too close to her."

I notice the fairies as they swoop into my hair, causing it to glow bright colors of red and green. I can hear them whisper in my ears saying, "Summon the Ancient Frost Dragon." I hesitate because I don't want to kill her. She was just a pawn in his sick game.

The colossal snake slammed its massive head into the ground where Heris and some of Niara's clones were standing. The impact made the ground shake, knocking them clear across the courtyard. Before anyone could react, the serpentine beast Xara was turned into, reared back and spat a stream of luminous green venom. The venom caught Iscana in the eyes. She screamed a sharp, piercing sound of pure agony while stumbling backward. Her hands clamped desperately over her face as the acid began to burn her skin and sight.

Just then a wave of displaced water hit the courtyard, the mermaids arrived! They didn't come in peace. Merlissa was at the forefront, directing her sisters to launch electromagnetic bursts of water and razor-sharp, magically enchanted seashells at the snake's massive body. The snake recoiled, distracted, its attention pulled from Iscana to the unexpected aquatic assault. Merlissa paused only for a moment, her eyes fixed on Nedos, the memory of her betrayed heart fueling her rage before she intensified her attacks. He doesn't seem to notice her.

Iscana is in terrible amounts of pain. I rushed to her side, pressing my hand against her burning eyes. A faint blue frost radiated from my palm, immediately cooling the agonizing sensation, but not stopping the damage. Rylo was already moving, sprinting to the pool and scooping up water in his hands to flush the venom from her eyes. As I watch Iscana lay helpless as Rylo and Violet tend to her, I become enraged. I summon the Ancient Frost Dragon from my hand, but it doesn't seem to work. I continue focusing on the thought, but nothing. I then remember the image of the dragon from under the floorboards in the castle.

As soon as the image came to my mind, a thunderous, agonizing crash sounded from the side of the castle. Stone exploded outward, and the Ancient Frost Dragon, a creature of pure towering ice flew toward us, finally freed from its centuries-long prison. It was a terrifying sight. Vex, who had been lurking in the shadows of the castle leaped onto the dragon's back as it descended, using it as a springboard to join the fight safely.

I didn't speak the command; I projected it into the dragon's mind. I pointed to the massive snake that was once Xara. The Ancient Frost Dragon landed with ground-shaking force, positioning itself between the snake and my friends, an imposing, chilling wall of muscle and frost. Niara watches the dragon as her eyes glisten. It stood in front of the snake as it tried to intimidate it.

The mermaids maintained their relentless assault, tossing electric orbs and shards of seashell into the snake's scales. Merlissa moved with the cold precision of a general, directing the attacks, making sure none of her sisters were caught off guard by the snake's unpredictable lunges. I can feel the magnetic pull trying to force me against my friends and attack them. Nedos is trying hard to take over my brain again, keeping me under his control. I still have these memories coming in and out of my head of being Queen Hexia. For a slight moment, I don't know what's real anymore.

Ceju holds Nedos in a force-field bubble, stopping him from entering my mind. As I come back to my senses and notice Ceju holding Nedos captive with all his strength, I order the Ancient Frost Dragon to freeze the whole castle, including the snake and Nedos. Everything around us filled with ice and snow, as if we were in another location completely. It didn't feel as it did once before. Niara walked toward the Ancient Frost Dragon. It bowed down, allowing her to touch its head.

"I'm glad to see you again, friend," Niara spoke as she remembered a time when it was only a Koi fish in her pond.

A row of icicles formed by the dungeon entrance with a glistening shine that caught my attention. It was the ring Nedos gave me that I tossed in the bushes, now up in the air with ice attached to it. I broke off the ring and placed it in my pocket. Watching as Nedos and the snake were frozen within the castle area, I ran over to Iscana to see if she was okay. Everyone looked worried as she continued to yell in pain. Heris formed a fire around her to keep her warm from the icy area that now enveloped Wormwood Castle.

CHAPTER 31

Royal Awakening

The spinning smoke barrier around the castle dissolved, leaving behind a haze of soot in the air. A thick, gummy web of residue clung to the icicles and spread across the other surfaces. A pungent smell of scorched pine needles and thick, boiling resin lingered throughout the castle. Everyone gathered around Iscana. Ferna ran over and gently placed something over her eyes.

"Iscana went blind," Ferna whispered softly.

Iscana now had a red ribbon covering her eyes, one that had been holding together one of Ferna's braids. Ferna unraveled the other braid and tied the second red ribbon on Iscana's wrist, letting her long, gray hair flow free in the breeze.

"Let's take her to Nexus, the raccoon who replaced your eye, Ceju," I said, taking Iscana's hand. Without her sight, she wouldn't be able to summon any doors or portals.

The mermaids at the castle pool remained there, watching over the frozen area until we returned. I assured Merlissa I would contact her through the mirror periodically to make sure everything was okay.

Ceju led us to the nearest black ribbon tied around a lamppost, pulled it off, and spoke the incantation, "Jessu Dessu Kessu Lak."

The guardian of the dead arrived in front of us. I hopped on with Ferna and Iscana.

"Vex, I think you should come along with us. There's someone I'm sure you'd want to see," I said, trying not to be too obvious about reuniting him with his father.

I told the others to head back to the castle and for Ceju to use his force field on Nedos until we got back, just to be safe. I really wanted Ceju to come along, but I needed him to ensure Nedos didn't escape. I gave a droplet of my blood to the guardian, and we were transported to Desert Driftia. We headed to Nexus in the desert to see if we could find a pair of eyes suitable for Iscana. He rummaged through his belongings and then came across a vibrant glow. He pulled out a jar and explained he would give her two cat eyes in exchange for her voice.

"These are rare Abyssinian cat eyes, held for this exact moment," he said.

"These are drawn to you. And although you might not know this or understand it, this is your destiny."

Iscana considered the decision that would follow her for the rest of her life. She decided her sight was more valuable than her voice and entered the tent alone, with Nexus following behind her. I could see the shadows from outside as he reached his hand down her throat, grabbing and pulling a piece of her insides from her body. Iscana screamed in agonizing pain for a brief moment, then everything went silent.

I heard the mechanical noises of the eye implant, a sound I was already used to from the time Ceju had his eye replaced. Iscana came out, tears of blood streaming down her face. Her piercing green cat eyes glowed in the night. "If only there was another way, I'm so sorry, Iscana," I said, crying with her.

"Something good will come of this, I promise you," Ferna assured her, braiding her hair and securing it with the ribbons Iscana gave back.

Vex stood there in silence, watching as Nexus finished his work. Nexus stopped and noticed him.

"My son, Vex, it's you!" Nexus exclaimed, walking toward him with his arms held out.

They embraced, extremely delighted to be reunited once again.

"I thought I'd never see you again," Vex said, hugging him tightly.

"We will never be far apart again, my son," Nexus told Vex.

As we stood there in silence for a moment, I saw Iscana adjusting to her new eyes, paying attention to every micro-movement. She silently summoned a door back to Wormwood Castle.

"Vex, stay here and catch up with your father. When everything is over and done with, I'll come and get you both out of here, where you can finally live together with every other magical being," I said.

"Thank you, thank you. You don't know how much this means to me," Nexus said, shedding a tear.

"No worries, friend," I replied as we headed off into the portal.

When we got back to the castle, I noticed the ice was slowly melting away. Rylo was keeping the snake frozen by holding his hands over it, creating a barrier making sure it wouldn't melt. Ceju was using up all his energy holding Nedos in his force field as he remained semi-frozen.

"We can't kill Nedos because of his immortality," I thought out loud. "We can bind him, as he's done with people in the past. But instead of keeping him in the dungeon, we can set a special place aside just for him."

I tried to think of a way to confine him but also be able to see him. Then the idea suddenly hit me. I shook my hands through my hair, making the fairies come out from hiding.

"Can you lead us to the largest mirror in the castle?"

"I think you guys might appreciate this," I said to them without any further explanation.

I was going to trap Nedos in the mirror, just like he did to my friends. As we approached the mirror I could see its reflection gave off a sapphire blue tint. I held a hand against it while asking Iscana if she could open a portal within the mirror. She turned her new, bright, glowing cat eyes toward the mirror, and a bright green light shot from her vision into the glass, burning a hole in the center. The mirror-portal opened, and inside was complete darkness. I thought about trapping Nedos there. For a moment, I began to feel sorry for him. I couldn't understand his reasoning for things.

Then, out of the darkness inside the mirror, three dark shadows emerged and formed into the shapes of three black-hooded figures. I turned to Iscana, hand out and ready to attack. The familiar hooded figures removed their cloaks, revealing their faces. They were the same blue figures I saw when I passed out in the forest with Ceju—the same blue-haired, blue-shadowed women that were once invisible: the Sapphire Mora. I started to have a flashback memory of the three black-hooded figures who led me into a door, guiding me down this spiral of events.

"We knew it was you all along. That's why we helped you along the way while working together with your fairy friends as we communicated through the mirrors we were trapped in."

"We are the three eldest sisters who were brave enough to venture out in disguise and guide you to your destiny."

"What are you talking about?"

"Astra is your name given at Starfall, you're being awakened, and soon your power will overflow within you."

"I don't understand."

The three sisters of the Sapphire Mora replied, "Every time Nedos has successfully killed you it weakens your soul's strength, making it difficult for it to be tested properly. The fire-filled alley is the beginning point you fall back to each time, with our guidance."

"You are who you are, and we're certain: Queen Hexia."

The polished surface of the mirror rippled like water as a single, shadowy hand, reached out from its depths. Before I could react, it clamped around my wrist, cold as ice, and yanked me into the mirror. A kaleidoscope of shimmering light and agonizing pressure overwhelmed the area around me. Inside the mirror's void, there was nothing but a crushing silence. My curly textured hair began to straighten, stretching out as if by an unseen force, turning a shining jet black —with red and green highlights that absorbed the light.

Each strand became sleek and impossibly straight, falling far past my shoulders. I began to feel a sickening stretch, a sudden pull within my bones as my limbs began extending, contouring my body into the lean frame of an adult. I could feel a vibration in my throat causing me to yell in a high-pitched cry that suddenly became deeper. My eyes began shifting into a brightened shade of purple, looking mystical and somewhat familiar to me. Pushing out the mirror, I watch as the Sapphire Mora all bow their heads and kneel on the ground.

"You've completed your soul's journey. This is your destiny and your true self."

"All hail Queen Hexia," they all said in unison.

While everyone bowed, I saw numerous blue-shadowed women of the Sapphire Mora filling the room, their piercing blue eyes staring down at the ground. Iscana and the others were kneeling with their heads bowed down as well. I could feel the shift in my spirit begin. Nedos was telling the truth: I really was his Queen. But I didn't need him to complete me, he's already shown me how he truly felt about me. I wouldn't let him deceive me again.

I watched Ceju until he felt me staring. He looked up for a moment, making eye contact with the one eye that remained. I winked at him, trying not to feel so guilty for him losing an eye. The Sapphire Mora became a part of Wormwood Castle. They protected us and helped bring order. I had them serve as guards, cooks, knights, farmers, entertainers, winemakers, and craftsmen, to give them a sense of belonging and purpose while living in the castle.

The Sapphire Mora brought us to a room at the very top of the castle, near the roof, where a door was blended into the brick wall. They opened it, and we placed Nedos inside with magic binding shackles around his arms and legs, chaining him to the walls, but with just enough room to barely move.

This would serve as his punishment for all eternity. They closed the door, and a padlock appeared. I watched as they entered the code 52495. I could hear the different sounds each number made, creating a tune resembling the music I'd heard from the young man while in Starfall.

The wreckage from summoning the Ancient Frost Dragon left a huge hole in the side of Wormwood Castle. Fixing it was going to be a project, but I'm sure it was nothing a few magical creatures couldn't handle.

I called over the raven that once served Nedos. It now saw me as its master. I commanded it to bring materials to fix the castle as it aided in repairing it.

The castle retained its icy exterior as I began realizing the change was strangely perfect for it. The structure had a frozen, chilling exterior but no longer gave off any cold temperatures. The Ancient Frost Dragon's power had permanently affected its structure. I felt as if it were always meant to be this way, an icy gleaming monument forged by magic it once concealed, a form of its true self. It felt more like home than the old stone walls ever had.

I couldn't tear my eyes away from the sheer beauty it had achieved. Its surface is smooth and milky in some places, jagged and diamond-sharp in others, but also warm to the touch. Glistening under the sky, the shimmering sapphire and silver ice formations were flawless. The mermaids were full of joy and longed for the day they would find the love they'd avoided for so long. The portal Iscana summoned in the castle's front pool remained intact. Heading back outside of the castle, I asked Ceju for a huge favor.

"Ceju, do you remember when you traded your eye to save Ferna?"

"Of course. Why do you ask?"

"Well, I think we can save my friend Xara. It isn't her fault she's been under Nedos' control. Can you see if maybe this star eye you acquired would bring her back? Please," I said, my voice worried.

Ceju removed the eye from its socket and dropped it down the frozen snake's mouth. Rylo stepped back, and we watched as the ice around the snake's body melted away, leaving behind Xara lying still on the ground. I grabbed her head and placed it under my arm as I held her limp body on the ground. Her short, dark brown hair spread across my arm as I began to shake her softly.

"Xara, wake up," I said, as tears from my face splashed onto her neck, soaking into her clothing.

"Why isn't it working? Why isn't it working?" I cried out toward Ceju.

Everyone watched with sorrow as I mourned my dear friend. The Sapphire Mora levitated her lifeless body to a shallow area near Ferna's destroyed cottage. They buried her, with a stick poking out of the ground, its metal end wrapped in orange fur. The tip of the stick lit up with fire, burning into the ground like a candle melting down into the wax. Something began tearing through the ground under where Xara was buried. She emerged, her body, eyes and hair stained blue, just like the Sapphire Mora who buried her.

Death was her fate, but seeing her transformed by the Sapphire Mora made the cracks in my heart mend. She didn't look any different from the others, with the same long blue hairstyle. I walked up to Xara with excitement. I cut off a small piece of my hair from each side—red and green—and braided it into her hair, securing the small braid with a thin piece of string wrapped around it multiple times.

Now I could tell her apart from the rest, and she'd always have a piece of me with her. I loved her like a sister, and it hurt me deeply when I thought she was against me. But why didn't the Well of Oversight show me she was being controlled by Nedos? Dwelling on it made no sense, either way. Had I known, it wouldn't have stopped Nedos from turning her into that snake. I came to terms with the new reality set before us.

I gave Xara an important position in Wormwood Castle: she would be the one to oversee the maintenance and repair of the castle and its defenses. Heris was also given an important role in the castle as the liaison between the guards and the newly assigned citizens, the Sapphire Mora.

CHAPTER 32

The Ties That Bind

It was now safe for Iscana to open the portal, leading Niara back to her many children. I watched as Iscana opened the door. Niara knelt to the ground as the ladybugs in her hair flew around her, morphing into clones of herself. They all began running inside, with Nii by her side, to greet everyone. It was such a beautiful sight to see them all safe and finally together again. The tranquility inside of their new oasis was overwhelming.

Iscana kept the portal open permanently for Niara and her family, should they choose to live there. It was a nice escape, especially being close to the castle. She also opened the portal that held all the other magical beings who were trapped in Aetheria Castle at Stillhold, where we found the Sword of Majesty. Everyone celebrated together, and the energy around us became static, as if Genesis Veil somehow knew peace had finally arrived.

The green fox roamed Wormwood Castle freely, uniting with the other green animal spirits released from the hidden area Niara had placed them in to protect them from Nedos. We all used our magic to bring the broken forest back to its former self. Ferna replanted some of the trees with Rylo, and I helped Heris remove any remaining traps and illusions used to hide from Nedos.

The Tree of Life was no longer hidden deep within the forest but out in the open. We created a space around it for all to gather and visit whenever they pleased. The magical properties and roots of the tree spread throughout the land causing great health and immortality to everyone that lived there. One of the very things that made Genesis Veil so special, was its diverse mixture of creatures and magical beings from all around.

The green spirit animals created a grove. Niara's children made many paths leading to the tree, similar to how they had lived hidden underground. Small mushrooms lit up the way, guiding visitors to the tree. Food became exceedingly abundant. Her children continued to grow crops, and they used the door Iscana summoned at the crop fields to manage everything they needed, as she kept the door open and accessible.

The mermaids often visited us through the coral-covered door Iscana summoned. Merlissa got engaged to a human, as she had always dreamed. Things were slowly returning back to how they once were, where the human and magic realms lived in peace together.

She wanted to have her wedding here at Wormwood Castle. I made sure the entrance around the castle was fully supplied with fresh saltwater before having Iscana summon a door for her and her family and friends to attend. As she swam down a path while her soon-to-be husband walked alongside, I watched with contentment, knowing that I had enriched the lives of those around me. Their happiness spread throughout the castle. Her sisters all watched, their top halves of their bodies floating above the water, while starfish and seaweed were thrown into the air in celebration of the marriage before us.

Violet began teaching magic to the younger generation, passing on the knowledge while finding her new purpose in life. The intense conflicts of the past had subsided, leaving a vital need to educate. She focused on the ethical foundations of power, ensuring that the next generation understood the responsibility that came with their gifts. In mentoring these young minds, she realized that this was her true calling. She established a small, quiet academy within the woods near Wormwood Castle.

Time continued to pass, and I was slowly tempted to check on Nedos. One late full moon night, I headed towards the room where he was imprisoned. I began longing for his affection again. Two guards stood on each side of the door at all times. How could I possibly get inside? I could easily order them to move—after all, I was the Queen—but I wanted a moment fully alone with him without anyone else knowing or interrupting.

I drew a diamond shape into my palm and conjured up a pair of iced cats chasing each other through the halls. I drew the guards attention to them, having them try to capture the illusory creatures as they raced through the halls. When both guards were out of sight, I began to mess with the wall until the padlock presented itself.

Right at that moment, I forgot the code to the door. I started to punch in... 5... 3... 2... 4... 5... but it was denied. I remembered the tune the code made, closed my eyes, and pressed each button, focusing on the sound. Playing around with it as if it were a musical instrument, I finally unlocked it without knowing the code numbers, but by the tune.

I could see Nedos lying on the floor, spinning the chain from his wrist with no purpose. The look on his face was filled with remorse and despair. "I can't believe I allowed the evil thoughts in my head to try and kill you," he said. "I'm truly sorry and deserve everything coming my way."

I began to feel darkness overcome me. "I hex you, from touching anyone other than me. I hex you to be bound to my love. I hex you from having any magical abilities. I hex you to be a servant bound to my every command. I hex you under my spell," I said to him.

"Yes, My Queen," he responded.

I could see the light being sucked from his eyes, leaving behind a voided emptiness. Being Queen Hexia came with powers I didn't fully understand yet, but I knew this power would be designed and destined for greatness. The shift inside me slowly started feeling more comfortable.

Everyone came back together, surprised and shocked, as I took over the castle with Nedos by my side. In light of everything that happened, I decided to start the victory off with a new light.

"From now forward, Astra is no longer, but your Queen. Queen Hexia. Ruler of this castle now to be known as Wyrmfrost Castle."

Iscana often spent most of her time in Cloud Fairy. The fairies taught her how to speak telepathically, which was exactly the loophole she'd been searching for since trading her voice for her vision. She became the fairies official guardian and used her summoning powers to guide them to crying humans easier. Instead of having to search, she could just summon doors where tragedy and despair were in Starfall, making the fairies' lives so much easier. After they took the time teaching her telepathy, she felt more than lucky to have such an honorable gift bestowed on her. Serving them was only a sliver of the gratitude she could convey to them.

Iscana drank from the tear-shaped sparkling potion given to her by the fairies, just as I once drank, causing wings to tear through her back. She never wanted to retract the wings, even when it caused her immense pain. She would often fly down to have Ferna apply a slab of cooled aloe mixed with crushed lavender from the front of the castle.

Sitting in Ferna's cottage, having a drink of mixed herbal tea one night, I stared across towards the sundial sitting in the distance. Her cottage wasn't fully complete; most structures were just up without walls. Nedos helped fix the cottage along with the others, but this time he used nothing but his own physical strength, as his powers were stripped from him. Although his mind was controlled by my power, I knew he was glad he was out here, powerless and bound to my commands, rather than stuck chained inside a darkened room for all eternity. This punishment suited him better.

One night at Ferna's cottage, with just the two of us enjoying each other's company, Ferna mentioned she had something important to tell me.

"What is it, Ferna? Are you alright?" I asked, leaning forward.

Ferna sighed, placing her ball of yarn and knitting needles onto the table. "Yes, my dear, I'm alright. But I have something I should have told you a long time ago. Please, just bear with me for a moment."

I swallowed hard, a knot of nervousness tightening in my throat. I gathered a section of my hair, twirling it between my fingers, waiting in breathless anticipation.

"I'm not who you think I am, Queen Hexia."

I looked at her, confusion clouding my face, and opened my mouth to speak. She quickly held up her hand.

"I'm Your Mother," she confessed, her expression filled with both guilt and deep love.

"My... Mother?" The word was barely a whisper before I erupted. "What?!" I threw myself onto her, hugging her fiercely, nearly toppling both of us off her chair.

Pulling back slightly, I gripped her arms. "How is this possible? And why are you only telling me this now?"

"I couldn't risk you knowing the truth earlier," she explained gently. "It would have distracted you from your true purpose as Queen."

"I don't understand. How can this be one of my lives?"

"This is one of your many lives, my Queen. Your spirit has been persistent. It lived on and traveled to different bodies after your first death, always searching for a way to become Queen and lock your spirit within its destiny."

Ferna's gaze hardened slightly. "And every time Nedos found you, he would kill you, just to prevent you from becoming Queen Hexia. He was always jealous of your destiny. He wanted it all for himself. That's why he banished me to the X-Graves. He didn't want me around to help you, but he knew as long as I was alive, your spirit would continue to find its way back towards the castle where we all lived."

My hands were trembling as she explained.

"The random visions you've had sometimes? They're glimpses of our history. It's because we're part of the Holy Ancients bloodline."

She took my hands in hers. "Every event leading up to this moment—every struggle, every loss—was meant to happen. It all led to your spirit finding the body it needed, guiding you toward your ultimate transformation."

I was left speechless. But suddenly, everything clicked into place. Ferna is my mother. That explained the deep connection, the immediate trust, and why she helped me without hesitating in the X-Graves. As I looked into her eyes, I saw the exact same intense, perfectly matching purple eyes that stared back at me when I first looked in the mirror as Queen Hexia.

"Thank you," I managed, hugging her again, trying to hold in the surge of powerful emotions.

"This is the best feeling I've felt in a long time. I always had a special bond with you, Ferna, but knowing that we share the same blood and that you're my mother... it makes everything feel complete."

"Thank you for finally telling me the truth."

As I processed everything, I thought for a split second: Everything Nedos said and showed me wasn't a lie. It was me in the photos, it was me he looked for and searched for—but only to kill me and put an end to my soul's purpose. I couldn't help but feel enraged. I quickly brushed it off once I realized that there was nothing he could do to change things now. I was exactly where I was meant to be, at the right time. Everything worked out.

Every full moon night from then on, I would have a big dinner with everyone invited, underneath the stars in front of the castle. Mermaids would splash around in the pool, catching cooked fish we would toss over, as they preferred catching their food rather than having it handed to them. The fairies all fluttered around as colorful orbs of light, creating a most magical feel.

Ferna got up and mentioned to everyone that we should join hands and bow our heads while she led in prayer. We didn't know what she was talking about. She began to educate us about the King of Kings: Jesus Christ. She reminded us that we were wearing his cross around our necks and that his love and protection for us would continue to follow us as long as we honored him and believed.

CHAPTER 33

A New Dawn

Finally, life began to feel meaningful. We all had a sense of purpose and belonging. Even Nedos, after all, was still my right-hand man under my curse. Anyone would consider this an honor to be the Queen's mindless servant. I would sometimes believe that we were the happy couple he used to envision with me. Whether the memories with him were real or not, I created new ones in my head. He was better off this way. Everything happens for a reason.

After Nedos was under my control and powerless, the magic barrier he created to infiltrate Genesis Veil began to drop, allowing others to finally travel here again. Iscana went to her bridge hideout, where the shipwrecks blocked entry and transported the wreckage to a deserted area through a portal. Merlissa and her sisters swam freely in the area once again, with nothing but fond memories of when they were younger. That area soon became a place of joy that they frequently visited.

The fairies began to reopen the portal that allowed Starfall to connect with Genesis Veil. For the longest time, we'd been secluded and living in fear. Now everyone could be at peace. Magical creatures from all around soon started to enter and start a new life at Genesis Veil. Many of them had fled to Starfall, living in disguise until this very moment arrived. The fairies explained to me that humans came through the portal as well, but only the ones who were chosen by dreams and fairies.

Not every human would be able to understand the magic abilities within them. Some fought the feeling away or simply brushed it aside. It was those who questioned their existence and believed in the impossible. The ones who stood out and were rejected by the rest. Those who felt with all their heart that they were different and destined for something greater than their understanding.

Only they would get the calling deep within them. If they chose to follow the fairy lights that are used to guide them out of Starfall, they would be free of their bondage and given a chance to live among us—to learn magic and discover a new version of their soul's purpose.

Genesis Veil was now at peace. The area is filled with hybrids, magical beings, creatures, humans, spirits and shadows of all kinds, living in harmony as they once did. It was a breathtaking sight—a tapestry of differences woven together by shared purpose and hard-won understanding. Everything felt as if I'd been here before with things being this way, a deep sense of familiarity washing over me like a long-forgotten memory. In the wake of this newfound unity, I started to think of how much I appreciated all the friends I'd made along the way, recognizing that this bliss was their legacy as much as it was mine.

Nexus and Vex were safe with us, having left Desert Driftia behind them. They had plans of starting their own business together in an actual shop, not a tiny, hidden tent. Vex still had the book he took from the shop we destroyed in Starfall. I felt it was in good hands with him and his father. If ever its magic was needed, they would be the perfect ones to use it.

Ceju and Rylo were getting ready to travel together to another realm of magic, a place called Chroma, where Ceju is originally from. Ceju wanted to let his family know he was safe and sound—alive—and that his mission of aiding in the revival of Genesis Veil was complete.

"It's time to bring peace home."

"Whenever you settle down, come visit us," Ceju said, handing over a smooth, thickened glass card. A fingerprint was clearly stamped onto the surface, glowing faintly for a moment.

"Travel using this; press onto the fingerprint, it will open a portal directly to Chroma. If anyone gives you any trouble, just show them the Chroma Card."

The Chroma Card felt warm in my hands, radiating a subtle pulse of power. Tucked behind the swirl of the fingerprint, a finely etched image of a map glinted in the light. Ceju pointed with a steady finger to the area where his family home was located so that I could find him and Rylo easily when the time came.

Ceju took out a piece of shimmering glass from his leather pouch and transformed it into a custom eyepatch, attaching a small circular mirror to the center. He gently placed it over his missing eye. The new eyepatch was almost like a final farewell. Rylo placed a hand on his shoulder for support.

"We'll see you when you're settled," Ceju said, his voice filled with a quiet certainty.

"I'm going to miss you two. Be safe out there," I said, pulling them into a tight hug.

Then, a glowing distortion formed in the air between us as Ceju pressed onto the fingerprint on the Chroma Card he'd given me, and then he and Rylo stepped through, disappearing into the light.

Ferna began spreading the knowledge and word of Jesus throughout Genesis Veil, allowing others to experience his great love and build a relationship with him, knowing the truth. There was a gravitational pull against those who were stuck in their ways and refused to allow Jesus into their lives. She would stay in her cottage, making small cross necklaces and bracelets to give away to whoever she came across. She never forced them onto anyone; she simply offered the small gift with a gentle, sincere smile, and the weight of that sincerity often seemed to soften the hardest hearts she encountered.

Some nights, while at her cottage, I would help her organize and sort her creations. I often watched her hands, quick and practiced, transforming simple materials into emblems of hope, feeling privileged to be a partner in her tireless ministry. Each piece she crafted was not merely jewelry, but a silent prayer and a small act of defiance against the spiritual stagnation she sensed in Genesis Veil.

Everyone has a choice to make in this life, regardless of their origins. Whether you were born into a certain way of life or from a particular bloodline, the path you take is ultimately decided by you. The choice to follow Jesus is yours to make, independent of any inherited circumstances or past influences. This decision rests on individual will and faith, leading to a spiritual transformation.

I headed back to Starfall with the fairies guidance, my heart heavy as I revisited the orphanage where I once grew up. My face flushed with embarrassment and anger as I saw the harsh living conditions. The peeling paint, the worn-out mattresses, the distant, hollow cries of children – it was worse than I remembered. I wanted so badly to do something good for this place.

Instead, I consulted with some of the kind humans learning magic at Genesis Veil, hoping they knew someone at Starfall who could help us. Violet immediately suggested I speak with Merlissa, whose husband was human. Merlissa then brightly recommended her husband, Orion, who had extensive experience building large ships. His experience in construction was exactly what we needed.

Orion was able to come back to Starfall with me, bringing along some of his friends to help with remodeling the orphanage. Before we got to work, I spoke with the Mistress in charge. She was a stern woman with a perpetually unimpressed expression, completely unbothered by the squalor, acting as if the children's suffering wasn't an issue. I insisted that the repairs would be free of charge and would genuinely enrich the lives of everyone who walked through these doors. After much convincing, and perhaps a subtle hint of my royal presence, we finally secured her grudging approval.

The next morning, with the Mistress' reluctant supervision, I took all the children to a nearby park, a small patch of green amidst the concrete, to get them out of the house so the men could begin their work. The children played for a while, their laughter a fragile sound in the stale air, until one small girl, no older than eight, came up to me. She was a wisp of a child, with skin the color of warm honey and a mass of dark, tightly coiled, unruly curls that seemed to defy gravity. Her eyes, large and a startlingly bright hazel, held a deep, quiet intelligence far beyond her years.

"Thank you," she whispered, her voice surprisingly strong.

I smiled, sitting down on the grassy ground, and she sat beside me. Soon, other children, drawn by her boldness, gathered around, listening intently. I couldn't help but be reminded of my younger self in this child—her hair, her quiet intensity, her unwavering gaze.

"This place you're living in," I began, sweeping my hand towards the distant orphanage, "will no longer feel like a place where you don't want to be. It will always be full of love, as long as you keep that love alive within yourselves."

The Mistress, standing a short distance away, watched me with thinly veiled disgust, as if I were foolish for even wasting my breath speaking to them. But I ignored her. I felt such a strong connection with these children, a profound desire for this to be a turning point in their lives. Maybe one day, I will meet them again in Genesis Veil, I thought. Maybe they will soon be guided by the fairies that once guided me.

Over the next few days, Orion and his friends worked tirelessly. The men painted the inside of the orphanage in vibrant, cheerful colors—sunny yellows, sky blues, and gentle greens—to brighten up the place and instill inner happiness. Every room was transformed, each wall adorned with a small, circular mirror, encouraging self-reflection and confidence. The children, when they returned, gasped with delight.

Entering the orphanage as if for the first time, they felt a pure, unadulterated joy. I knew it would only continue to get better from here. Eventually, the bright, welcoming colors of the orphanage attracted potential parents, and many children were adopted into loving families soon after. A group of wonderful chefs even agreed to work at the orphanage, ridding the children of their starvation. It seemed everything was turning out better than we planned.

Before I left, I wrote a note, inscribing a simple but powerful message: "Don't be afraid to be yourself, even if it means standing out from the rest." I framed it and hung it prominently on a wall. As I turned to leave, the small child, the one who so reminded me of my younger self, approached me again. She carefully handed me a small, crinkled piece of aluminum foil. I took it, confused.

"Thank you," I said, not knowing what it was.

"It's chocolate, eat it," the young girl instructed, her hazel eyes sparkling.

Chocolate? I've never heard of such a thing back in Genesis Veil. I placed the whole, wrapped thing in my mouth, tasting the strange, metallic texture.

The girl giggled, a bright, melodic sound. "No, you have to unwrap it first!"

I quickly pulled the foil apart, revealing a dark, gleaming brown nugget. I brought it to my nose, inhaling deeply; it smelled richly of sweetness, a hint of vanilla, and something wonderful. A wave of intense curiosity washed over me. I took a small bite of this mysterious chocolate, and as soon as it hit my tongue, it began to melt, coating my mouth in a velvety richness. An explosion of deep, sweet, slightly bitter flavors burst forth. My mouth began to salivate and tingle with delight. I had never tasted anything so wonderfully complex and satisfying before. I wanted so badly to have more.

"Where did you get this from?" I asked, my voice hushed with wonder.

"It's magic," she simply replied, a secret smile playing on her lips. I thought she was truly special for having such an ability.

She then explained how she would often walk around on the streets at night, hungry and begging for scraps. No one ever gave her anything with love; she was always fed like a wild animal. During those desperate times, she would imagine some of the most wonderful foods she was never able to have. She would imagine it hard every day, focusing so intensely that she would feel fully satisfied just by the thought. Then one day, she saw what she'd imagined appear right before her eyes, a real, tangible treat. She had stirred up the ability to conjure food, but she had kept it a secret from everyone, knowing she was different and could be hurt for such a gift.

She had even been leaving extravagant dishes around the house for her friends in the orphanage to eat, little acts of kindness in a harsh reality. The Mistress barely gave them enough food, and what she did provide was often cold and tasted of cardboard. At that moment, listening to her story, I knew I couldn't leave her behind. Not only did she remind me so much of myself, but she had been able to trust me with her deepest secret, her extraordinary gift. And to me, that meant more than anything. I went straight to the Mistress to inquire about adopting her.

The Mistress, surprisingly eager to be rid of another mouth to feed, explained that as long as I was willing to care for the girl permanently, there wouldn't be any issue. I returned to the young girl and asked if she wanted to come along on a journey with me and be adopted. Her bright hazel eyes widened, and her face lit up with overwhelming happiness. I quickly signed the few papers at the Mistress' desk, and we were ready to head out. As the other children waved their goodbyes, we headed to the ocean, where Merlissa's husband, Orion, waited with his ship.

Aboard his sturdy vessel, we sailed out towards the shimmering portal that connected both realms. Upon entering Genesis Veil, I turned to the child, a deep sense of joy filling my chest.

"What would you like your new name to be, my dear?" I asked softly. "You have a new life ahead of you to look forward to."

"Seven," she replied quickly, without a moment's hesitation.

"Seven, like the number? Is that what you said?"

"Yes, Seven," she confirmed, her gaze steady. "I had fought for this day to happen my whole life. Six times I fought to stay alive. The seventh time was a gift sent to me—being you. The day we met, you came right on time."

Tears welled in my eyes. I cried and grabbed her close, hugging her tightly against me. "I'm so thankful to have you in my life, Seven. We will do great things together."

Seven was enrolled in Violet's magic classes, eager to learn more abilities. She became one of the most well-rounded beings who practiced magic in Genesis Veil. Everyone knew of her kindness and her quiet strength. As a surprise, a special chocolate area—a little wonderland of cocoa delights—was built just for her in Wyrmfrost Castle. Ferna helped her choose decorations for the room, while Niara gathered everyone to show her the surprise. Seven was happiest, not because she finally had a space of her own, but because she had found something even more precious: a family, the loving support of friends, and a home that was finally safe.

I hung the mirror that Merlissa gave me in my room in the castle and was obsessed with it. My obsession wasn't only due to its magical properties, but rather to its exquisite craft, to possess such a beautiful object near me. Thanks to the many crops from Starfall being introduced to Genesis Veil, different foods became accessible. I planted the seed the green guard woman gave me, retrieved from her stomach, near the front of Wyrmfrost Castle, toward the entrance of the forest.

The seed began to sprout a small leaf as soon as it was covered with soil. I wondered what would come of the seed and how it would save the race of the Viridiani Tribe. As the days went by, the planted seed began to sprout into a beautiful green tree. The leaves hung down as if in large cocoons, protecting what was inside. Green people began coming out of them every so often, regrowing the race. I recognized the face of the green woman who gave me the seed back at Aetheria Castle and gave her a warm hug.

"It's good to see you again," I said.

"I knew it was you Queen Hexia, My name is Olivine the leader of the Viridiani Tribe." she said as she bowed down.

I watched as she gathered the rest of her tribe from the cocoons that opened up. They all began singing a beautiful melody which caused the leaves of the tree to rise back up into itself. The tree had a section underneath it that snow fell from. I stood under it for a while thinking about what a great magical tree it was. I felt like it was part of a memory I couldn't quite grasp and it made me satisfied knowing it was thriving around us.

The shadows that gifted me the ability to travel in spirit form would visit me occasionally. I'd see them pass by the mirrors of Wyrmfrost Castle, their dark forms distorting the reflection. They would sometimes spread out from my shadow, rapidly expanding to cover the walls and fly around the castle like silent guardians. Knowing they weren't there to harm but to protect me, I always felt a sense of peace whenever they visited. Their presence was noticed only by my eyes, making our bond that much more special.

I recognized the cross around my neck that Ferna had given me. The metal it was made of was heavy and bound with a thin, tarnished silver wire. A fresh wave of relief washed over me as my fingers instinctively gripped onto its familiar shape. This had remained my most treasured possession; a tangible link to Ferna's love and the protection from our savior, Jesus, the King of Kings. It had repelled restless spirits in Starfall, acting as a shield to the overwhelming darkness. It had saved me from death's door more than once, and held strong through the dangers of our final battle, helping to keep everyone safe.

As Nedos and I sat atop the castle one late night, watching the sunrise together, I laid my head on his shoulder as he laid his head onto mine. The ghost child that I had spotted in the castle a few times flew over us and dropped something from the sky. I caught it in my hand, not realizing what it was until I turned it around. I examined it to realize it was a pocket watch, I couldn't tell if it was the same one I threw into the fire; it looked untouched and completely new. A frantic pulse throbbed in my throat and chest, a dizzying percussion against my ribs, while Nedos turned his head, making eye contact with me.